HUNTER FROM HELL

Last night Lucifer had gone adventuring for the first time in two weeks.

It had been time to let another woman find him. There were many women who wanted him, who were awaiting him, and he respected every one of them. He respected them so much that after he took them to the mountain top and showed them his kingdom, the kingdom that would be theirs, the kingdom of pain and horror and desolation and despair and hopelessness. After he taught them that the terror of the day was greater than the terror of the night, he would wash them and dress them and take them to a place where they could sleep until the Time of Renewal. He could do that because he was Lucifer, the Son of the Morning Star.

He was the Light Bearer.

Pandemonium was his kingdom.

KILL THE ANGELS

Robert Coram

A SIGNET BOOK

SIGNET
Published by the Penguin Group
Penguin Books USA Inc., 375 Hudson Street,
New York, New York 10014, U.S.A.
Penguin Books Ltd, 27 Wrights Lane,
London W8 5TZ, England
Penguin Books Australia Ltd, Ringwood,
Victoria, Australia
Penguin Books Canada Ltd, 10 Alcorn Avenue,
Toronto, Ontario, Canada M4V 3B2
Penguin Books (N.Z.) Ltd, 182–190 Wairau Road,
Auckland 10, New Zealand

Penguin Books Ltd, Registered Offices:
Harmondsworth, Middlesex, England

First published by Signet, an imprint of Dutton Signet,
a division of Penguin Books USA Inc.

First Printing, July, 1996
10 9 8 7 6 5 4 3 2 1

 REGISTERED TRADEMARK—MARCA REGISTRADA

Printed in the United States of America

PUBLISHER'S NOTE
This is a work of fiction. Names, characters, places, and incidents either are
the product of the author's imagination or are used fictitiously, and any resemblance to actual persons, living or dead, events, or locales is entirely
coincidental.

*For Nigel Fullick, who once saved my
life in the Bahamas. Nige is the best cop
ever to strap on a gun—even if he did wear it
on the wrong side—and he is my compadre forever.*

Acknowledgments

First and foremost, I thank Roy Hazelwood of The Academy Group. This book rests in large part upon his work as an FBI agent with the Behavioral Science Unit. I have borrowed liberally from his books and articles as well as from his classroom.

At the Atlanta Police Department, Major Mickey Lloyd, the man who brought profiling to the APD and who has investigated many Lucifers, provided guidance. Homicide detective Carl Lee Price helped from beginning to end. Sergeant Gordon Earls allowed me to ride with the evening watch of the sex crimes squad, and investigator Robert Ford shared cases past. Numerous other APD officers I thank for their patience and willingness to share their knowledge of the street.

Ed Medlin knows Emory is a great university and that this is a novel.

Dr. Randy Hanzlick taught me to listen when the dead speak.

Pete and Janice Charette I thank for the "Peteyisms."

Finally, my deepest gratitude to those rape victims who fought through the pain to tell of their experiences.

Be sober, be vigilant; because your adversary the devil, as a roaring lion, walketh about, seeking whom he may devour.

I Peter 5:8

1

Major Norris Morris stopped his unmarked police car and squinted up at the square box of a brick apartment building. "What a dump," he mumbled, putting off what he had to do. He sighed, slid out of the car, and looked around as he adjusted the weight of the 9mm Smith & Wesson on his right hip. Morris took a final drag off the cigarette hanging out of his mouth and flicked the butt across the parking lot. He wiped a few ashes off his shirt and sighed. It was June, and Atlanta's temperature and humidity were fighting somewhere in the high eighties. Morris was wearing sunglasses, but the mid-morning sun was so bright that he squinted.

Morris was a big man—six feet tall and 230 pounds—and was neatly dressed in the bland civilian uniform of high-ranking police officers: dark suit, white shirt, dark tie. His suit would draw no attention. But his face would. His face lurched and jumped like an old boot inhabited by a panic-stricken cat as his expressions flitted from frown to squint, from grimace to glower.

He ambled down the cracked sidewalk between rows of scraggly red geraniums, his eyes roving over the numbers on the apartment doors until he found the door with a faded brass 7. The patch of dirt on either side of the door was jammed with a lush, over-flowing growth of multicolored lantana, dark purple daylilies, white cleome, and brilliant yellow europsis. Underneath was a tight blanket of vinca covered with tiny blue flowers. It was a postage-stamp garden that showed loving attention.

But Morris saw only the door of the ground-floor apartment. He shook his head in disapproval. The Roach knew better than to live in a ground-floor apartment.

Morris paused in front of the door. He looked around, pushed his sunglasses higher on his nose, and knocked. He stepped back.

When the door opened and a tall man appeared, Morris was struck by how much the Roach had aged in the past three years. Autumn was in his eyes and the white of winter in his hair. The skin around his eyes was wrinkled, and Morris realized it was more than age he saw. The man's eyes were those of an anchorite—the eyes of a man who has seen too much of the world and experienced too much pain and had withdrawn.

The man stepped outside and closed the door. For a moment his eyes brightened, and he almost smiled. But then, like a wise old dog, his eyes dulled and his face went flat.

"Major," he said casually. His voice was softer than Morris remembered.

Morris grinned and stuck out his hand. "Hello, Roach."

The two men shook hands and stared at each other. Then the tall man slowly shook his head. "Been a long time since anyone called me that."

"Yeah, well, maybe it's because you don't see your old friends anymore. We talk about you from time to time."

The man nodded but said nothing.

Morris paused, still putting off the reason for his visit. "How's the back?"

"Fine. No problems."

Morris rubbed his hands together. "Yeah? Good to hear that." He looked around as if searching for something to talk about. "You know I just got off. I'm working morning watch. Traffic out there is bump to bump. And vice versa."

Nigel smiled. He had forgotten how the major sometimes mauled his mother tongue. The major had moved upward through almost every office in the department and throughout his career his goal had been constant: to wrestle the English language into submission. He kept trying.

Some thought, usually to their regret, that because Norris Morris mangled his native tongue he was ... well, backward or even a bit of a clown. But Morris had risen to the rank of major, and that was no small accomplishment for a white police officer in an overwhelmingly black city government. He had done it by knowing and following every rule in the ever changing police bureaucracy; by being unswervingly loyal to his superiors and unswervingly demanding of his troops.

For a moment there was silence. Morris knew he had to get to the point. "Nigel, this is not a social call. The chief sent me." He looked at the door as if he wanted to go inside.

Nigel's eyes narrowed. In the decades they had known each other, Morris had never called him by name unless they were huddled over a beer at Manuel's Tavern. Nigel Trench, ever since he went to work in the sex crimes unit of the Atlanta Police Department some twenty-five years ago, had been known as the Roach. Morris had given him the nickname. It was not the sort of flattering or humorous nickname police officers usually give one another, and it did not have the good-natured edge to it that means only a cop's closest colleagues are allowed to use it. No, the Roach was a special nickname. To an outsider it sounded pejorative. But as used by Atlanta cops it had overtones of near reverence.

"I can't invite you in, Norris. Rachel is ..." His voice dribbled away.

Morris nodded. "How is she?"

Nigel shrugged. "Every week or so she comes home from the ... from the hospital for a day ... sometimes two days. The doctor doesn't like it, but I think being at home is good for her." He paused. "She's very fragile."

"I'm sorry."

Nigel waved a hand in dismissal. He looked over his shoulder at the door. "When she's here she wants me close by. I can stay only a minute."

"The chief sent me."

"You said that."

"Yeah, I did, didn't I?" Morris cleared his throat. "Nigel, we've got a serial rapist on the loose."

"All rapes, except date rapes, are committed by serial rapists. Some of the rapists happen to get caught early in their careers."

"Yeah. But I mean a real serial rapist."

Nigel stared at Morris for a long moment. "I'm no longer a police officer, Major." He reached for the doorknob.

"Just listen for a minute. This guy is different. He's a sicko. A pervert."

For a moment Nigel almost said that to so describe an offender is to bias one's self toward the offender. A serial rapist, by definition, is good at what he does. Otherwise he would be arrested after the first offense. Nigel shrugged and said, "Not interested."

"Nigel, hear me out."

Nigel's hand was still on the doorknob.

"Nigel, just listen a minute," Morris importuned. "Please." His voice had taken on a bit of an edge.

"How do you know it's not a series of rapes?"

"Same M.O."

"Any anal attacks?"

"No."

"Bondage?"

"No."

"Did the offender transport the victim?"

"No."

"Then he doesn't appear to be a sexual sadist." Nigel paused. "How many victims?"

"Three."

Nigel's eyebrows rose a fraction. "Over what time period?"

"About five weeks. The first one was in early May. The last two were close together. He's stepping up his pace."

"I haven't heard anything about this."

Morris shook his head from side to side. He wanted a cigarette, but he knew Nigel hated the smell. "This thing is like a snowball that rolled down the hill, gathered moss, and when it got to the bottom it was a big mushroom. We're sitting on it like you wouldn't believe. Even officers who have reporters as friends are not talking."

Nigel smiled. It was a tight, ironic smile. He had been through this before. "The great city of Atlanta still worried about its image, huh? It couldn't have anything to do with the Olympics, could it?"

Morris glared. "That's a low blow between the belt." He paused, shrugged, and added, "Well, that's part of it. Or vice versa."

"Part?"

"The victims are the same physical type, Nigel. He's targeting a certain type female."

Nigel paused. Something wasn't right. In the back of his mind he wondered why Morris continued to call him Nigel rather than by his nickname. Why was everything on a personal basis? What did Morris want? But what Morris was saying pushed the thoughts away. Rapists almost always targeted their victims by location rather than by physical type. "Hunting for a physical type takes a lot of time and effort. He must be finding them all at or near a certain location?"

Morris looked down at his shoes and nodded. "Emory University is the common element. That's his hunting ground. The victims were Emory students."

Nigel whipped his head toward Morris. "I read about only one. It was"—he paused and his eyes widened—"about five weeks ago. Right after graduation."

"That was the first one."

"Sarah hasn't called me about this."

"She doesn't know. The students only know of the first victim; the one attacked on campus. After that the perp began attacking students in their off-campus apartments. His M.O. began evolving. This boy's a work in progress."

Nigel stepped closer. His voice was a whisper. "Listen to me, Major. You people better do your jobs. If anything happens to my daughter, I'm coming after somebody."

Morris nodded. He had expected this. Sarah was an only child, and she was her father's daughter, especially since what had happened to Nigel's wife. The day Sarah won a full academic scholarship at Emory, Nigel had taken everyone on his shift to Manuel's Tavern for a roaring evening. It seemed like yesterday. And now she was a senior.

"What do you want, Major?"

"Help."

Nigel slowly shook his head. "I can't help you. Go talk to the people at Emory. Go talk to the DeKalb County P.D. Go talk to the parents of those girls." He looked away. "They are the ones who need help."

"I'm talking to you."

"Major, you know me and you know I don't do cover-ups. Emory is keeping quiet when three students have been raped. Three young girls. Emory wants the parents to think their kids are at Happy Valley. The parents are paying more than twenty thousand dollars a year for their kids to go there. For that amount of money, don't you think they deserve the truth?"

"Nigel, the first rape occurred on campus. The others have been off campus. One was in DeKalb County, and one was in Atlanta. The three kids dropped out of school. They had to. They were so traumatized and so brutalized they probably will never come back to school."

The pain on Nigel's face caused Morris to stop. He

bit his lip. "Nigel, I didn't want to be the one to come out here."

Nigel did not speak for a long moment. "What have you got? Obviously not enough to arrest anyone. Any leads?"

Morris shook his head. "Nothing. No blood. No semen. No physical evidence. No witnesses. It's all behavioral."

"Victims can't ID him?"

"He either wore a ski mask or covered the eyes of his victims. We know he's white. Young. Muscular. Educated. Savvy about investigative techniques. And mean as hell."

"You got nothing. Emory is not even in your jurisdiction. It's in DeKalb County. I'm asking you again, why are you here?"

Morris shifted his feet. His face tightened. "We got a task force working on this thing. Since I'm running Sex Crimes, the task force is under my command. I was sent here because I used to be your supervisor, because we were friends and because of some, uh, special aspects to this case. We need your help. . . ." His voice dwindled away. "It's more than the Olympics, Nigel. Give us a little credit."

Nigel's jaw jutted forward and his body tensed. When he spoke his voice was hardly more than a whisper. "I ought to knock you on your ass. You come out here knowing what happened to my wife, and you use my daughter as leverage to try to get me to do your work." He snorted in disgust. "Get away from my house . . . from my apartment, before I—"

"Nigel, after he rapes them, he combs their pubic hair."

A shadow flitted across Nigel's face. He took a deep

breath. "So you got a smart rapist. Your boy knows a little bit about forensics and doesn't want his pubic hair in the lab."

Morris continued in a flat, unemotional voice: "He's using a condom, Nigel. Either that or he makes his victims douche after he rapes them. If he uses a condom, he takes it with him."

Nigel closed his eyes.

"He wears rubber gloves, Nigel. Disposable latex gloves like doctors use."

Nigel was frozen.

"He makes them talk to him, Nigel. He makes them say things."

Nigel's shoulders slumped. "He's scripting," he whispered involuntarily.

"After he has sex with them, he beats them, Nigel. Viciously."

Nigel shook his head.

"He talks to them about God, Nigel. He knows the Bible."

"It's not him." Nigel's voice was pained.

"Why? Because I haven't mentioned bus stops?"

Nigel's last defense had been breached, and he could not speak.

"He's not going to bus stops the way he did before, Nigel. But we're certain it's the same guy. Same general physical description. And he can't change his signature. Sure, some rapists use a condom or make the victims douche. Some wear rubber gloves and some comb the pubic hair and beat the victims. Some might even talk to their victims about heaven and hell and about God. But all those things together? How many rapists are that smart and that mean? For God's sake, Nigel, do I have to say it?"

"No," Nigel whispered. "No. No." He shook his head. "You don't have to say it." He took a long, shuddering breath. "As my friend, Norris, is this righteous? Everything you've told me?"

"It's righteous."

Nigel's shoulders bent in pain, and when he spoke his voice was so soft that Morris could hardly hear him.

"He's back."

2

Nigel leaned against the brick wall and closed his eyes. When he spoke he had difficulty controlling his voice. "I know this individual. His demons are powerful. His level of violence is increasing with each victim, isn't it?"

"Yes," Morris said. "How do you know that?"

"If he isn't caught, he will begin killing his victims."

Morris smiled and shook his head. "He's a rapist. Don't get your eggs before the chicken, Nigel."

Nigel put his hands over his eyes. "You said that after the first victim, he changed his M.O., presumably to keep the word from getting out about what he was doing. Did he call the girls' parents and tell them where they could find their daughters?"

Morris nodded.

"And by the time the parents got to their daughters, found out what happened, took them to a doctor, and then called a police officer, it was hours later, maybe a day, maybe two days?"

Morris nodded again.

"By then the victims had taken showers and thrown out the clothing they were wearing when they were attacked?"

"Yes. In fact, one of the victims douched again after the perp made her douche. Both of them threw away

their night clothes. But it's more than that. The fathers
of the second and third victims wouldn't let an officer
interview their daughters."

"He asked the girls where they were from," Nigel
said. It was as if he were talking to himself. "Or he
knew in advance where they were from. He probably
knew in advance. After he assaulted the girls, he
called the parents and told them where they could find
their daughters. He has to relive the crime, Norris.
The victims' unconscious bodies were lying where he
could see them as he talked to the parents."

Nigel's voice became even softer. "People who commit sex crimes are different from criminals whose mo-
tivation is money. People who commit sex crimes seek
emotional satisfaction. They have a fantasy. You must
listen to the fantasy. You must try to understand what
they are saying to you. And you must understand that
no matter what they do to a victim, the experience is
never as good as the fantasy. So they keep going. On
and on and on. They have to. They never stop."

Nigel paused. "He's a planner. All he thinks about,
twenty-four hours a day, is the next victim. This is
what he does. Some men go to the neighborhood bar,
some play tennis, some have a little workroom in the
basement. This guy rapes. And after he rapes, when
the victims think the ordeal is over, when they think
the guy got what he came for, when they think he is
about to leave, he beats them."

Morris stared at him.

"Any of the victims from New York, Pennsylvania,
or New Jersey?" Nigel asked.

"Jesus, Joseph, Mary, and the donkey. How do you
know that?"

Nigel's voice was patient. "Major, my daughter goes

to Emory. I made it my business to know about the students. Many are from those states."

"One from Pennsylvania and one from New York." Morris paused. "You know, people up there don't think much of Atlanta police officers."

"The other victim, the first one, was closer."

Morris nodded. "South Carolina." The Roach had not lost his touch.

The years disappeared and the two men fell into a decades-old closeness, one that had begun when they were rookies chasing a rape suspect through an alley. Nigel jumped from a roof and got a compression fracture. Morris charged ahead and got a bullet in the side. The perpetrator got away.

"A four- or five-hour drive for the parents. Enough time for him in the beginning. Later, this individual needed more time. It took him longer to work on his fantasies. That's why the later victims were an airplane ride away, eight or ten hours, maybe a day."

Morris waited. When the Roach was rolling, it was a sight to behold.

"He's going to need even more time," Nigel said. "His needs will increase incrementally. He will stop calling the parents. Raping and beating will not be enough. He will kill. Probably by strangulation or stabbing. He's an up-close and personal kind of guy. When he kills he will realize why he has been unfulfilled all these years."

Morris paused. When he spoke it was in a slow and careful fashion. "Roach, I know what happened with Rachel. There's still an open file on that case. I remember how you work, and I don't want to pull the rug out in the middle of the stream, but how do you know this?"

"I don't."

"You don't? Then what the—?"

"Not in the way you mean. It's not written in stone. There is no formula, no checklist that I follow. We're dealing with human behavior, and there are countless variations of that behavior. In addition, an offender's behavior can change."

"So what makes you think it might go down this way?"

Nigel sighed. And then he spoke very slowly, as if trying for the first time to articulate primal feelings. "After Rachel went to the hospital ... I-I had a lot of time, Norris. I wanted to do two things. First, I wanted to try to make some—some sense out of what happened ... I had to understand what it meant."

He spread his hands wide as if in supplication.

Morris waited a long moment. When Nigel did not speak, he asked, "Do any good?"

"No."

"What was the second thing?"

"I studied this individual. I read everything from the DSM Four to the Bible. I read theology, angelology, and every other '-ology' I could find. Doctoral theses, abnormal psychology textbooks, I read them all. I wanted to learn all I could about the man who ... the man who attacked Rachel. Ever hear of Roy Hazelwood?"

Morris shook his head. "What's a DSM Four?"

"It's the bible for mental health professionals. Everything you would ever want to know about any sort of mental disorder."

Morris nodded. "So who is Hazelwood?"

"Former FBI guy. He was one of the first members of the Behavioral Science Unit. Expert on sexual violence. I read his articles and books. I talked to him. I even attended one of the classes he teaches."

Morris shook his head. His face shifted into a scowl. He sighed. "Roach, Roach, Roach. We been around long enough to know you can't get answers from the feds. I want to know what *you* think."

Nigel did not answer for a long moment. Then he said softly, "It's going to get worse."

Morris stuck his tongue in his cheek and pushed it around. The chief was not going to like this. He did not even want to think about how the mayor would react.

Nigel was caught between anger and anticipation and pain. The man who had changed his wife's life forever, the man who had changed his life forever, was back in Atlanta. This time he would catch the man. He knew that. But to do so he would have to go for a toboggan ride inside the skull of the rapist, and that would cause him the greatest pain he had ever known.

Nigel seized Morris's arm and squeezed.

"I'm going to catch him," he said.

Morris nodded. "I know you are. If he gets away this time, that will be the day God freezes over. I don't know where he's been for the past few years, but—"

"It hasn't been a *few* years, Norris." Nigel's eyes lasered into Morris, and his voice was harsh.

"What?"

"It has been three years and six days."

Morris nodded numbly. My God, he thought, The Roach knows how long it has been right to the day. I bet he knows the hours. He cleared his throat. "As I said, Roach, everything we have is behavioral. But it all checks out. It is enough. The same sexual aspects as seen by the victims, the same verbal behavior, the same physical force."

"Check VICAP. When this guy left Atlanta he went somewhere, and he didn't stop doing what he does."

"We already checked. Nothing."

Nigel nodded. The Violent Criminal Apprehension Program had never worked as it was designed to do. Primarily because many jurisdictions, particularly smaller ones, did not always enter information on violent perpetrators. He sighed and looked away as if in deep thought.

The attack on Rachel, her hospitalization and breakdown, came rushing back. Rachel had tried to be strong, God knows she tried. She even thought it was her fault that her car broke down that day and she had to go to a bus stop. She was raped and beaten and she couldn't cope and she was a cop's wife and she believed it was her fault. She spent a month in the hospital. She remembered nothing of her attacker. Pain and fear and shock and denial had blocked his face from her memory. It was her way of coping.

But when the nightmares began and she awakened screaming about a blond young man and what he did to her and what he said to her and what he made her do and say, the detectives knew her attacker had been blond. They also learned that he had peculiar eyes and an unusual body odor.

There were therapy sessions, but they were not enough and she entered a private mental institution. The insurance ran out and Nigel sold the house. Rachel was relieved. She never wanted to go there again. That was where it happened. The man forced her into his car and drove her to her house and raped her in the bed she and Nigel shared and he bathed in her shower and he made her douche and he watched her. He turned on the radio and the television, turned them up loud, and began beating her. He toyed with her, beating her in the kitchen, then letting her run into the dining room and beating her there and letting her run into the living room and beating her again. While she was half-conscious he roamed through the closets and found Nigel's police uniform and looked at the name tag. He came to her and said, "Well, Mrs. Police Officer Trench." He beat her again, and this time he did not let her run away.

Now when she spent an occasional night at the apartment, Nigel never knew how she would act. There were times when she was almost normal, when she could talk to her husband about how their life had once been. And there were times when she retreated into a psychic haven. There were times when she talked of the future and cried softly, times when she talked of her daughter and whimpered in fear. She lived on the edge. The blond man was only a nightmare away.

A sound or an odor or a color of clothing or a phrase of music on the radio or a floating image on television triggered the nightmare and caused every brittle moment of that day to come rushing back in a cascade of pain. The slightest push could send her into the darkness. And there was always the chance that she would find such comfort in the darkness that she might never return.

Morris interrupted Nigel's reverie. "You need to know everything that's going on. The chief in DeKalb County talked to his commissioners. Then he called my chief. Emory is involved. They all agreed that ju-

risdictions are not the most important thing right now.
In a few weeks somewhere around two million people
from all over the world are coming here for the Olympics. For fourteen days Atlanta will be the center of
the universe. And if the reporters who come here talk
about crime, they won't make a distinction between
DeKalb County and Atlanta. You can't throw stones
if you own a house. It's *all* Atlanta. That's why the
mayor wants this thing solved *quickly* and *quietly*."
Morris paused for emphasis. "The mayor talked to the
chief, and the chief asked for the name of the best
man to work the case. I said the best man no longer
worked for the department, that he had ... that he
had ..."

"Quit," Nigel said.

Morris nodded. "That he had quit. She had you in
mind even before she came to me. She wants you
back. I told her if we could get you, you would insist
on doing this your way. She agreed. On paper, you
report to me. My job is to get you anything you want.
DeKalb County will assist, and so will Emory."

"Why did DeKalb County agree to let APD work
this? You know how DeKalb is about other jurisdictions, especially Atlanta."

Morris shrugged. "DeKalb commissioners need tickets to Olympic events. Atlanta has the tickets."

Nigel raised his eyebrows.

"You're a consultant," Morris said. "You name
your fee. Emory pays it."

"That means Coca-Cola is paying," Nigel said. He
knew of the close connection between Emory University and Coca-Cola and the Sun Trust Bank—the business triumvirate that had run the city for decades. The

three were inseparable, the business equivalent of being joined at the hip.

He chewed this over for a minute. "The mayor is involved?"

Like most police officers, Nigel did not like Atlanta's mayor. The man was a former assistant U.S. attorney, an unctuous man who had far more concern for the rights of criminals than for the rights of victims. When he was elected, his first decision regarding the police department had been to dismantle the Red Dogs, the black-suited squad of officers that created hell and destruction by kicking in the doors of crack houses and knocking in the heads of crack dealers. The mayor was not concerned that the Dogs had demonstrably lowered the level of drug dealing in Atlanta; he was concerned that the Dogs were violating the rights of crack dealers. Within a few weeks large parts of Atlanta were taken over by crack users—rock stars, the cops called them—and by crack dealers, and the mayor was forced to bring back the Dogs. But the fact he had wanted to leash them was forever stuck in the craw of Atlanta cops.

"The chief didn't say so, but I got the idea the mayor signed off on every member of the task force. They came from all over. I got a few good people. Dr. Mengele is there from Sex Crimes. But most of them are as useless as tits on a horse."

Another reason many cops did not like the mayor was that he had taken over management of the police department; he had preempted control from the chief.

Morris paused. "I'll be straight with you, Roach. With the mayor, it's strictly the Olympics. He wants to be known as the man who was mayor during the Olympics, not as the man who was mayor during a

string of rapes. He doesn't know about your ... about
your past experience with the guy."

"Is the crime lab plugged into this thing?"

Morris nodded. "Yes. Ralph Stone, the guy who
does psychological profiles, and Liz Quarles, the serol-
ogist, will drop whatever they're doing to help. All
you have to do is call."

"Good. They're the best." Nigel looked away into
the middle distance. "The city wants to avoid a public
relations problem. Emory wants to avoid a public relations problem. But isn't anyone concerned about the
victims?"

Morris did not answer.

Nigel sighed. After a while he pointed at the geraniums along the sidewalk. "Getting ratty-looking, aren't
they?" He stared at the flowers. "It's the heat. In the
fall the manager will replace them. Probably with pansies. Pansies bloom through the winter and into the
spring. Did you know that?"

Morris shrugged. "Six of one and three dozen of
another if you ask me. Or vice versa."

"We call someone a pansy, and we mean he is weak
or effeminate. But pansies are one of the toughest
flowers you can plant. I'll take these geraniums out in
the fall and plant pansies. Very hardy." Nigel looked
at Morris. "You notice those things when you are
home all day."

"I guess so."

"When I sold the house to pay Rachel's medical
bills, it didn't bother me. I can live anywhere. All that
mattered was I had enough money to pay the bills.
But I didn't because the goddamn insurance company
wouldn't come through. Now I miss not having a

house. Not so much that particular house—just the idea of a house. I want to live in a house."

"You had a nice house, Nigel."

"Norris, I miss not having a lawn to mow." Nigel's voice was intense. He looked at the cracked sidewalks, the oil-stained parking lot, and the splotchy patches of brown grass.

"Nobody likes mowing the grass," Morris said. "Even people who work at landscape companies hate mowing the grass." He shrugged. "But every dog has his pony."

Nigel shook his head. He pointed at the flowers on either side of the door. "I miss it, Norris. I love to put my hands in the dirt. It ... it does something ... it's therapy ... I need it."

For a long moment neither man spoke.

"Rachel must not know about this, Norris. She must never know this individual is back and that he's working Emory. She must never know. She's not strong enough."

Morris nodded.

"She's been home two days, but this afternoon she goes back to the hospital. I visit her every day or so. She comes first. Anytime she needs me, I'll be there. I don't want anything said about it."

Morris nodded in agreement. "Like I told you, it's your case. The only thing the mayor asks is that the situation doesn't go public."

Nigel shook his head. "That's unrealistic."

"We have to try."

"The mayor second-guesses me one time and I walk."

Morris spread his hands wide. "It's your show."

"Set me up an office. Tomorrow at six a.m. I want

the crime scene video, the still pictures, all the reports, and all the transcribed interviews. Everything."

"I forgot how early you go to work."

Nigel continued as if he had not heard. "I want to see the crime scene at Emory."

"I'll call the director and tell him you're coming. The DeKalb chief says he's okay."

"I want to interview the victims. All of them. Especially the two who would not talk to you."

"I'll set it up."

"No, just get the numbers. I'll do it."

"Okay."

"Put some plainclothes people at Emory. Men and women. Young ones right out of the academy. Have them keep an eye on the students. Day and night. Cover the campus."

"Roach, that's going to take a hell of a lot of manpower. The type he prefers is . . ."

Nigel stared. "Yes?"

Morris had hoped to hold back on a few details until later. "Nigel, the three victims had black hair and olive complexions. There are a lot of students like that at Emory."

Nigel smiled. "Emory is in summer session, and not many students are there. You can do it."

Morris shrugged. "Okay." He paused. "You want them to . . . ?"

Nigel shook his head. "No. Nothing special for my daughter. I'll take care of that. The undercover people—" Nigel stopped and looked at Morris. "Sarah is the type of victim he favors." It was a flat statement.

Morris cleared his throat. "Yes."

Nigel stared at Morris. When he spoke his voice

was very soft. "Why didn't you call me at home weeks ago and tell me this?"

"Like I told you, we're sitting on this one." Morris shrugged. "I don't like everything I have to do on this job, Nigel."

Nigel clenched his fist. "I'll talk to my daughter," he said. "I'll have her move into the apartment."

"You need anything else?"

Nigel shook his head.

Morris was relieved. "See you in the morning."

Nigel looked at the door. "Rachel must be wondering what I'm doing."

Morris moved a few steps away and stopped. He grinned.

"What's the matter with you?" Nigel asked.

"I'm just thinking of what some of the guys will say when I tell them."

"Tell them what?"

"The Roach is back."

3

The task force squad room was filled with morning watch officers waiting for the end of the shift when Nigel walked in at 5:50 A.M. Uniformed officers from down the hall were talking over cases with detectives, and everyone was watching the clock. Another hour and the day watch officers would arrive. Then, after both shifts shared a half hour of coffee and insults, the morning watch troops would straggle out into the early morning heat and find their cars and drive home.

Conversations began to wind down when Nigel appeared in the doorway. The investigator, who was a legend among old-time detectives, stood there dressed in a navy suit and wearing a pair of black cap-toed shoes that had been polished until they looked like patent leather. His still damp white hair was neatly combed. He looked like someone's sad-faced uncle rather than a cop.

The bulletin board by the door caught his eye. He remembered the camaraderie of the squad room, and without thinking he moved a few steps and began reading. The first thing he saw was a newspaper clipping; a column written by the major's wife.

Major Morris had a bigger problem with his wife than he had with his mother tongue. Marie Morris had gone to law school at night and then became a public defender. Norris Morris thought being a public defender was the worst thing she could do—that is, until she went to work for the ACLU. Nothing was lower than an ACLU lawyer. Then she began writing op-ed columns for *The Atlanta Constitution*. It was a time when the *Constitution* was trying to showcase women writers and to open up the pages to more voices from the community. The editors loved Marie Morris and ran everything she wrote, sometimes two columns a week.

After the first Emory student was attacked, Major Morris had told a newspaper reporter, "When we find out why the perpetrator raped the victim, then we'll have a motive." Whereupon his wife wrote a column saying her husband needed a course in remedial English plus at least two weeks of sensitivity training. When the clipping appeared on the bulletin board, he appended a note saying, "I'd divorce the bitch if she wasn't so good in bed."

The silence in the squad room caused by Nigel's presence prompted Major Morris to emerge from his office. He was wearing his uniform. His white shirt was starched, and the gold oak leaves on his shoulder glistened. His hands were on his hips, and his cheeks were stretched in a fierce glower. A squad room filled with police officers is like a schoolroom filled with second-graders: silence is not good. Morris's face was wreathed in cigarette smoke. "I can count the reasons on ten toes why this place is quiet, and I don't like any of them. Or vice versa."

"The toes or the reasons?" asked Dr. Mengele. Dr. Mengele, whose real name was Herman Manhold, was the grandson of a German soldier who had served in World War II. When Herman's sister married an American, he came to the States and became a cop. With his stereotypical attention to detail and devotion to following orders, he became an outstanding investigator. His problem was a propensity for giving stiff-armed Nazi salutes and muttering "Sieg heil."

Major Morris ignored him and looked at the next desk, where the Undertaker sat. The Undertaker was in his late forties and was one of the few skinny cops in Atlanta. He was cadaverous. He was called the Undertaker because when his wife died five years ago, he had her cremated and never could decide what to do with the ashes. The urn sat atop his desk. When he went on a call, he took it with him and locked it in the car. At night the urn went home with him. The Undertaker was thorough at preparing cases, and he wrote excellent reports. His problem as a cop was that he could not interrogate suspects. The moment a suspect denied being involved in a crime—and most of them did—the Undertaker was unable to press forward.

Popcorn, an alcoholic at thirty-five, looked at Morris through bleary eyes. His black-rimmed glasses rested halfway down a nose etched like a Calcutta street map. "I'm off the sauce. Dry as a popcorn fart," he announced at least once a week. He thought no one knew about the bottle he kept in the space above the ceiling tiles.

Maggot was the only woman on the task force. Her name was Rita Durian, but even the name plate on her desk said "Maggot." She had come over from Sex Crimes and was a slender woman of thirty-six who weighed about a hundred and twenty pounds. She carried the biggest pistol of anyone on the task force, a

10mm that she wore in a shoulder holster. Unlike other officers, who put their weapons in their desk when they were in the office, she wore her 10mm all the time. She had a loud voice and was second only to Maytag in the harshness of her judgment of rape victims.

Maytag was a special case. He got his name because he was a perpetual agitator; he was always stirring a bucket of crap. He stood about five feet six, had a red, pockmarked face, and long blond hair that indicated he had transferred either from dope or Vice. It was Vice. He had worked there since he graduated from the academy four years earlier. Usually a certain camaraderie exists between prostitutes and the recognizable members of the vice squad. But even easygoing prostitutes disliked Maytag. On his desk was a small statue of a monk. When the top of the monk's head was twisted, an erect penis poked from beneath the robes. And on the wall behind his desk was a pair of black panties, a black bra, and a sign that said, "No pain. No gain."

Not many people are perfect, but Maytag was a perfect asshole.

"Major, we got a visitor," Maytag said.

Morris reluctantly looked at Maytag. The young detective raised a forefinger and pointed toward the door.

Morris turned and his eyes lit up. He waved, stubbed out his cigarette, and walked across the room. "Roach, glad you're here. Everything's ready."

"Morning Major."

"Hey, see you're reading one of Marie's columns. The woman couldn't write a laundry list." He looked Nigel up and down. "You're looking great, Roach.

Just like the old days." He pointed down the hall. "Come on. I'll show you your office."

The two men walked down the hall, and Morris ushered Nigel into a small office. "I have your badge and ID," he said. "We used your old photo for the ID card so you wouldn't have to wait. You can pick them up when you leave." He pointed at the desk. Three case files were lined up on the desk and surrounded by records and papers. "Everything you wanted."

"Thanks, Major."

Nigel took off his coat, hung it on the back of a chair, and stared at the desk. It had been more than three years—a lifetime. He sat down and stared for a long moment at the three folders. He swallowed, opened the first folder, and began reading.

As Morris returned to the squad room, Maytag was thumbing through photos of nude victims in old rape cases and talking, as if to himself. "So that's the famous Roach." His voice indicated he was not impressed.

"Don't you be a smartass where the Roach is concerned," Morris said. "I won't stand for it. The Roach was making felony busts when you were still crapping in your diapers."

Dr. Mengele nodded. "I worked the case involving his wife, and I can tell you that is one impressive woman."

Maytag snorted. "So what'd she do? Squeal extra loud?"

Morris shook his head in disgust and waved a finger at Dr. Mengele. "Don't talk to him about that."

"Excuse me, Major. But Maytag needs to know he is full of shit." Dr. Mengele turned to Maytag. "Listen,

Detective," he said. "After the offender raped her, he forced her to climb into the tub and douche. Rather than flushing out the fluids, she let them drain back into the douche bag. The perpetrator's semen was diluted, but we managed to get a good DNA. How many woman would be that smart and that much on top of the situation?"

"All that mechanical stuff would impress a kraut. But, hey, I thought the perp was on top." He waved a picture of a nude victim.

Dr. Mengele turned away.

"So you got a DNA," Maytag said. "Big hairy deal. Because unless you got somebody to match it with, all you got is a bunch of numbers."

"That might be the only thing you said today that makes any sense," Morris said. "But you know whose fault that is? The General Assembly. Because of the case involving Roach's wife, the Atlanta Police Department asked a local legislator to introduce a bill to create a DNA data bank. Any convicted sex offender would have to give a blood sample before he is released from prison. When those guys get out, most of them are gonna do it again. And if we had their DNA on file, we could nail their asses and send them away forever."

"So what happened?" Maytag said.

"The goddamn defense lawyers who are legislators, that's what happened. They changed the bill to affect only child molesters. And then they withheld financing for that. Our legislators are in favor of fucker butts and rapists and child molesters. Half the legislators are fucker butts themselves. When the legislature comes to town, you better put one hand over your eyes and one hand over your asshole."

For a moment there was silence in the squad room. Then the officers broke out in applause. It was the longest speech they had ever heard from Morris. And most of it made sense.

But Maytag shook his head. He threw his arms wide. "So maybe she did a good deed for herself by playing with her douche bag. What's that got to do with the Roach? He's an old man."

"Maytag, I'm trying to be patient, but you don't understand about something," Morris said. He pointed down the hall. "The Roach is doing what he was put on earth to do. He is not only the best man for his job, he is the only one. I've seen him cry when he interviews victims."

"I can do that," Maytag said. He sounded aggrieved. "It really gets to 'em."

"Sieg heil," Dr. Mengele said.

"Yeah, but you don't give a damn about the victim," Morris said. "The Roach is on a different plane. He's got ideas he ain't even thought of."

"Musta been a rapist in a former life," Maytag said.

Morris looked at the ceiling. "God. Help me not to kill him."

Maytag grinned. "So somebody tell me. What does the mighty Roach man do on his off-duty time?" He looked around the squad room.

"That's enough," Morris said. "I didn't want you over here. Nobody else wanted you, either. They ordered me to take you on the task force because you're a little fuck. But lemme tell you something. The streets of this town are littered with the bones of young police officers who thought they could fuck with me. Some of you people are like goddamn Yankee tourists; you think because somebody talks funny that they're stupid. Well, mister, I'm a walking, fucking supervisor, and I will do what I gotta do. You better not forget that."

He turned to leave. Then he spun back and raised a finger. "The Roach and I are the same age. You think I'm an old guy?"

Maytag held up his hands to mollify the major. "No, sir. Didn't mean to say that." He smiled. "Hey, I'm happy wherever I go. Okay?"

Morris stared at the young officer for a moment. He nodded abruptly and was again turning to leave when Maytag spoke.

"Major, let me ask one more question. Why do you call him the Roach?"

Morris smiled, walked to Maytag's desk, leaned over, and with a bony, authoritarian finger he poked the officer in the chest. "Because he understands the night creatures."

Except for the case file of the rape on the Emory campus, the folders on Nigel's desk were slim and contained little more than the name and age of the victim, a picture, and a brief physical description. Victoria Kennedy had been the first victim, Jan Archangeli the second and Monaco Jackson the third. Nigel made a note to ask Emory for additional information on the students.

Nigel picked up Victoria Kennedy's file and began going through it again. He had looked at an inventory of material taken from her room, photographs, a lab report regarding the sheets and towels and washcloths, and an analysis of the contents of the sink and shower drains. Nothing. The victim's photograph showed dark eyes and short hair, an exotic face that needed no makeup.

Victoria Kennedy was a black student, but she was of such a light complexion and such sharp features that she looked Spanish. She was a beautiful young woman with a direct, almost challenging gaze. Nigel leaned closer, staring at her eyes, searching for information—victimology, he called it. A prostitute, a night clerk at a convenience store, or a waitress at an all-night diner are high on the victimology scale. College students are low on the scale, as there is little in their habits or lifestyle to put them in harm's way. Their friends are other students. Their professors are concerned about publishing and tenure and other cosmic subjects—sometimes even with teaching.

Nigel continued staring at the photograph. What was in her eyes? Defiance? Insecurity? Both? She was a freshman, eighteen years old, and at the time of the attack had lived in Calhoun Hall. Her room had been located two doors down the hall from the rear entrance of the dorm. She said she had been out the evening of the attack and had "a few drinks" at P.J. Haley's, a nearby bar known among underage fraternity boys as a great hangout.

Nigel shrugged. One of the first accoutrements acquired by a college freshman was a driver's license showing the holder to be twenty-one. As for "a few drinks," Nigel suspected it was far more. College students drink only to get drunk. Moderation is not in their vocabulary. Had she really been in a bar? Could it have been a fraternity house? He made a note in his leather-bound legal pad.

The girl's statement was brief. She had been awakened in the middle of the night—she didn't know the time—when a hand clamped over her mouth and a voice whispered in her ear. The man pressed something cold to her cheek and said it was a knife. It was dark and the shades were drawn, and all she could see was a shadow. She said the man was clean and smelled of soap.

"He said he didn't want to hurt me, but he would if I made a noise," the statement said. "He told me to be quiet and he would leave in a few minutes. He told me he was there to give me what I wanted, and when I said the only thing I wanted was for him to leave he laughed. He said he knew I wanted him to make love to me, and he asked me if I had a douche bag and when I said no, he said he would use a condom. He took off my nightgown and made me have sex with him."

The statement said that after a while the man stopped, pulled a pillow case over her head, and told her that he would not hurt her unless she pulled the pillow case up and saw him. She heard a click and realized the lamp on her desk was on, and then she heard the rustle of coat hangers and knew her closet door had been opened. "He came back to the bed and told me to remain quiet and not to remove the pillow case. He went back to the closet. I don't know what he was looking for. Then he made me have sex with him again. He told me to put my arms and legs around him and to act as if I was enjoying it. He made me tell him that I loved him."

Afterward, the attacker removed the pillow case and she saw him. He was wearing a black ski mask, latex gloves, and a condom. The knife was in his right hand. He held her arm tightly and said he would not hurt her unless she made a noise. Again, he pressed the knife against her cheek. "He told me I was pretty and it would be a shame if he had to cut my face," the statement said.

He picked up a comb from her dresser and walked her into the bathroom. Nigel paused. He remembered that when his daughter was a freshman, she had been in a dorm with bathrooms at the end of the hall. He wondered how many dorms had individual bathrooms. How did a freshman get a single room with an attached bath? He made another note and returned to the report.

The perpetrator made the student stand by the sink. "He leaned over the toilet, took off his condom, and wrapped it in a towel," the statement said.

She thought the man was a few years older than she, perhaps twenty-five. He was very muscular. He turned on the shower and pushed her under the water until she was soaked. Then he turned off the shower and washed her, using a lot of soap and paying particular attention to her pubic area.

He turned on the shower again, making sure his head remained clear of the water, and washed his body and watched as she rinsed off. Then he turned off the shower and made sure the drain at the bottom was clear. He kneeled in front of her and slowly combed her pubic hair. He pulled hair from the comb, dropped it into the commode, and flushed it.

He marched her back to the bed. "I don't want to gag you, but you can't make any noise when I leave," he told her.

"I told him I would be quiet," the statement said. "I asked him if I could get dressed and he told me no. Then I said, 'It's over. You got what you wanted. Now please get out of my room.' He smiled at me in

a funny way and said, 'It's not over. It's only beginning.' He turned off the light and raised the shade and
made me stand in the window with him. He just made
me stand there in the open window. Several cars went
by. We saw three students. They walked only a few
feet away but did not see us. He talked for a long
time about heaven and hell. He asked me if I believed
in God and if I had been saved. 'We must bend to
God's will,' he told me several times. I don't remember exactly what else he said. I was too scared. He
just talked about God. Then he dressed. He went to
the bathroom and picked up the towel with the condom and put it in a little bag he was carrying. It was
like a tool bag. It was black. he put it by the door
and left the bag open and then he said he was going
to take off his ski mask and leave, but that first I
would have to put on the pillow slip. He said he would
be outside the door listening for a moment, and if he
heard a sound he would use the knife on me.''

The attacker asked her what she would do when
he left.

"I told him I would take another shower and call a
doctor. He asked me if he had hurt me, and I told
him yes. He said he thought I would call the police
as soon as he left but that it didn't matter because the
police would never catch him. He said the police were
dumb. He told me to be quiet and not to move for five
minutes, and then I could do whatever I wanted to.''

Nigel stopped for a moment. Even though he had
read the statement several times, he sighed at what
was coming.

"I wanted to put on some clothes, but he wouldn't
let me. He kissed me. He still had on the ski mask.
He made me put my arms around his neck. I had to

tell him again that I loved him and that he had given me the best sex I would ever have. He made me say, 'I'll miss you. Please call me again.''

Nigel gritted his teeth and pressed on.

"Then he turned off the light. He pulled the pillow slip over my head and made sure it was down over my shoulders so I couldn't see. I heard him moving around his bag and thought he was about to leave. Then I heard several clicks and there was music. He had a CD player or tape deck. He was playing classical music. Suddenly he hit me very hard. He hit me in the stomach. He hit my breasts. I would have fallen, but he held me up with one hand and hit me with the other. I tried to scream, but I couldn't. Each time I opened my mouth to scream, he hit me in the stomach again. I passed out. When I awakened it was almost daylight. I called the Emory police and told them I had been raped and beaten up and that I was in a lot of pain. I asked them to send a doctor to my room. But they sent a policewoman, and she took me to the hospital.''

Nigel put down the file and shut his eyes. After a moment he picked up the second file, opened it, and looked at the photograph.

Jan Archangeli wore a Duke University sweatshirt. Nigel sighed. Emory students were said to have the highest SATs relative to their GPAs of any students in the country—relatively bright but somewhat lazy students who, almost to a person, had applied to Duke or Vanderbilt or Harvard or Yale or Princeton before being accepted at Emory.

Jan Archangeli, twenty, a junior from Sewickley, Pennsylvania, had been attacked off campus in her apartment. The offender had called her parents and said their daughter was ill and that they should fly down to Atlanta. He recommended Delta over USAir and even gave them the flight schedule. He sounded like a friend calling on her behalf.

The third girl, Monaco Jackson, also twenty and also a junior, was from Manhattan. She was still hospitalized with a broken leg and cracked ribs. She had told her father a story that he relayed to the police, a story similar to that of Victoria Kennedy's. Nigel knew that one man was the perpetrator in all three cases.

He knew because even though the records of each case were sparse, those records shouted out to him.

He knew because for three years and seven days he had lived with the results of the man's work.

He closed the files and picked up the videotape of the crime scene from the first assault. Like most crime scene videotapes, it was useless for anything but background information. The commentary by a DeKalb officer was erratic and of poor quality. There was far too much extraneous noise—police radios, horns, the sound of traffic, numerous pieces of conversation, and various opinions from officers. Toward the end of the tape the DeKalb County chief wandered onto the scene, picked up a picture of the victim, and studied it closely. She was wearing a bathing suit and was posing on a beach somewhere. The chief shook his head and said, "Would you look at the knockers on this kid?" The tape could never be introduced as evidence in a court of law.

Nigel pushed the tape aside. He looked at his watch, stood up, and grabbed his coat. He walked down the hall.

Maytag was waving another picture. He showed it to Maggot. "This one gave the perp a blow job."

Maggot laughed. "Was it a good one?"

It did not register with Nigel that he was the reason the squad room was crowded. Ordinarily the morning watch officers would have gone. But today the Roach was there, and they wanted to see what was going to happen. The heavy-eyed morning watch officers lingered over their coffee. Everyone watched Nigel cross the room toward Major Morris's office.

He opened the door and stepped into a room filled with cigarette smoke. He blew out his breath in disgust, then picked up a badge and his police identification. He backed up a step. "Major, your cigarettes are going to kill us all."

"You got to die of something." Morris handed him a pager. "Here, take this, too. We need to keep in touch with you." Morris paused. "Need anything else?"

Nigel looked at the pager, then snugged it over his belt. "Yes. Would you call the uniformed division, everyone on the task force, plus Homicide and the medical examiner's office. Do it now and back it up with a fax for the record. I'm to be notified immediately of any rape, attempted rape, missing-person case, suspected kidnapping, or any assault or homicide involving a young woman. The crime scene is to be locked down until I get there. I get the crime scene first. Before Sex Crimes. Before Homicide. No one questions a victim except me."

Morris looked as if he were in pain. "Roach, Homicide won't buy that. Maybe you can work with them. At the same time. Or vice versa."

Nigel looked at Morris.

"Okay, I'll call the chief."

"One other thing."

"Yeah?"

"That officer with the big mouth. The one who was talking about a blow job."

"Maytag. The little shit."

"Would you tell him the proper terminology, the only acceptable terminology, is fellatio?"

"Roach, it's the squad room."

"All the more reason to be professional. And that stuff on his desk and the wall behind his desk have to come down. What if a victim was brought here for an interview and saw that? I won't have it. If he's working for me on the task force, either he gets professional or he gets out."

Morris stared at Nigel. His cheeks rolled and twisted, showing an emotion somewhere between impatience and anger. He took a deep puff off his cigarette. "Roach, you haven't changed. You're still crossing your bridges before you burn them."

"This is non-negotiable."

Morris waved his hands in a placating gesture. "Okay. Okay. I'll make it happen."

"I'm going to Emory," Nigel said.

Morris followed him to the squad room.

At the door, Nigel turned. "See you later, Major."

"Keep in touch."

Nigel folded his coat over his arm and walked out the door.

"Well, I see the famous Mr. Roach doesn't carry a weapon," Maytag said.

"Andy Griffith didn't wear a gun," the Undertaker said.

"Yeah, but that was Mayberry. This is Atlanta."

"What is Mayberry?" Dr. Mengele asked.

"He's a self-confident guy," Morris said, staring at the door. He looked at his watch. "Well, the old lady has gone to work by now and is writing some of her left-wing crap. After I make a few quick phone calls and send those faxes for the Roach, I can go home. It takes two to play tango."

Maytag smirked.

Morris pointed at him. "You. You got all the earmarks of an eyesore. Clean that . . . that thing off your desk and take that shit off the wall. This is a professional operation."

Dr. Mengele laughed. "Sieg heil."

Maytag bowed up like a rooster. "It's been here ever since I got here." He looked at the door through which Nigel had gone. "Whose idea is this?"

"I run this office, dammit. If I'm lying, I'm standing here."

4

Nigel drove through the main gate of Emory University and made a quick left into the visitors' parking lot. He looked at the parking booth and shook his head. The thing never ceased to amaze him. It was covered with marble and must have cost as much as a three-bedroom house. Oh, well, that was Emory. The university that Coca-Cola built.

Nigel drove behind the Boisfeuillet Jones Building—the one students called the Buffalo Jones—and parked his five-year-old white Ford halfway down the hill. This part of the campus had been a dense pine grove until a few years ago when the president—who was called "the builder pharaoh" because he built something on every available piece of dirt—cut down the trees and paved the hillside. Nigel walked up the hill and crossed the street toward the white marble Administration Building. Rather than climbing the steps and entering the front door, he walked to the left and entered at the end of the building on the ground floor. Two doors down the hall on the right was the Emory Police Department. Or where the Emory Police Department was supposed to be. A secretary saw his expression, figured he was a police officer, and said, "Are you looking for Director Medlin?" She directed him to the new North Decatur Building several blocks away. Nigel sighed. Another new building. He decided to walk across campus rather than give up his parking space. Five minutes later, he was in the basement of the new building.

"Nigel Trench with APD to see Director Medlin," he told the blond secretary.

"He said send you in as soon as you got here," she said, pointing at an open door. Nigel crossed the office, turned right, and was met by a big man whose boyish smile cut through a thick beard. The man was wearing a white shirt, red tie, pinstripe suit, and polished black wing tips.

Nigel stuck out his hand. "Nigel Trench. APD."

"Ed Medlin. Come in, Officer." The Emory chief closed the door. "Do I call you officer or detective?"

Nigel laughed. "I'm not sure what my category is. Call me Nigel."

"Okay, Nigel. I'm Ed."

Medlin closed the door and walked to his desk. Nigel looked at the office. A Picasso print on one wall. Another wall with floor-to-ceiling books—all appearing to be well read and on topics ranging from identification of weapons to search and seizure to philosophy. Part of one bookcase was a cabinet with locked doors. Weapons stored there. A computer sat on Medlin's desk and another on the credenza.

"I was glad to hear you were coming over," Medlin said. "We will cooperate with you in every way. In fact . . ." He paused. "We have a student who may be missing, and I'm afraid she could be another victim of this fellow we're looking for."

Nigel was about to sit down. He paused in midair

and stared at Medlin. His stomach roiled and he felt a flash of nausea. He had not known it would be so soon. The husband in him, the father in him, spoke calmly and told him a girl who was a college student was missing and she could be away for a dozen reasons. The long-time police officer in him screamed that this was another victim.

The police officer won. Nigel knew the offender had struck again.

He knew.

Nigel sat down. When he spoke his voice was calm. "How long has she been missing?"

"About two weeks. Her parents called from New Jersey last night. I sent an officer to her apartment. It is obvious no one has been there in some time. And she hasn't attended class in two weeks."

Nigel waited. Medlin knew what was on his mind.

"Nigel, you have a daughter here, so you must accept what I'm about to say as an academic observation. It is background information from one police officer to another. Then I'll tell you more about the missing student."

Nigel nodded. Medlin knew his daughter was an Emory student. Score one for Medlin.

Medlin pursed his lips, laced his fingers together atop the desk, and leaned forward. "First, I have thirty-seven sworn officers, including five detectives. One of my sergeants has written more than a hundred articles for law enforcement journals. Another has a Ph.D. from Emory and was a college professor. One-third of my officers are certified as instructors. My officers get five times as much annual training as the state requires—about a hundred hours. When we do building-entry exercises, we use live ammunition. Last

year we had three job openings. I got more than two
hundred applications."

"You are not a rent-a-cop operation."

Medlin nodded. "We are the best-qualified police
force in this state."

"Okay."

"Now, having said that, I'll tell you this university
is a petri dish for crime. In that respect it is no
different from most other universities. The academic
community is self-centered, impractical, and trusting. Our students are at an age when they consider
themselves immortal when, in fact, they are walking
security risks. They think the campus is an extension
of their yard at home. They come on campus thinking we're all going to school together, we're all in
the same place, we're all family. They are too young
and too trusting. Our dormitories are coed, and coed
dorms drastically degrade the level of campus security because no longer is the presence of a man in
a woman's dorm room unusual. Plagiarism used to
be the worst crime on a campus. No more. We are
a little city-state, and we have the same crimes as
the real world."

"Aren't the dormitories locked?"

Medlin ruefully shook his head. "You could walk
around campus now or at midnight, and you would
find almost every door is propped open, wedged open,
or unlocked. If by some chance it was locked and if
you were younger, you could easily find a student who
would open it for you."

"What about roommates? Don't the students look
out for each other? And don't the professors know
when a student is not in class?"

"Many Emory students come from relatively

wealthy homes. They have lots of money and lots of hormones—a powerful combination—and they keep a dorm room in name only. Many of them live off campus with a boyfriend or a girlfriend. Those students check the answering machine in their dorm room in case their parents call, but they might go for weeks without spending a night in the room. As for class, the reality is that some of then often skip class, especially freshmen and sophomores. And students are always leaving the university. They flunk out, drop out, become homesick, have relationship problems, family problems, you name it. Oftentimes they leave quickly and their classmates rarely know the reasons. Professors think of absenteeism in terms of academics, not in terms of safety." He shook his head. "No, it is not at all unusual for students to leave unexpectedly."

"When there is an incident, like the first student who was attacked, don't other students become concerned? Aren't they more aware?"

"Maybe for a few days. But the reality is that in the dorms, particularly freshmen and sophomore dorms, many students are drunk almost every night. If something happens and one of my officers questions a student, the student's point of reference is whether the event happened before or after he vomited."

Nigel shook his head. "It's been a long time. I'd forgotten."

"My jurisdiction extends five hundred yards beyond the limits of the campus. That covers some of the apartments where students live. But if something happens in one of those apartments, the nine-one-one call goes to DeKalb P.D., not to the university. If the student lives in Atlanta, as did one of the victims, the call goes to APD."

Nigel nodded. "Those crimes are not reflected in crime reports for Emory? They are listed in DeKalb or Atlanta?"

"You got it. Not all of Ted Bundy's victims were in sorority houses. Danny Rolling killed five students at the University of Florida, all of them off-campus in their apartments. Those homicides are not listed on university crime reports."

"We wouldn't want the parents to think the university has a crime problem."

"Does APD file reports on incidents in DeKalb County or anywhere else outside its jurisdiction?"

Nigel nodded. "Point taken. But I think it's different when the victim is a student. However, that's another issue. Tell me about the student who has been missing for two weeks, and then I want to talk with you about the one who was attacked on campus."

Medlin picked up a folder on his desk and passed it across the desk to Nigel. "The university attorney said I could give you any information we have about any students involved in these incidents. We don't usually do that, even for law enforcement agencies. Privacy laws."

Nigel opened the folder and began reading. "Thank you."

Medlin studied Nigel for a moment. "I have to ask you something else. How is it that a retired APD officer is the lead investigator on this case? How did you get DeKalb to agree to that?"

Nigel shrugged and continued to read. "I didn't," he murmured. "I told the chief's representative how I worked. He agreed." Nigel tapped the folder. "Kathleen Powers. Eighteen. Freshman from Trenton, New Jersey."

His eyes widened as he flipped a page and saw the student's photograph. The resemblance to his daughter was startling. "My major would say she fits the profile."

Medlin nodded. "That's why I think she may be a victim. All the problems I just mentioned to you are compounded during the two summer sessions. No one knows anyone else. The sessions are brief. Students from other campuses are here. Freshmen who want to start college early are here. And those freshmen who arrive early will not go to freshman orientation or the freshman seminar until September. The campus is very quiet. Even lonely. Frankly, we might not have missed Kathleen Powers for another week or so if her parents had not called."

"Refresh my memory. What is freshman seminar?"

"Professors and upperclassmen sit down with the freshmen, tell them about the college and what to be careful of when they go off campus. It's a way to help kids adjust to life at a big urban university."

Nigel nodded. He closed the folder. "Not much here."

"You won't find anything but good news in a student's application."

"Calls on her answering machine?"

"Nothing except a half-dozen calls from her parents."

"Anything else?"

"No. Her parents are on the way down. Do you want to see the room?"

"Have your men examined it?"

"My *officers* examined it," Medlin corrected with a smile. "The lead detective on the case is a woman."

Nigel nodded but said nothing.

"We found the usual things you find in an Emory student's room. Stereo, computer, TV, VCR, photographs, videotapes ... you get the idea. We inventoried everything. DeKalb County also examined it."

Nigel paused. His daughter had none of those things. "Find anything?"

"Nothing."

Nigel nodded as if he expected this. "I'd like to see the report. But I don't think the crime took place there. He's started taking his victims someplace, his house, a special place, a slave chamber. I'll alert the task force and Missing Persons. We'll keep it low-ley."

Medlin was aghast. "A slave chamber?"

Nigel nodded. "Ed, we have to catch this guy. And soon."

"You think this potential victim is more than an assault?"

"She's been gone two weeks."

For a moment neither man spoke.

"Let's go back to the first victim, the student who was attacked here on campus. I've seen the reports. What else can you tell me?"

Medlin smiled. "Usually, if a student has been on campus during the summer for several weeks, she has met only a few people and her professors do not know her well enough to remember much about her. But Angel was different."

"Angel?" Nigel's brow wrinkled. "I thought her name was Victoria."

"Victoria Kennedy. You're right. But she told everyone to call her Angel. She said her daddy gave her that nickname. She came in here, met my officers, and told them she was in a dorm with only a few other students. She said she knew she would be okay, but she asked them to look in on her from time to time. She has a smile that will light up a room. One of those young people everyone likes."

"Why was she in a dorm with so few people?"

"She came on campus early. I think it was the day after graduation, so all the students from last semester were still here. That's an old dorm; it's not air-conditioned. It's all we had at the time. We wanted her to wait a week until the first summer session started. But she was adamant about coming early."

"Why did you let her do that?"

"Her father is a prominent lawyer in Columbia, South Carolina. An alumnus. A *contributing* alumnus. He and his wife were traveling in Europe, and we made a concession for her."

"She didn't have a roommate?"

"No. We planned to move her when the summer session started. She would have had a roommate then. But she liked having a single room and decided to stay there."

"How many other students are in that dorm?"

Medlin wrinkled his brow. "Not many. Calhoun Hall is not air-conditioned. I think six students were there at the time. Most of them were graduate students who, like Angel, came on campus early."

Nigel stared at the wall. "I'd like to see the room."

Medlin reached into his desk and pulled out a key. He looked at the tag attached to the key. "I'll have one of my officers unlock it for you."

"I know the campus. I'd prefer to do it by myself."

"You can. One of my officers will unlock the dorm and the room and leave you alone."

Nigel reached across the desk and shook hands with Medlin. "Thank for your help. I'll be in touch."

"Good to meet you." Medlin nodded. "Before you leave, may I say something?" He paused, weighing Nigel with his eyes, wondering how far he could go with this officer who had come out of retirement to work the case. The bow wave of political influence spreading from this officer was unprecedented. Even federal agents who came to the campus were not allowed to see students' records. Yet despite the obvious political power behind this man, he seemed focused only on his work.

"Yes."

"I think we should go public with these cases."

Nigel did not respond.

"It has never been my policy, and it has never been the policy of this university, to hide this sort of information from the community. But the word came down from somewhere—I don't know where—that these are DeKalb cases or Atlanta cases and that we would compromise the investigation if we issued a news release." He stopped and stared at Nigel. "That's nonsense, and you and I both know it."

Nigel said nothing.

"I think political decisions are taking precedence over the welfare of students," Medlin continued. "I don't like that."

Finally Nigel spoke. "Neither do I, Ed. Neither do I."

Medlin followed Nigel to the door. His eyes followed Nigel and an Emory officer down the hall. Then he turned to his secretary and said, "Call the registrar's office. Get me every file the university has on a student named Sarah Trench."

"Wear your badge," the Emory cop told Nigel. "Otherwise you might get reported as a suspicious person."

Nigel opened the new leather case and stuck it into his coat pocket so his badge dangled from the pocket.

"I'll unlock the back door and the room," the Emory officer said. "When you leave, turn the latch."

Nigel nodded. The officer walked away, and Nigel stood on the curb looking at Calhoun Hall. It was across the street from the railroad track on the edge of the campus. Most freshmen dorms were more centrally located, closer to the Dobbs University Center— the building students referred to as the "DUC"—and to the cafeterias and library and classroom buildings. Calhoun was remote.

Nigel continued studying the building. Anytime there is a serial rapist or a serial murderer, the first crime scene is of crucial importance—in many ways far more important than subsequent crime scenes. When committing the first attack, the perpetrator is more nervous or frightened than in following attacks. He often reveals more of himself than he does later when he becomes more confident and more skilled.

Okay, Nigel mused, *you're a good rapist, so you have to be a good burglar. I know you left by the door, but my guess is that you came into the dormitory the way a burglar would. I don't believe you picked your first victim at random. You don't do anything at random.*

Nigel made a note on his legal pad. He crossed the street and slowly walked around to the rear of the building. A yard of shimmering green grass and the parking lot for the medical school separated Calhoun from other buildings on two sides. How did Emory manage always to have green grass—even during a blistering early summer—when everyone else had lawns of mottled brown?

The physical plant and deserted train depot across the street added to the remoteness. Even though the dormitory was not the most distant residential hall from the DUC, it was one of the most isolated.

Nigel counted the windows until he found the second room from the rear door. He approached slowly, his eyes sweeping the ground. Five weeks was a long time for evidence to remain. He saw nothing. He moved closer to the room and carefully examined the screen. He slid his fingers along the edge and paused near the corner when he encountered a small nick. In the corner, near the clasp, was a scrape. He rubbed it. Rusty. And there, over the clasp, the mesh was widened by the slightest amount, no more than it would be had an ice pick gone though to open the clasp. He slid down the screen to the second clasp and examined it closely. Not as noticeable as the other, but the mesh had been stretched in a matter hardly discernible. Had the student done it? Maintenance people? Did it mean anything?

Nigel stood on his toes. No marks on the windowsill.

He walked around the dorm and stood on the curb in front, looking up and down the street.

He went to the door of the dormitory. It was propped open with a waste can, and a note was taped to the handle. "Pizza man. Bring it to 207."

Nigel shook his head. Pizza at 8:30 A.M.?

The hall was empty.

Nigel took a few steps down the hall, opened the second door, and stepped inside. As he looked around, he reached behind and locked the door. For a long time he stood still, only his eyes moving as he studied the tiny room, feeling it, soaking it into his pores, *knowing* it.

You stood here by the door. You waited a moment, didn't you, while you savored the moment. You knew she was in your power, and you knew what you were going to do. There was no need to hurry.

Nigel's eyes widened.

You were here before. At least once. You came in by the window during the night. You stood here and watched her sleeping, but you did nothing. You knew you would be back.

Nigel moved slowly across the room toward the bed.

He stopped and looked around. The room was small and cramped, and to him it was dismal. But to a freshman away from home for the first time it would have been wonderful. He stared at the narrow bed for a long time. The mattress was a plastic-covered piece of foam. He moved around the bed and opened the closet door. A mirror was on the back of the door. He stepped aside and slowly moved the door back and forth. He returned to the bed.

He sat down. For a long moment he was still, almost as if he were a person in great pain who knew that to lie back would cause even more pain. Then very slowly he turned and stretched out, eyes closed, brow wrinkled. He did not move for a long time.

You smelled the latex. That was your first sensation on awakening. There was a man in your bed, and you were petrified with fear. Then the hand behind your head shifted and there was a knife at your throat and the man whispered in your ear. You did not want to be mutilated. Young women are terrified of knives and mutilation.

He cut off your nightgown, didn't he? You threw it away and you wouldn't talk to us about it, but he cut it off.

Nigel put his arm across his eyes. Anyone watching him would have thought him in great pain.

You talked to her about God, but what did you say? What were your exact words? And why did you stand with her in the window with nothing but the screen between you and the outside?

Slowly Nigel turned his head to the right. He saw himself in the mirror on the closet door.

You watched yourself as you molested her. You watched yourself perform. It was almost as if you were watching someone else. You critiqued your performance, and when it was over, when you had bathed and cleansed her, when she thought it was all over, you beat her. It was so unexpected for her. That was the best part for you. You had power. You had control.

It all came back to him. It all washed over him in a great tidal wave of pain, and he closed his eyes tightly. He had seen the report on his wife, Rachel. He was not supposed to, but he had. And he remembered every word.

The same thing happened to Rachel, to my Rachel, to my wife.

Nigel lay on the bed with his right arm over his eyes. It was long minutes later before he swung his feet over the side of the bed and stood up and strode across the tiny room. He locked the door and walked rapidly toward his car.

5

Wilbur and Walt were in their mid-twenties and dressed alike in T-shirts, faded jeans, and heavy tan boots with lug soles. Both were wiry and both had dull eyes that indicated the cheese had fallen off their crackers. The most obvious difference between the two was that Wilbur's hair was red and Walt's was brown. But that was a small difference because each man's hair was so dirty that an observer could describe it only as dark and greasy.

On this July morning they sat in the cab of a concrete truck and motored entirely too fast as they drove from a plant in northeast Atlanta toward the Carter Presidential Center, where a new parking lot was being built.

The container on the back of the truck turned slowly and relentlessly as the truck turned off Ponce de Leon toward the gently rolling kudzu-covered hills where the Carter Center was nestled. Wilbur liked to drive fast and watch the expressions on the faces of approaching drivers as he drifted across the center line. Goddamn, it was fun. Some of them people suddenly got eyes big as dinner plates.

"Hand me a Coke," Wilbur shouted.

Walt leaned forward, lifted the top of a small styrofoam cooler, and pulled out two cans. "Think I'll have one, too." He laughed. "Damn it's gonna be hot today. Seven o'clock and seventy degrees. By eight o'clock it'll be eighty. Nine o'clock, ninety. This place is hotter than a blistered pussy in a pepper patch. Gonna be a million degrees this afternoon." He flipped a can to Wilbur who deftly caught it, held it against the steering wheel with one hand, and pulled the tab with the other. He quickly put it to his mouth and sucked at the fizzing soda, then turned the can up and drained half the contents in several gulps. His large Adam's apple rhythmically yo-yoed up and down his scrawny neck.

Wilbur passed his Coke can to Walt and pointed at a copse of oak trees. "Throw it hard enough it'll stay off the road. I don't need no ticket."

"Hah," Walt said. He took the can, turned, and half stood as he stretched out the window. He pulled his arm close to his stomach as he prepared to fling the can.

"Say when." Walt was rocking his shoulders in time with the music.

"Get ready." Wilbur swerved toward the side of the road. "Now," he shouted.

Walt's body froze. He was half out the window, eyes locked on what he had seen. His head turned, keeping the spot in view as the truck thundered down the road.

Wilbur laughed. "Get your crazy ass back inside."

Walt suddenly ducked inside, sat down, and turned to stare at Wilbur with widened eyes.

Wilbur looked at the can in Walt's hand. "Why didn't you chunk it?"

"They's a body back there."

Wilbur laughed, looked at Walt, and looked in the rearview mirror. "What in hell you talking about?"

"Back up, man. I saw a body."

"We on a schedule here. I ain't stopping for no foolishness."

Walt hammered his fist against the dash. "Wilbur, I saw it."

Wilbur pressed on the brakes and with much wheezing and groaning the truck slowly ground to a halt. He shifted into reverse and a strident *"beep . . . beep . . . beep"* began as the truck backed up.

"What kinda body was it?" Wilbur said, eyes moving between the rearview mirrors on either side of the truck.

"I don't know. I saw it for just a minute."

Walt leaned away from the truck. "Stop. There it is." He jumped down and ran toward the woods.

"Wait a minute," Wilbur shouted as he maneuvered the big truck until the outside wheels were on the grass. He turned on the caution lights, opened the door, and jumped to the ground.

No sign of Walt. "Hey, Walt. Where you?" he shouted.

"Up here. Go through that kudzu patch and the bushes to them oaks." Walt's voice was about thirty yards away. As Wilbur climbed through the bushes, he saw Walt staring at the ground.

"Is it a body?"

Wilbur found Walt stooped over a figure on the ground, a dark, human-like figure that seemed to be shifting and moving. Wilbur walked slower. His brows wrinkled. The figure had a long nose, a broken nose that had been pushed off center.

An unspeakable odor from the thing on the ground

wrapped around his head, and he involuntarily let out a loud noise of disgust and revulsion. It was not the body that was moving; it was millions of maggots covering the body.

Walt spun away, clasped his hands over his mouth, and lurched stiff-legged toward the other side of the clearing, vomit spewing from between his fingers. He bounced a few steps farther and continued vomiting.

Then Wilbur realized what was wrong. That was not a nose. It was the handle of a screwdriver protruding from the left eye of the thing on the ground. Wilbur backed up, eyes locked on the collapsed flesh, the maggots, and the gaping holes that indicated rodents or birds, or both, had been feasting upon what had once been a human. Even though he didn't know about these things, he knew the body had been there for weeks.

"Damn, Walt. You see that? A screwdriver in the eye socket. Son of a bitch."

There was no sound from Walt. Wilbur looked around. Walt had pulled a red bandanna from his pocket and was wiping his hands and his face and staring into a patch of kudzu.

"Come on, Walt. We got to call the police."

Walt stared at the ground.

"Walt, we got to get out of here."

"Hey, Wilbur. Guess what?" Walt's voice was soft. He continued wiping his hands.

"What, man?"

"They's another one over here."

"Another what?"

"Another body. This one's fresh."

"No shit?"

"Yep. It's a blonde."

6

Last night Lucifer had gone adventuring for the first time in two weeks.

It had been time to let another woman find him. There were many women who wanted him, who were awaiting him, and he respected every one of them. He respected them so much that after he took them to the mountaintop and showed them his kingdom, the kingdom that would be theirs, the kingdom of pain and horror and desolation and despair and hopelessness, after he taught them the terror of the day was greater than the terror of the night, he would wash them and dress them and take them to a place where they could sleep until the Time of Renewal. He could do that, because he was Lucifer, the Son of the Morning Star. He was the Light Bearer. And Pandemonium was his kingdom.

Lucifer was not his real name. But that was the name his mother and his five halfsisters had called him from the beginning, and it was how he referred to himself. He was the sixth child and he had been born on the sixth day of the sixth month in 1966. Yes, the mark of the devil was upon him. His mother and his halfsisters had told him so many times. He believed them because they read the Bible often and they made him read the Bible. He could recite the names of the books of the Bible when he was six years old, and he knew most of the Old Testament stories by the time he was twelve.

He sat in the living room of the house he had recently rented. The house—actually, it was a converted barn behind one of the stately old homes on Lullwater Road about a mile from Emory University—perched on a knoll at the rear of a deep lot. The barn was about ninety years old and solid and well built. What had been a large second-story door into the hay loft was now an enormous expanse of windows through which flooded the morning light. The front of the house was approached by a narrow driveway that cut through a thick stand of old pines. The rear of the house was on the edge of a ravine that had eroded to a depth of about sixty feet. The ravine was a deep gash in the red clay and was bereft of vegetation. Not even kudzu grew there.

The minute he heard about the barn he knew it would be perfect for his needs. It was even better than he anticipated. He particularly liked the view from the large open second-story window. He looked over the sixty-foot drop—actually, from the second story it was closer to eighty feet—and across the golf course, and it seemed he was closer to the heaven where once he had been second only to Him.

Lucifer was a fair young man and very handsome. He had wide shoulders and a deep chest and a ridged stomach and oak-tree legs. He wore only a pair of blue silk shorts, very light and soft they were, and he rested his feet atop the chest containing trophies from years of adventuring and stared at his reflection in the window. He had yellow eyes; sometimes they were a pale, almost watery shade of yellow. At other times they burned with a flame of brilliant yellow. His lips compressed as he thought of his mother and his sisters.

When he was six years old, he and his mother had been standing at a bus stop in his home town of Dahlonega, a small town in the north Georgia mountains, when a smiling man walked up and began talking. He was a charming man. When there were no cars on the street and no one was nearby, the man stopped smiling and lost his charm. He grabbed Lucifer's mother and pulled her into a thick patch of woods a few feet away. Lucifer followed, crying and begging the man not to hurt his mother.

"Make a sound and the boy dies," the man snarled.

"Oh, God, he's my only son," she whimpered. She turned to the boy. "Don't say anything. Please don't say anything."

The man pushed his mother down into the grass, then took Lucifer's belt and tied Lucifer's arm to his mother's arm. Lucifer lay there and listened and watched as his mother was raped.

She never reported the rape. She simply walked back home that day and went to bed. When Lucifer told one of the girls he then thought of as his sisters, she was almost cavalier. "How do you think you got here?" she asked smugly.

He did not understand.

"Same thing happened about seven years ago," the girl said. "Happened at the same place. At the bus stop." She shook her head. "Mama don't have good luck at bus stops."

Lucifer stared at her.

"Why you think you got blond hair and you so pale when Mama and Daddy is dark as Indians and all of us is dark and have black hair?" She paused. "You our *halfbrother*."

Lucifer could not speak.

"You yellow-eyed little turd. Why you think Daddy don't like you? Why you think he don't want you calling him daddy?"

After that Lucifer made an extra effort to be a good child and a needed member of the family. He had always been a neat child. His older sisters taught him early that he should sit down when he went to the bathroom so he would not wet the seat.

In the weeks after his mother was attacked he watched her morning sickness progress. He was sleeping with her the night she miscarried and hemorrhaged, and he awakened awash in warm blood and sticky gore. He washed the sheets and cleaned the floor. But he could not wash away his guilt, and he could not cleanse his conscience. If he had been older and bigger and stronger he could have protected his mother from the man at the bus stop.

It seemed that the more Lucifer did, the more he was required to do. He cleaned house, washed dishes, and did most of the housework. As he grew older he ironed his sisters' clothes and his mother's clothes, and he learned to cook. He was a good cook, but his sisters and his mother were never pleased. "You little turd. Do this." Or, "You little bug. Do this." Or "Sit here and do not move."

The one sister who did not ridicule him was Fiona, the youngest girl in the family and the one closest to him in age. Fiona had polio and spent most of her time in bed. She was very weak. But occasionally she would get out of bed, slowly put her crutches under her spindly arms, and move about the house. "You a smart boy," she often told him. Fiona was even more religious than her older sisters. She believed God would straighten and strengthen her legs and that one day she would be a normal woman. She often said to him, "I am God's child. I am the true child of God, and nothing that happens to me, not even this polio, can really hurt me."

Lucifer did not understand.

He wanted to please the man who lived with his mother, the man who was father to his halfsisters. But that man was rarely home. Then Lucifer heard his mother tell the girls that their daddy was in jail down in Atlanta. Something about a robbery. Lucifer never saw the man again.

He tried even harder to please his mother and his sisters. He began working in the small garden behind the house.

The young man closed his eyes as he remembered.

It was my favorite work because I could spray poison on the plants and watch the bugs fall off and die. I spent many happy hours in the garden. Picking out a bug and following it around a plant for a half hour before spraying it brought unimaginable pleasure. I was in control of that bug. I experimented endlessly with them. A small amount of spray immobilized the bug and enabled me to draw closer and examine every convulsion and every spasm and every futile attempt to escape. And then, when I decided it was time, came the final spurt of poison. I decided how long it lived, and I decided when it died.

Sometimes when I thought of my life and my sisters and my mother, I destroyed parts of the garden. I broke off or uprooted the vegetables. I told them someone must have come into the garden and done that just to make us mad.

It was very hot working in the summer garden. I'd come in wearing only a pair of shorts and covered with sweat. After being cooped up in that little house all winter, my sisters were wild.

I spent many hours with my older sisters. I watched them dress in all different clothes and act grown-up. They all liked to wear scarves. "Nothing makes a woman more of a lady than a scarf," I heard them say a thousand times. They made scarves out of everything from feed sacks to their old slips.

My sisters talked and acted as if I were one of them. They often were nude around me, prancing around the house in nothing but a scarf. All of them but Fiona. They laughed when I told them it was a sinful thing they were doing. Fiona didn't do that. Fiona enabled me to see my proper place in the world. She said that I, too, was the true child of God, and nothing they were doing to me could hurt me.

I don't remember the first time one of my sisters—I think it was Edwina—ordered me to perform cunnilingus. "We gonna have an adventure," she said. One by one, over the next few weeks, all my sisters made me do it. Over and over until I did it just the way they liked. And then they all wanted me to do it frequently.

Occasionally, one of my sisters would fellate me. But it was not to bring me pleasure. Each time I ejaculated, my sister criticized the size of my penis and laughed at the noise I made and ridiculed the way my body jerked. They mocked me. Orgasm brought no release for me, only shame and anger.

After we had sex, my sisters would hold me down on the floor. They called my penis "a little piece of string." *Sometimes they would tie string around my penis and tie the other end around the doorknob, and they would hold me down while they slowly opened the door, pulling on it until even the pillow over my mouth did not muffle my screams.*

My sisters always laughed at me. But they said that when I got older I would remember our dates as days of heaven. "We are making your dreams come true," one of them said. "We are your personal angels, you little turd, and you don't even realize it."

I told Fiona about all of this. "If they are angels, they are not God's angels," she said. "Everything has a reason," she told me. "God is letting this happen to you for a reason. Even if you can't see it and even if you don't understand it, it is happening for a reason. You have to accept that. If you are going to do God's work, you have to bend to God's will."

Bend to God's will.

Bend to God's will.

Mama found out what my sisters were doing and wanted me to do the same for her. But Mama did not know everything. One of my sisters made a penis-shaped object and showed me how to insert it in the place between her legs and how to move it. Two other sisters liked for me to use the object in another orifice. Then they began demanding the real thing. Keeping up with my older sisters, even when I was very young, was difficult. And every time I had an orgasm, my sisters giggled and ridiculed me and tied that string to me. I tried not to have an orgasm, but I was too young and my sisters were too skillful.

Then Mama found out that my sisters and I were adventuring, and all that summer my time was spent in Mama's bed.

After I had been in bed with my mama, she would take me by the hand and say, "Let's go to the florida room." That's what she called the screened-in back porch, the florida room. We would stand there together and look off into the woods, and then my mama would stretch out on a wooden bench and I would brush her hair. When her black hair was smooth and silky, I would take a comb and slowly part her hair and then, using the tip of the comb, gently scrape her scalp and loosen the dandruff. Then another slow part all the way across her head and again the gentle loosening of dandruff. And on and on until I had picked my way across my mama's head and a little pile of dandruff was on the floor.

Afterward I brushed her hair until no sign of dandruff remained, until her beautiful black hair glistened with good health.

If she drifted off to sleep, as she often did when I was combing her hair, I sat quietly, not moving, until she awakened. Then she would stand up and stretch and pat me on the head, and she would say to me, "Lucifer, you a good boy."

Lucifer's hand crept upward and curled around the gold cross on the chain around his neck. The cross was small and delicate and feminine. He blinked his eyes rapidly but was unsuccessful in holding back his tears.

After a moment he sniffed and wiped them away. He stood up and took the new tape, the one he had recorded last night, and inserted it into the tape player. He had wanted to listen to it when he came in from adventuring, but he was tired. He was so tired. He fell into bed and slept soundly as he always did after an adventure. Now he would listen. He could listen and remember.

He walked across the room and covered his hands with lotion. He rubbed and rubbed. The only way to have soft hands was lotion, and lots of it. Mama told him so years ago.

He sat down and pushed the Play button on the tape recorder and then leaned back and rubbed his hands together. He closed his eyes and listened to the sweeping epic music of Wagner. And he listened for the stifled sobs and tape-muffled groans serving as a soft counterpoint to the horns and drums.

He rubbed his hands and he listened and the expression on his face was rapt.

7

Nigel walked down Clifton Road, past Emory Hospital, and continued toward Harris Hall. Long known as "The Virgin Vault" because it was the last women-only dormitory on campus, Harris had gone coed several years ago. Because of its central location, Harris was open during the summer sessions. Other than its location the dormitory had little to recommend it. The H-shaped building was nondescript and decrepit and had the slightly seedy air of a building too long in the hot southern sun. In addition, the building was jammed up so tightly against busy Clifton Road that there was room only for a small half-moon-shaped driveway.

Nigel shook his head as he approached Harris Hall. that a university could have a marble-covered parking booth in the visitors' parking lot and a warehouse of a dormitory for students struck him as ironic.

Sarah was living in Harris this summer. Nigel slowed as he approached the building. He noticed the alleyway between the hospital and the dormitory. Lots of low trees there. Overgrown. Easy for a man to hide there. To the side of the dorm was a small, unpaved parking lot. How did the university president overlook an unpaved piece of dirt? Nigel veered to his right,

walked across the small parking lot, and examined the
side entrance of the dorm. The top half of the wooden
door was glass. The door had one lock. Nigel pressed
his face against the window and peered inside. The
dead-bolt lock had a lever so it could be opened from
the inside without a key. That meant a pane of glass
could be cut or broken, and anyone could reach inside
and open the door. He looked over his shoulder. No
one passing by on the sidewalk would notice. He
shook his head in disgust. Emory University had the
security of a chicken coop. And students left dormitory doors open for the pizza man.

Nigel returned to the sidewalk and walked toward
the front door. As he reached for it, a young man
carrying a book bag walked through. When the young
man, obviously a student, saw Nigel, he paused and
held the door open.

"You shouldn't do that," Nigel said.

The student looked at him in bewilderment.

"You always let strangers in your dormitory?"

"Hey, man, I was just trying to be nice."

"Do you know me?"

"No." The young man backed away. Nigel caught
the door before it closed.

"Then, goddammit, don't be nice. What if I were
here to beat the hell out of you and burn down the
dorm?"

The student backed up another step. "Man, I'm calling the cops."

"My name is Nigel Trench. I'm with the Atlanta
Police Department."

The student turned and rapidly walked down the
driveway. Over his shoulder he said, "I'm still calling
the cops."

"Good."

Nigel walked into the dorm. The hall was bleak and institutional and far darker than he would have liked. He walked slowly down the hall, reading the names on the doors. Many of them were open. Nigel looked up when he heard a dog barking. A young woman was trotting down the hall toward him. She wore a black halter and red spandex running shorts. Her eyes were on a small dog that ran beside her. She sensed his presence and looked up and stopped, startled. Then she recognized him.

"Daddy, what are you doing here?" She looked him up and down. "And aren't you dressed up? I'd forgotten how great you look in a suit. What's the occasion?"

"Speaking of dress, where are you going dressed like that?"

She laughed. "Oh, Daddy. You're so stuffy. I'm going jogging in Lullwater Park. You want me to dress like you?"

He grunted. "Don't I get a hug?"

"Yes." She threw her arms around his neck and gave him an enthusiastic squeeze.

"How are you, Sarah?"

"I'm great, Daddy. I'm having a great summer." She paused. "Why are you here? Is Mom okay?"

"Yes. She's fine. She went back to the hospital. But she's fine." He looked at the dog. "Who's this?"

Sarah's face broke into a radiant smile. She stooped and scooped the small dog up in her arms. It was a black and brown dog of indeterminate origin, a mutt, a creature with no pride of ancestry but with a big promise of posterity. The dog weighed maybe thirty pounds and had the lolling tongue and bright eyes of a hound whose only goal in life was to love someone. Anyone.

"This is Pepsi," Sarah said. She laughed as the dog licked her face. "I was coming across campus the other day and he followed me." She looked around. "We can't have animals in the dorms, but I brought him in to feed him. He loves nachos. I bring them from the cafeteria, and he doesn't care if they're cold." She nuzzled the dog. Pepsi again licked her face. "I was about to take him out for a walk." She laughed. "He thinks I'm his mother."

"Pepsi?"

"Yeah, he doesn't belong on campus, so I call him Pepsi."

In spite of himself, Nigel grinned.

Sarah let Pepsi slide out of her arms. She stood up. Sarah was a tall girl, about five feet eight. Her thick black hair was cut in a pageboy and surrounded a face darkened by the summer sun. She wore no makeup. Her jogging outfit revealed far more of her body than her father liked. She was a dark, shimmering young woman who radiated sexuality.

"You didn't tell me why you're here."

"Can we go to your room? I need to talk to you.'

She looked at him quizzically. He had not visited her dorm this summer.

"Sure. Pepsi can go without his walk for a while. He loves my room. He sleeps on the empty bed."

She led the way down the hall. As they rounded the corner they met a young man rushing down the hall. Clearly he was late for class. But not too late to take notice of Sarah. The boy's eyes widened, and as he passed he turned to watch, his thoughts etched on his face. Nigel glared. The boy was a pervert in the making. Nigel would have said something had not Sarah stopped and pushed open a door.

"Here it is." Pepsi scampered through the door, ran across the room, and jumped on the lower bunk. He spun around once and dropped, head on his paws, eyes riveted on Sarah.

Nigel paused. "Your door was not locked?"

"I was just going out jogging. I can't carry a bunch of keys." She laughed and slapped her hips. "No pockets."

Nigel sighed.

Sarah threw out her right hand. "Be it ever so humble."

Nigel was struck with the similarity between this room and the room in Calhoun he had just visited. Perhaps college dorm rooms were universally cramped and tight and depressing and dismal to all but the students who lived in them.

"Daddy, why don't you sit there at my desk?" Sarah sat on the bed beside Pepsi and patted him several times before looking expectantly at her father. Pepsi licked her hand.

Nigel sat down and crossed his legs. "Sarah, I'd like for you to come home." He was trying to be low-key about this.

"You mean move into the apartment?"

"Yes. For the remainder of this summer."

"Why?" She stopped patting Pepsi. "Does this have something to do with Mom?"

"No, your mother is okay. I'd just like for you to come home for a while."

"Why?"

"Sarah, humor me. It's only for a few weeks." Nigel was growing impatient.

"Daddy, I like it here. I like my room. I like the dorm. And the campus in summer is so laid-back. The classes are small. I get to know my professors. They know me. I like it."

Nigel sensed his daughter's defenses going up. He had to control his anger; she must see the reason he wanted her to come home. He moved across the room and sat down on the edge of the bed near her. Pepsi was between them.

He stared at her for a long moment. "Sarah, I've been asked to come back to work."

"Where?"

And then it registered.

"You mean with the police department?"

"Yes."

"But why? You retired when ... when Mom ..."

"Yes, I did," he interrupted. "But I've been asked to help with an investigation."

"Where you worked before? The same department?"

"Yes."

"Does Mom know?"

"No. Of course not."

Sarah stood up, clasped her hands together and moved across the room, spun around and looked at her father. "And you're here because you're worried about me? It has something to do with the Emory student who was attacked this summer."

Nigel rubbed his mouth. Sarah had long ago grown impatient with what she called his paranoia. He was like most police officers: everyone was guilty of something. His job had taught him the depths of depravity to which humans can sink. He knew the mindless and limitless horror that humans inflict on one another.

He had seen it happen to his wife. He desperately wanted to protect his daughter.

"Daddy, I'm going to summer school so I can graduate early. After fall semester I'll graduate and be on my own. You can't look after me forever." She threw her arms wide. "I'm grown."

The only man on earth who would have contested that was the man with whom she was talking. To him she would always be his little girl, his only child.

"I know you are, Sarah. But ..." He paused and looked at her for a long moment. "A serial rapist is targeting Emory students."

Sarah looked at him for a long moment and then laughed. "Oh, Daddy, you never change. One student was attacked. But she lived over in Calhoun on the edge of the campus. And there have been some questions about what happened to her. I've heard several things."

Nigel stared at his daughter. Would it never end, this belief that the victim must have done something to bring on the attack, the feeling that somehow the victim was responsible for being brutalized? Now he was hearing it even from his daughter, from a bright and educated young woman whose mother had been attacked.

"Three students have been raped, Sarah. Not one. Three. Another has been missing for two weeks. We don't know what's happened to her."

Sarah gasped and stared at her father. She sat down and pulled Pepsi closer. "Three? Three? Why haven't we been told?"

"Two of them were off campus. It happened in their apartments. It's being kept quiet."

"Who's missing now? What's her name?"

"You don't know her."

"Tell me her name. I want to know."

"Kathleen Powers. She's from—"

"I know her. I do know her. She's in my Yeats class. I thought she ..."

"You thought what?"

Sarah did not answer for a moment. The idea that a student whom she knew was among the missing had stunned her. She waved her hands. "I thought she was partying. I thought she was having boyfriend problems. I thought she might be out of town. I don't know. I just never thought ..."

"She has an olive complexion and black hair."

Sarah looked at her father in amazement. "How do you know that?"

"Sarah, not only is the perpetrator targeting Emory students. He likes a certain type."

Nigel paused.

His daughter stared at him expectantly.

"You are that type," he said softly.

Sarah jumped up and began pacing the room. Three steps one direction. Three steps in another. Pepsi's eyes followed her every move. After several minutes she glanced defiantly at her father. She kept pacing.

"You tried to look after Mom."

Nigel shook his head. "Sarah." His voice was tight.

"You bought her a gun and a cellular telephone, and you made her believe every man out there was a potential rapist." Sarah's voice was bitter. "She was always looking over her shoulder. She told me she was afraid if anything ever happened to her that you would blame her. She thought it would be her fault if she was attacked."

Nigel said nothing.

"And look what happened. All that stuff you filled her head with didn't help. Now look at her."

Nigel was mute.

"Daddy, I'm staying. I can look out for myself." She laughed almost scornfully. "Didn't you teach me to lock the doors and make sure no one was following me and to be aware of my surroundings and all that police stuff?"

Nigel wanted to say she had not locked the door when she left the room earlier. He wanted to tell his daughter that the same man who had attacked her mother had returned to Atlanta, that he was the man suspected of attacking Emory students. But her straight back and her crossed arms and defiant look on her face told him not to bother.

"Daddy, I graduate in December. I'm staying." She glared. "And don't give me a pistol to carry around like you did Mom. They're not allowed on campus." She pointed at Pepsi. "I've got a dog. He'll bark if anyone comes around."

Nigel looked at the scrawny dog. Pepsi had eyes anxious to please and a tail anxious to wag. The only thing he could do to a trespasser would be to lick him into submission.

Nigel nodded. "He's a good dog."

Nigel knew he had lost. But still he groped for something to say, for some bit of logic or emotion that would make Sarah sense the danger she was in. He wanted to tell her how desolate his life would be if anything happened to her. But it was too late. He could not order her to come home. She was too old and too independent and too proud.

Suddenly a strident sound filled the room. Nigel and Sarah jumped. Pepsi's ears tried vainly to stand erect as he looked about trying to fix the source of the sound. Nigel's pager was sounding off. It had been so long since he had carried a pager that for a few seconds he did not recognize the noise. He opened his coat and peered at the numbers being displayed atop the beeper. Major Morris.

Nigel stood up, looked around, and reached for the phone on the desk.

Sarah looked away and shook her head in resignation. "Of course, you're welcome to use my phone," she muttered. "Thank you for asking."

Nigel did not hear. He picked up the receiver and punched in the numbers.

"Major, Nigel here." He listened intently for a few moments. He turned his back to Sarah and with his left hand rubbed his eyes. "What's the twenty?" He repeated an address. Then the straightened fingers of his right hand stabbed the air. And a voice Sarah knew only too well rose in command. "That's my crime scene. I want it secured. Nobody crosses the tape. Nobody. I'll be there in ten minutes."

He hung up the phone and took a deep breath. His hand remained on the phone as he stared at the wall.

"Daddy, what is it?"

"It's him."

"Him? Who?"

Nigel reached out and gently grasped Sarah by the shoulders. He shook his head. "Two bodies—they think they're women—have been found. I have to go."

Sarah was struck by the pain in her father's eyes. For a moment she was almost frightened.

"Two? But I thought only one was ..."

"I did, too."

"Is one of them the girl in my Yeats class?"

"I don't know."

He looked at her for a long moment, an unasked question in his eyes.

She pulled away and shook her head as if to throw off the shock. She backed up a step. "I'm staying."

Nigel nodded. He looked at her for a long moment, then turned and walked from the room. As he hurried down the hall his pace increased. By the time he reached the door he was almost running.

He was sliding into his car when he realized the young man he had met as he entered the dorm had not called the campus police.

8

My great joy, and the only thing more fun than work-ing in the garden and killing bugs and tearing up vegetables, was reading. I read everything. My teach-ers learned early on that when the other students did not know the answers to their questions, they could always call on me. I even helped the teachers grade papers. The other students did not like me because I was rigid and demanding in my grading system, far stricter than the teacher. I knew how to perform the job.

I was thirteen when I had my first adventure with a girl who was not my sister. It was summer and she was wearing a sleeveless dress that enabled me to see the swell of her breast. She was tempting me. So I reached over, pulled up her skirt, and took a long look. That was the way boys played with girls. While I was holding her, somehow her bra fell off, and she was so well developed that she felt offended. She resisted, but I knew she was seeking me so we had a date. Her parents did not know about their daughter, and they charged me with rape. That was a misconception on their part. And the girl later put out a lot of negative information about me and tried to discredit me.

At the juvenile center down in Gainesville, a woman

interviewed me and showed me the ink blots and asked what I thought. She gave me IQ tests and thematic perception tests and vocabulary tests. But those were not the real tests. All the time she was talking to me and all the time she was giving me those tests, her dress was over her knees, and every time I looked away she pulled her dress a little higher. On the second day she wore a much shorter dress. She crossed her legs every few seconds and occasionally put her hand inside her blouse and patted herself. She was in truth the Great Whore of Babylon, and she was trying to tempt me, trying to pull me out of myself. But I was able to resist the temptation she put before me.

Because I resisted her and because I did well on those silly tests and because I was considered the man of my family and because of a little talk I had with the girl who had falsely accused me, the rape charge was dropped. That was proper. God's work must be done.

My next adventure involved a waitress at a fast-food restaurant in Dahlonega where I worked part-time. One day when the evening shift was over she followed me. She said she was walking in the same direction as I, but in reality she was following me. She was another harlot and wanted what all women want. We were walking by the bus stop when I allowed her to take me into the woods and we had a date. No one ever knew. She said she could never talk of it to anyone. When we came out of the woods, she was crying and saying, "I'll never forget this. Oh, my God, my God, I can't believe this happened. I'll never forget this."

I went home and did not remember doing anything. It obviously meant more to her than it did to me.

In those days Fiona and I often talked about our

dreams. Hers was to go to college. Perhaps because she knew she would never realize her dream, she talked of the most distant and expensive college she knew about: Emory University in Atlanta. Emory was a school for rich kids. We would be talking and she would cradle that little gold cross she wore around her neck. A faraway look would come into her eyes, and she would grin and say, "I want to go down to Atlanta and drink tea with them rich people at Emory."

I always encouraged her dream, but she did not encourage mine. When I told Fiona about my dreams, she said I was growing up too fast, that I needed to go into the desert like Moses. She said I needed to experience the fiery furnace before I could understand God's will. "It's like Mama says," she told me. "You got to bend to God's will."

She talked of how Joshua blew his trumpet and the walls fell, and she said when I heard God's trumpet the walls around my heart would fall and I would find victory. I knew then she had been possessed. I knew what she was really talking about.

We were out on the porch that day. It was a good day for Fiona. She had gone out there on her crutches and was sitting in the sun. When I realized she was talking of sending me to jail, I walked over to her, put my hands around her shoulders, and said, "Fiona, it is time for you to meet your God."

She looked up and I saw in her eyes that she knew what I was talking about. "I know my God," she said. "I am a true child of God, and nothing you can do will really hurt me."

It was an accident when she died. I know she did not feel any pain. She died very quickly.

I went inside and sat at the table and was trying to

figure out what had happened when my mama walked by and said, "Lucifer, why you sitting there like a bump on a log? Ain't you got things to do?"

And I said, "If you think I'm a bump on a log, you ought to go out there on the porch and see Fiona." She did. I told Mama and my sisters that Fiona had just up and died. She had always been sickly, so they believed me. But later that day they called the police. By then Fiona had been dressed and laid out in her bed, and one of my sisters had gone down the road to ask a preacher to come by and funeralize her.

I told the policeman I had found Fiona on the front porch. He looked hard at me, and I knew what he was thinking. But all he had to go on was my word. Fiona sure wasn't talking.

A few days later the juvenile people came by, and they told Mama it would be best if I went down to the juvenile prison at Alto. They told her they suspected I had killed Fiona. They said I had violated Fiona's civil rights, blah, blah, blah. They had no proof, but they said since I was a juvenile that if she signed the papers they would take me to Alto.

The juvenile authorities told the people at Alto that my childhood was responsible for whatever I had done. The mind-set of the juvenile authorities combined with my grades resulted in my getting a good job at Alto, working as an assistant to the counselor. I watched the guards every day; that was my first awareness of what law enforcement could be like. And after several months the authorities sent me to school in the little town near Alto.

I received a HOPE scholarship to college, and because my sister had died when I was a juvenile, that record was sealed and put away. The college admis-

sions people never knew of it; they knew only that I
had a fully paid state scholarship. I went to Atlanta
with a fresh start as a student at Georgia State
University.

I was a good boy for the first year or so. I held down
my Awakening. But I knew that in Atlanta I would be
shown the way to the light. It was in Atlanta that I
went to my first X-rated movie. The sexual perversity I
saw there was overpowering. It was Sodom and Go-
morrah. I was eating popcorn and a few seats away a
couple was hugging. On the other side was a couple,
and her dress was up and his hand was in her. I could
hear her moaning. I left the theater and went to a bus
stop to go to my boarding house, and there was a girl
there. She was a few years older than I. All the things
I saw in the movie were in my mind, and I grabbed
her and pulled her into the woods and we had a date.
After it was over, she began mumbling and I believe
she said she wanted to see me again.

"I don't even know you," I said. I was very angry
with her. So I had to discipline her so she would not
be so abandoned with the next man she met. I disci-
plined her more than I meant to, and there was an
accident.

Sometimes I awakened at four a.m. with the rituals
sizzling in my mind, and I knew I had to go to a bus
stop and find someone who wanted to go adventuring.
So I would walk to a bus stop and it would be my
place. I would say to myself: "This is mine." And when
a woman came along I would say to her, "This is my
place. What are you doing here?" When she said she
could be there, I knew she was seeking me and I took
her into the woods. Many women never told anyone
about our dates. That's because they were attracted to

*me and because they knew they had been looking for
me. I have always been kind, nice, understanding, and
respectful of women. I am mindful of them.*

*The newspapers in Atlanta wrote about some of my
dates One reporter in particular, the crime reporter for
The Atlanta Constitution, a fellow named Dan Buchanan. He put out a lot of malicious gossip about me.
He didn't know the mental anguish and the pain I was
going through. He did not know how much my teachers
had always admired me and how jealous the other students were of me.*

*The biggest problem was the police officer's wife. She
never understood about me. Because she was unmindful of my pride and respect, she caused me to leave
college a year before I graduated and to go into the
army. But God protected me during my sojourn. I
sometimes wondered if Fiona had been right, if the
three years in the army were the purifying years in the
desert. Because wearing a uniform and being a military
policeman taught me so much. It enabled me to continue my work and at a much higher level. It enabled
me to move upward along the path, ever closer to the
day when I shall return to my rightful place on the
right hand of Him, when I shall again be His most
favored, when I shall rule over all the heavenly hosts
and be second only to Him.*

Thinking of the army and the uniform and his life's
work made Lucifer suddenly remember his job. He
jumped up and walked to a closet and removed a
crisply creased blue uniform and hung it on the door.
A polished badge was over the left breast pocket and
a name tag over the right. He pulled a pair of sparkling black corfam shoes from the closet, blew away
a speck of imaginary dust, and set them on the floor.

When everything was in its proper place, he began
dressing. Then he stood in front of the mirror. His gig
line was straight. His hat sat at the proper angle. The
creases in his uniform were knifelike. The shoulder
patch identifying his employer was creased precisely
through the middle. He turned from side to side. So
many police officers did not care about their appearance. But he did. He was a fine-looking officer.

*I learned so much when I was away. Many women
sought me out, and I had many dates. My adventuring
reached new levels. And my work resumed when I returned to Atlanta. I did what Fiona had always wanted
to do: I came to Emory University. The first women
were wonderful dates. Five of them so far and four
more to go. I am in a period of great growth and development and understanding, and I know the remaining
women will help my work and my return to glory.*

*At work today I will make another selection among
the women who are searching for me, the women who
want to go adventuring. I know who wants me, and it
is time for another date. One of my recent dates was not
respectful of me and fought me to cover her pleasure. I
had been doing some improvements on my new house
and carelessly left a screwdriver on the floor. She
picked up the screwdriver and lunged at me. The screwdriver dug deeply into my arm and may have even
scarred me. To my shame, I reacted in anger. She collapsed on the floor, shuddered a few times, and died,
and I realized what I had been missing all those years.*

*Then I had another date and I did not realize how
great was the strength of God's chosen one. The experience escorted her into the kingdom. It hastened my
return. And it taught me that adventuring is not enough.*

Adventuring will never again be enough. Because now I know.

In their fears I am fed.
In their suffering I am nourished.
In their accidents I am fulfilled.

9

Nigel sat on his heels and stared at the corpse.

Unlike cops in movies or novels, he did not cover his upper lip with menthol or any other strong-smelling agent to diffuse the odor of the corpse. Nor did he wear a filtered mask. Like most real-life homicide cops who find a stinker in an open field, he took it straight and he endured it. He had never gotten used to it, but he had learned to put up with it. The miasma of death would be in his hair and in his clothes. It would be absorbed into his skin, and it would crawl far back into his nose and deep into his throat. One reason so few homicide cops have beards or mustaches is that the syrupy odor of death lurks there for days. Bathing will not remove it. Nigel would stand in the shower for a half hour tonight, soaping and rinsing and soaping and rinsing. But all the soap at Caswell & Massey would not begin to wash away the singular odor of rotting human flesh. Only time would do that. The clothes he was wearing he would hang on the screen porch tonight. Tomorrow the clothes would go to the cleaners. He would wait a week, maybe two, before picking them up. But when they came back and he removed the plastic bag, the odor would leap forth.

Nigel's eyes were fixed on the face of the corpse. Or the remains of the face. He studied it intently and tried to put the rampaging thoughts of the other body out of his head. He had seen both when he first arrived. Now he did not want to think of the second one, the young blonde, because her pale body and golden hair were unmistakable signs that the perpetrator was not targeting his victims because they had dark skin and dark hair. But if the first three rape victims and this homicide were not chosen because they had dark skin and dark hair, how were they chosen? What were the criteria?

Nigel realized he was back at square one.

Three rapes and two deaths, and he was still at square one.

He fought hard, tightening down the screws in his mind so this revelation would not make him confused and jangled.

You are my instructor. You have put a problem before me, a problem for me to solve. But what is it that you want to teach me here?

Nigel studied the body. He knew it was a woman because the hair was long and surprisingly neat, the skeleton gracile, the brow ridge smooth, and the subpubic angle was quite wide. A silk scarf was around the cervical vertebrae.

You are his first homicide. You are a transition for him. Through you, he graduated from rape to murder. And once he killed you the clock was ticking. He had to move you far enough away that when you were found, your death would not be associated with him. Yet it had to be close enough to minimize the chances of his being caught with your body in his car. An offender usually will move a victim's body no more than

*six miles from where he killed the victim. So the of-
fender probably lives within a six-mile circle of the Carter Center.*

*Transporting the victim is one of the danger signs. It
indicates a sexual sadist may be at work.*

*He will learn as he goes. Later, as he gets better at
this and becomes more confident, he will hide the bodies better. They will be farther away from where he
lives or works.*

*Why did he put you at the Carter Center? Why here
on this hillside so near several major roads? The prox-
imity to the road is another sign that this was his first
kill. He made little effort to hide your body. In fact, he
wanted us to find you. Why?*

*Why didn't he drop you into the Chattahoochee?
Why didn't he put you in a black section of town so
we might think you had been killed by a black person? Did he put you here because he wanted us to
think the offender is among the homeless people who
live under the bridges around the Carter Center? Was
it because he was proud of what he had done and
wanted to put you on display? Was it closure of some
sort? If so, why did there have to be closure?*

Nigel shook his head, and a feeling of ineffable
sadness filled him. He was nauseous, and not just
from the odor that slammed him. What he felt was
more than an olfactory assault; it was a psychic revulsion, a primal, visceral feeling that what he was
doing was unnatural. Man was not meant to hover
over the rotting remains of a fellow man. But he
had to do it because by listening to what the corpse
had to tell him, he would find the offender.

*I have to study this violence. I must be absorbed by
the violence. If I was studying Picasso, I would examine*

his art. If I was studying John Steinbeck, I would read his books. If I was studying Frank Lloyd Wright, I would contemplate his buildings. Rape and murder are what you do. I must become more familiar with your work.

He stared at the screwdriver in the woman's left eye socket, listening, watching, feeling, wondering about the vibrant young woman who once had inhabited this shrunken shell. He looked at the black putrefaction of her skin and the shriveled skeletonization of her once strong young body. He had been on The Job more than twenty years and thought he knew the dark, bosky vales of denigration and all the tangled fens of cruelty of which man is willing. Now he realized he was still learning. Real life is different from novels, even the most explicitly detailed crime novels. And it is different from movies, even with all their potential to form and influence. For neither novels nor movies can begin to convey the rampant reality, the soul-numbing horror, the raw, repulsive magnetism of the street. The author who even began to approach reality would be dismissed as taking his craft too far or laughed at as ludicrous or even considered as one who had let his dark side gain the ascendancy. The moviemaker who portrayed the reality of the streets would be seen as a black-souled pornographer.

Nigel sighed. He knew he was about to begin a descent into the deepest horrors of the real world.

The screwdriver is the first piece of physical evidence you've left behind. Why didn't you pull it out? Did you feel a certain closeness to her? Was there a relationship with her? Going for the eye is going for a high degree of lethality. The shaft of the screwdriver

*went into her brain and killed her instantly. Do you
have a deep degree of guilt? Is there some biblical
thing here; an eye for an eye? Are you an avenger?
If so, whom are you really killing?*

A group of homicide detectives and uniformed officers stood twenty yards away and kept their eyes
on Nigel. They watched curiously as he stooped over
the almost bare bones of the rotted corpse. The uniformed officers were repulsed. They could smell the
remains from fifty yards away, and that guy was up
there leaning over the bones.

They would stay outside the yellow tape that
marked off the crime scene. The yellow tape was a
barrier of more than one kind. It separated Nigel and
the body from the world. It separated Nigel and the
body from the uniformed cops. Outside was one
world. Inside was another. Nigel was inside a *cordon
sanitaire*. And there with him, resting in a hillside
clearing among the oak trees, were the remains of two
young women.

This was a homicide scene.

This was sacred ground.

Not all the police officers felt that way. "Hey, Detective, what you got?" shouted a homicide detective.
The homicide squad was anxious to take over the
crime scene. There had been a brief confrontation
when Nigel arrived and told several of the younger
officers to stay outside the yellow tape until he was
through. They resented this white-haired guy taking
over. Then Lieutenant Kenny Raines, a senior homicide detective, arrived and put an end to that. He and
the Roach were old friends. Kenny Raines wanted
only to get the job done.

The press had turned out and were in full bay. It

had been the TV people who showed up first—five crews. They monitored police radios closely. Then the radio reporters came—four of them—followed by a half-dozen newspaper types. It was not every day that two bodies were found near the Carter Presidential Center. The reporters were clustered like a pack of hungry hounds waiting outside a kitchen window for someone to toss a biscuit. You could look at their faces and hear the gears clanking in their heads as they composed leads in which they could mention the two bodies and the Carter Center. They watched Nigel from a distance, and they eyed the homicide cops outside the yellow tape, their feral antennae searching for one who might talk. They wondered which ploy in their bottomless repertoire of guile and seduction and threats and cajolery would be most successful, and they chafed at the knowledge, at least the experienced ones did, that none of these worked too well with cops. If they didn't trust you—and what police officer in his right mind trusted a reporter?—you were out in the vastness of that hated desert of not knowing.

One reporter, a middle-aged guy, slouched apart from the others. He dressed as if he had fallen out of a CARE package. This was Dan Buchanan, who, even with a half-dozen martinis sloshing in his ample gut, could stumble into any assignment given him and waltz out with a first-rate story. Buchanan had once been the best big-city cop reporter in the country, but now he spent most of his time fleeing from beady-eyed thirty-year-old editors who, even on their best days, would not make a pimple on his big white ass. He had too many friends in high places and was close enough to retirement that they would

not fire him. But they were waiting him out for retirement and he knew it.

Buchanan stuck a cigarette between his teeth and
eyed the female TV reporters, hoping there was one
who did not know him as a middle-aged boozer and
whom he might, with promises of revelations that
would give her the lead story on the six o'clock news,
convince to give him something in return. But that
was all in the past. The South would rise again before
he did.

Buchanan's gaze shifted to the man working in the
clearing under the oaks. When the man stood up for
a better view of the crime scene, he turned sideways
and Buchanan gasped. He knew that profile. He
turned his back to the other reporters to cover his
excitement.

My God. It was the Roach.

But he retired three years ago.

What is he doing here?

At that moment Nigel waved at the closest homicide
detective. "Ask the M.E. to bring a disaster bag,"
he said.

He knew the homicide cops would have great interest in the physical evidence. But Nigel wanted to go
through books, papers, luggage, personal belongings,
and all the collateral material; everything he could find
to indicate the victim's state of mind. He wanted to
know her behavior and her daily habits while homicide detectives wanted the facts. "If it's not a fact, it's
not provable," they often said. And for purposes of
building a case that would stand up in court they
were right.

But there is no such thing as a scientific approach
to human behavior.

He stared at the body.

He is a very organized man, and he would not simply grab you on the spur of the moment.

Danny Rolling worked a college town, and he looked for women whose doors were open. His criteria were simple: age and availability.

Some woman wrote a book saying Ted Bundy looked for women who parted their hair down the middle, had pierced ears, and wore hoop earrings. But Bundy worked at a time when many young women parted their hair down the middle, had pierced ears, and wore hoop earrings. Bundy later said he picked women whom he thought were worthy of him. Anyone can get children or prostitutes, was his argument, but to get a bright, middle-class young woman, well, that takes style.

Did it come down to age and availability?

The prevailing wisdom was that David Berkowitz, the Son of Sam, looked for women sitting in parked cars.

Age and availability?

Was it because you are a college student and it was easy to get to you during the summer session? Or was it your appearance? Lifestyle? Clothing? Where do you hang out? What is your daily routine? Who would you likely meet or be with?

I don't believe he picked you solely because of age and availability.

Not much left of your body. Nevertheless, it contains secrets. The dead speak to the living. What will you tell me that will give me insight into the violent behavior that left you lying on this hillside?

Nigel closed his eyes.

Tell me about this individual's courting ritual. Give

*me the dialogue for the movie playing in his mind.
Show me the pictures he sees. Tell me about his sexual
DNA. Tell me what he left behind. No matter how
decomposed your body, no matter how careful he
thought he was, there are signs. He left something. He
took something and he left something. But what?
What?*

For long moments Nigel did not move. When he
opened his eyes his attention once again was drawn
to the screwdriver.

He heard a rustle of footsteps and knew it was not
one of the detectives. Then a voice said, "This one
has been here a while." The medical examiner, a surprisingly young man of wiry build with a full red
beard, squatted beside him.

"Hello, Randy," Nigel said.

Dr. Randy Hanzlick was surprised. "Nigel," he ex-
claimed. "I didn't recognize you for a minute. Your
hair has gotten lighter."

"I heard you moved over to Grady Hospital and
that you were doing research for the CDC. What are
you doing out here?"

"My office got a fax several hours ago about the
possibility of young female homicide victims. The fax
said you were in charge. So I assigned myself to answer any calls like that." He shook his head. "Had no
idea it would be so soon."

"Me, either. You bring a disaster bag?"

Dr. Hanzlick nodded. "Hey, we live in the world's
next great city. I always keep several in my car."

"You're not going to be able to tell me much about
this one, are you?"

The M.E. stared at the body. "Not much to work
with."

"When will you do the autopsy?"

"Early tomorrow morning."

"Randy, we've got a time problem on this one. What can you tell me now?"

The M.E. slipped on a pair of latex gloves and leaned closer to the body. He moved around to the other side and touched and probed and examined, all the while muttering polysyllabic words to himself. After a few minutes he sat back on his heels and gazed dispassionately at the body. Then, in a slow clinical voice, he began:

"First, some background. You know some of this. But I'll do it anyway. The first thing you notice about this body is the advanced decomposition. Decomposition is the result of two processes—autolysis and putrefaction. The first is the body's digestion of its own cells and organs, and the second is a bacterial breakdown. Both can be accelerated by heat."

Dr. Hanzlick pointed at the body. "Different insects are attracted at different stages of decomposition. Those insects follow a set pattern of development on or in the body. Three types of insects are found on human remains. Necrophagous insects such as these maggots feed on the body. Predators and parasites feed on the necrophagous insects. Finally, omnivorous species feed on the body and on other insects."

Dr. Hanzlick pointed at the victim's mouth. A removable dental bridgework had been pushed to the side of the oral cavity. "Maggots probably did that. They get on the job and get excited and exhibit remarkable strength."

Nigel said nothing.

The M.E. pointed at a particularly thick mass of

adult maggots. With a gloved finger he poked them. The motion prompted a reflex from the maggots. Clouds of them jumped as high as eighteen inches into the air.

Dr. Hanzlick nodded. "These are the most important in determining the time of death. Flies lay eggs, eggs hatch as maggots, maggots develop into pupa and then emerge as flies. We have several generations at work. And look at this." He pointed at a fly. "See the three black stripes down its back. That's a common house fly."

"And?"

"A house fly. They breed inside. That means she was killed inside, the body was there at least an hour or so. Then she was brought here."

"You can tell that from looking at flies?"

"Lots of variables in the process. You need an entomologist to nail it down precisely. But, in this heat, I'd estimate maggot to pupa in about seven or eight days. We're looking at flies, pupa, and maggots here. It appears to be all first-generation. The second generation of pupa has not hatched."

The M.E. gently moved the skeleton and poked into the soft earth. He pushed his fingers, and several hard-cased pupa were brought to the surface. "See. Second generation."

"Tell me about the victim," Nigel said.

Dr. Hanzlick paused. "Certainly." He looked at the body for a long moment. He bent closer and peered and examined and pulled and lifted. Then he spoke.

"Closures in the growth plates of the shoulder and the basilar synchrondrosis of the sphenoid and occipital bones are recent. Wisdom teeth are beginning to erupt. The pelvic growth plate is almost fused.

I'd say the victim is eighteen to twenty-two years of age. The hair is straight and black and of a texture that indicates she may be Caucasian. Cause of death appears to be the puncture wound in the left eye. Marked decomposition of the body, which is virtually skeletonized with massive maggot infestation. Facial soft tissue virtually destroyed. The femur has been pulled away several feet, probably by animal activity."

He paused and tilted his head. "Soft tissue examination is fruitless except for toxocology testing and tissue typing because of the advanced decomposition. She's been here ten days, maybe two weeks. After I scrape the bones free of decaying matter I'll look for fractures. X rays may reveal something I can't see with the naked eye. I'll make a note of her dentition so once you ID her we'll go for a favorable comparison. Dissection is not possible because of the decomposition. I can't examine the sexual parts. Hell, I can't even identify the sexual parts because of tissue loss and maggot infestation."

Dr. Hanzlick picked up the victim's hand. "Look at this. Fingers are mummified. They are wrinkled and brittle. Must have been exposed to more sun than other parts of the body."

"Can you lift prints?"

"Maybe. I'll soak the fingertips in a special solution to soften them and then try for prints. I doubt if it will work."

"I believe her name is Kathleen Powers," Nigel said softly. "I think she's an Emory student."

"How do you know?"

"A student who fits this general description has been missing about two weeks. I'll have her dental records sent to you." Nigel paused. "If this is who I believe it to be, she was in a Yeats class with my daughter." He shook his head. "Two weeks ago she was studying Yeats."

Dr. Hanzlick did not speak for a moment. Then he pointed. "The screwdriver?"

"I looked at it. Came from Home Depot. There are thousands just like it out there. But be careful. Send it to the crime lab."

"What do you expect to get from it? There's nothing there but the victims' blood."

"I know the guy who did this, Randy. He hasn't killed until now. He's a rapist."

"You think his blood is on the screwdriver? You're going for a DNA?"

Nigel did not answer.

The M.E. shook his head. "Won't happen. Even if you're right, his blood is too diluted for a DNA test. Not enough of it."

"We'll see."

"Never happen. But if it does, do you have a DNA from a suspect to match it with?"

After a long moment Nigel nodded. "Yes."

The M.E. stood up.

Nigel was staring at the body. He rubbed his back. "Horseman, pass by," he murmured.

The M.E. motioned to his assistant and pointed toward the body. "Turn this one over to Homicide. After they're through, take her to the morgue." He and Nigel moved across the clearing toward the second corpse.

A few yards away Lieutenant Raines nodded at two of his detectives. "Let's go," he said. He pointed at the victim. "When her day ends, our day begins."

10

Nigel and the medical examiner studied the second corpse. She was so blond and so neat. The sun ricocheted off her skin in shimmering waves of light. She was petite, no more than five feet one or two. Insect activity, which begins almost immediately when a body is left in the open heat of June, was obvious. Flies had deposited eggs in the mucosal folds of her eyes and nose and mouth. Rats had been here during the night. They had gone for her face. They always do. One eye and an inch or so of flesh around the eye was gone. A bit of early greening was obvious in the lower abdomen where the intestines touch the abdominal wall. But the greening had not climbed upward toward the thorax, and there was no marbling, clear signs she had been here fewer than thirty-six hours. She was not yet bloated. Lividity was well developed.

A bright blue and yellow scarf was tied around her neck, a disconcerting and incongruous touch for a nude and carefully laid-out body in a patch of woods. The festive scarf seemed almost obscene. The victim's face and neck above the scarf were not congested, but Nigel saw the petechial hemorrhaging on her nose and brow and cheeks and knew she had been strangled. Even though she died violently, there was a curious air of neatness about her. He could not get over that. Her hair appeared to have been combed after she was placed here. She was so neat.

And—a fact he could not escape—she was blond.

Nigel sighed. He was embarrassed at his relief that Sarah was no longer a target.

"She will tell us more than the other one," Nigel said.

The medical examiner looked at him in curiosity.

Nigel stared at the scarf.

"What will you find under the scarf, Doctor?"

The medical examiner paused and looked at the detective. This was not a question usually asked in ligature strangulation.

"If she was strangled with the scarf, the ligature mark may be preserved and, after the body dries a bit, more recognizable," he said. "Ligature marks resist decomposition because the ligature compresses the underlying blood vessels and acts as sort of a roadblock for the bacteria responsible for putrefaction."

The medical examiner pulled the edge of the scarf. "I don't want to take it off until we get to the morgue," he said. "Ligature marks vary considerably, depending on the type of ligature, the force used by the perpetrator, and the resistance offered by the victim." His fingers explored under the edges of the scarf. "No apparent fractures of the neck."

"You have any paper bags?" Nigel asked.

The doctor pointed at his bag. Nigel looked inside and pulled out two bags. Very slowly and very gently he slid them over the hands of the victim.

The medical examiner nodded. Hair is sometimes found clutched in the hands of victims of ligature strangulation. It usually is that of the victim. But it can be from the assailant. He returned to studying the neck of the victim. "The ligature mark is faint and blurred," he said.

"So he used something soft, and he probably loosened it or removed it immediately after she died."

The medical examiner nodded.

"The scarf?"

"Maybe. I can tell you more after the autopsy."

"Let's assume he did use something soft and that he removed it immediately. Would that explain why the ligature mark is not obvious?"

"Probably."

Nigel sighed. Medical examiners are scientists and very cautious. But some things cannot be quantified. Some things science cannot examine under a microscope. Some things, signs, are clear. And sometimes the corpse speaks in such a loud voice it cannot be ignored.

The medical examiner kneeled and turned the girl's head to the side. It took him a moment to work the stiffness of rigor mortis from her neck.

"Any slash marks on the back of her neck?"

The M.E. peered under the girl's hair. "No."

Nigel sighed in relief.

"But there are abrasions and contusions around the ligature mark."

"From her or the perpetrator?"

Sometimes a strangulation victim claws her neck in an effort to relieve the pressure of the ligature.

The medical examiner pulled one of the paper bags down and looked at the girl's fingernails. They appeared to be neat. He shook his head. "I don't see any broken nails. But I'll have to wait until we get back and take scrapings before I can say."

"Is that something on her wrist?" Nigel asked. "See it in the sun? A couple of little white flecks."

The doctor looked closely at the wrists of the victim. "Appears to be tape residue. There's usually more than this. He might have washed it off."

"So he taped her hands. That means the abrasions on her neck were made by the perpetrator as he twisted the ligature to tighten it?"

"Possibly."

Bondage. Another sign of a sexual sadist at work.

The medical examiner pointed at the victim's mouth. "See that faint redness around her mouth? He probably taped her mouth, too. Usually, when the hands are taped, the mouth is also."

Nigel nodded. Sensory bondage as well as physical bondage.

"What else can you tell me about the ligature?"

The medical examiner moved the girl's head again. "It may have slipped while he was asphyxiating her." He pointed at the blurred mark. "See here. Maybe she resisted and his hand slipped or maybe he relaxed a moment to get a better grip, but I think that's why the mark is rather indistinct. There is no clear single mark."

The M.E. pushed back the victim's eyelid on the remaining eye. "Marked petechial hemorrhages," he murmured. "Unusually large."

"She struggled quite a bit and he responded with great pressure?"

"That appears to be the case." The young doctor pushed back the eyelid even farther. "Ignore the rodent activity. Look closely. Scleral hemorrhage. Petechial hemorrhages not only on the bulbar conjunctivae and conjunctival sac, but also on the skin of the upper and lower eyelid. Same on the brow and cheeks."

"Meaning?"

Dr. Hanzlick did not answer. He was closely examining the girl's face.

"This is very interesting," Dr. Hanzlick said. "I don't know that I've ever seen this before."

Nigel waited.

"It takes maybe five to seven pounds of pressure to block the veins in the neck. Easy to do that. But it takes about fifteen pounds to block the arteries. Light or moderate pressure in a ligature strangulation causes hydrostatic pressure to build up in the head when it blocks the veins. The deeper arteries are carrying blood to the head, but the veins are blocked and it cannot leave. In layman's terms, it's something like a kink in a garden hose. The pressure build-up and poor oxygen flow cause the ocular petechia. On the other hand, if the guy really squeezes down, both the veins and arteries are blocked and there may be little or no petechial hemorrhaging."

"But she has petechial hemorrhaging, and there are indications that great strength was applied?"

"Yes." Dr. Hanzlick was palpating the neck. "I have to wait until I'm in the morgue. But there may be some fascial hemorrhaging and the tracheal cartilage may be fractured."

"What else?"

"The clear part of the eye is not yet clouded. That takes about a day. The eye is not swollen or collapsed, and eye pressure seems normal. I'd say she was put here late yesterday. In this heat, if she had been here longer, the eye would be collapsed and it would be difficult if not impossible to see the petechiae. Also,

after about a day and a half hemolysis would have
begun, and that would obscure the petechiae."

Nigel was hearing another voice.

*The ligature did not slip. He choked you uncon-
scious, then released it until you regained consciousness, and then he choked you unconscious again and
released it again. Your hands were taped. And your
mouth was taped to muffle your screams. He felt the
power. He felt God-like. How long did he toy with
you? How many times did he choke you unconscious
and revive you before he tired of the game and his
anger ruled and he applied all of his strength?*

*Why did he put your body here with the first one?
He knew the first one had not been found. He was
taking a big risk to bring you here. Is he that arrogant?*

Nigel looked at the body again. No rings. No jewelry. No watch. No clothes. No apparent weapon. The
homicide detectives would find no physical evidence.
There was nothing. Only the body of a young girl.

*What did he take from you? What did he keep as
a trophy?*

"Any evidence of sexual abuse?" Nigel asked.

"Lot of insect activity. Could be normal or it could
be due to labial bleeding that occurred during intercourse." The M.E. shook his head. "I can let you
know tomorrow."

He pointed at a faint sheen around the nipples. "See
that? Appears to be a thin crust. Maybe saliva residue.
I'll go for a DNA on the nipples, but I doubt if there's
enough sample to test."

Both men stood up and took a lingering last look
at the body.

"Doc, what strikes you as strange here?"

The M.E. backed up and studied the victim.

Nigel waved his hand the length of the body. "Being strangled is not the best way to go. Victims of ligature strangulation are not the neatest of victims. They put up a great deal of resistance. This girl should be bruised and sweaty and disheveled. But she's not."

The doctor backed up another step and continued studying the body. After a long moment he nodded. "Her hair."

"Right. It's too neat. Too well combed."

Dr. Hanzlick moved closer and again kneeled down near the body. He touched her hair. "He must have caught her just as she was about to go out."

"Why?"

"Hair spray."

Nigel did not speak for a moment. Then he said, "Are her injuries confined to the ligature mark and the bruises under the mark?"

"As far as I can determine at this point."

"Doctor, you're going to have to look very closely for evidence on this one. I know there appears to be little beyond what we've seen." He turned to the doctor, and his voice was earnest. "Look closely, Randy. She wants to tell you what happened. She can't tell me. But when you put her on the table, she will show you and she will tell you. All you have to do is look and listen."

"I'm a scientist, Nigel, not a necromancer." He paused. "Anything in particular you think I should look for?

Nigel shook his head.

"You have an ID on this one?"

"No. But I'm sure she's an Emory student. I'll send you her name later."

"Bad time to be an Emory student. What else?"

"Nothing. I'll come down for the autopsies tomorrow morning. Homicide can have her."

The doctor waved at Lieutenant Raines. The lieutenant nodded and two detectives followed him under the yellow tape. The reporters surged forward, maneuvering, cameras rolling.

Nigel nodded toward the reporters. "Lieutenant, would you mind not letting the reporters photograph the bodies?"

Raines turned and pointed at his sergeant. "Tell the uniformed guys to keep those goddamn slimy reporters away from here. Make them stay up the hill. In the sun. Somebody will talk to them in a few minutes."

"Thank you, Lieutenant," Nigel said.

"Hey, Roach, good to see you. Been a long time."

The two men shook hands. Nigel looked Kenny Raines up and down. The lieutenant was wearing a gray suit with a pink shirt and a paisley tie. "Kenny, you're the best-dressed homicide detective in Atlanta."

Kenny nodded. "Except for that white hair of yours, you look just like the old days."

Nigel smiled. "I'll copy you on every piece of paperwork on these two. Let's sing from the same page in the hymnal."

"No problem. We got a briefing on you at roll call. You got some big horses behind you. I'd help you anyway, but this makes it easier."

"Thanks, my friend." Nigel looked at his watch. "Got to run."

"Where you off to?" Kenny asked. "We need to go to Manuel's and catch up."

"Another day, Kenny. I'm going to see my wife."

Raines paused. "How is she?"

Nigel shrugged. He nodded at the medical examiner. "I'll be in your office tomorrow morning. What time?"

"We've got two of them. What time can you be there?"

"Six a.m."

The M.E.'s eyes widened. "How about seven?"

"Okay."

Lieutenant Raines held up his hand. "Roach, before you go, you want this place under surveillance in case your boy comes back?"

Nigel nodded. "Good thinking. Put the SWAT people here twenty-four hours a day."

As Nigel walked down the hill, he was ignored by the young reporters who clustered around a homicide sergeant. They were too young to have any institutional memory of the Atlanta Police Department, too young to know who he was. But one reporter, the middle-aged one who was slouching alone on the hillside with a cigarette in his mouth, saw Nigel and angled across the hillside to intercept him. Nigel did not notice. He was relieved that his daughter was safe.

And he was wondering again how the offender picked his victims.

"Hey, Roach, wait up," the reporter said. "I didn't know you were back."

Nigel looked over his shoulder. He and Dan Buchanan had started their respective careers about the same time and had worked many cases together. "Hello, Dan." He knew he was being watched by the homicide cops up the hill. He waved as if he were dismissing the reporter. "Call me at home tonight. After nine."

"That's past my deadline, Roach. You know that."

"After nine. Now get away from me."

The sharpness of his voice caused Dan to stop. Nigel continued striding down the hill. His back was beginning to hurt and he tried not to limp.

I don't know the fantasy he is chasing. I may not know until after he is caught. I don't know where the abduction took place. I don't know where the death took place. I may never know those two sites. All I have is where the bodies were found—the crime scene. It will tell me more than the other places. What I have are two bodies. And they tell me a lot.

You used rubber gloves and condoms, and you combed their pubic hair for one reason—to conceal your identity. Killing the victim is an advanced version of that same line of thought. You want to conceal the crime as well as your identity. Mutilating the bodies, even dismembering them and hiding the parts in different locations, is still another version. But yet you put the bodies on display as if you are proud of your work.

You're evolving and changing, victim by victim. And you'll continue to change. What will you do next?

Nigel had been a police officer long enough to discover a truth about human behavior: when in doubt, think evil thoughts; think the worst possible scenario and you will be right most of the time.

You've killed twice. Soon you will begin mutilating them before you kill them.

Nigel squeezed his lips together.

His pace increased.

11

In the late 1970s and early 1980s, Atlanta was brutally scarred by a series of twenty-four homicides known as the Missing and Murdered Children. Eleven children were killed before Atlanta police officials and city officials announced they were facing a serial killer. That delay, that denial, is forever implanted in the DNA makeup of Atlanta. Today, two or more similar homicides cause seismic shock waves to reverberate throughout the city. The city's deepest fear and greatest horror is that it once again has become the stalking ground for a serial killer.

Officers were standing in clusters and talking and waving copies of *The Atlanta Constitution* when Nigel walked in about ten-thirty. He reeked of autopsy smells, chemical smells, death smells. The closed door to Major Morris's office indicated his wife had written one of the stories being discussed. Nigel ignored the animated conversations and turned toward his office. The odor from yesterday's homicide scene was mixed with odors from this morning's autopsy, and for the first time in three years his lower back was hurting. He was not in a good mood.

Dr. Mengele saw Nigel and shouted, "Hey, Roach. You read the paper this morning?"

Nigel shook his head and continued down the hall.

"Your *unsolved* case is in there," Maytag said. "The mayor is pissed."

Nigel stopped. He turned and walked toward Maytag's desk, where he stopped and looked around. "Glad to see you've cleaned this area up," he said. He took the newspaper from Maytag's hands. The story was on the front page. It was written by Dan Buchanan.

Nigel skimmed the story, folded the paper, and dropped it on Maytag's desk. "Seems straightforward enough." He turned to Dr. Mengele. "Was it on TV?"

Maytag jumped in. "Lead story on every station. But TV didn't have anything except that two bodies were found. Buchanan's bit about the bodies being dumped at different times is what riled the mayor. He's afraid people will think we have a serial killer out there."

"We do," Nigel said flatly. He turned toward Dr. Mengele. "Who says the mayor is concerned?"

Again Maytag jumped in. "Mayor's called the chief twice. She's called Major Morris. Plus we been getting phone calls from Buchanan. He says he's got a story in the first edition of *The Journal* updating this. That means TV news at six will use his stuff."

"Major in?" Nigel asked.

Maytag laughed. "Yeah. He's in there on a cot. He should have gone home hours ago. But his wife gave his home phone number to every TV and radio reporter in town. Did you see what she wrote this morning?"

Nigel did not answer. He walked across the room, knocked once, and opened the door as Major Morris shouted, "I'm not in."

When Morris saw Nigel, he stood up from the couch, tried to straighten his uniform, and said, "Roach, am I glad to see you. Tell me what you got."

The major was a mess. His tie was tossed across a chair. His sweat-streaked shirt was rumpled. He needed a shave. The room was foggy with stale cigarette smoke.

"M.E. didn't get much from the first one. She'd been there too long. No physical evidence except for the murder weapon, a screwdriver sold in every hardware store and discount store in town. Second one had had intercourse recently. No semen found. Muscles and cartilage in her neck were crushed." Nigel paused. "The M.E. found hair spray on both bodies. Trace elements on the first, substantial amount on the second. Same kind of spray."

Morris threw his hands wide. "So?"

"College kids don't use hair spray. Older women use hair spray."

"I might spray it on my wife's computer," Morris mumbled. He looked at Nigel. "What does it mean?"

"I don't know."

"Roach, the chief's been calling me every fifteen minutes. She's raising hell. She wants results. The mayor is pushing her hard. The chief will protect you as much as she can, but she wants to know when you will have something. They're all afraid this thing is about to blow up."

"It is."

Morris's eyes widened. He lit a cigarette and puffed anxiously. "It is? What do you mean?"

"Norris, we have a double homicide here. The bodies of two Emory students were found in a patch of kudzu near the Carter Center. Does the mayor expect two murders to remain a secret?"

"No, but he doesn't want them connected to the three rapes at Emory. He wants you to find this guy before Buchanan ties it all together." Morris rubbed his eyes. "Chief said the mayor told her three times the Olympics are coming to Atlanta. What the hell? Does he think we don't know about the Olympics? Does he think I'm stupid? I'm shit? Or vice versa."

Before Nigel could respond, Morris picked up a newspaper from his desk and waved it above his head. "Know what my wife wrote this morning? My sweet wife. Did you see the poison she wrote? That woman has a computer stored in shit and warmed in hell." He looked at Nigel. "Did I tell you she's Italian?"

Nigel shook his head.

"Yep. She's of Italian distraction. Goddamn wop. I married a wop spaghetti-eating ACLU bitch."

He held the paper at arms length. "Only two things lower than an ACLU lawyer. One is whale shit. The other is a newspaper person." He opened the paper, looked at the column, then tossed the paper aside. "Well, I can tell you that what's good for the goose is good for the mice that play when the cat's away."

"Or vice versa."

Morris nodded. "Or vice versa. You can take it to the cleaners."

"You hear Buchanan's got more coming in the afternoon paper?"

Morris took a deep puff and sliced his hand dismissively. "Yeah, yeah, yeah. I wish I could nip that bull by the horns. He's got the home phone numbers of every officer on the force. And every one will talk to him." He looked at Nigel. "You got anything else? Anything new?"

"It's all in my notes and in the autopsy report. I'm taking everything out to Ralph Stone at the GBI. The blonde blew the profile out the window. After I go over my notes and the case files again, I'm going to try something to flush this guy out."

"Is this something I don't want to know about?"

Nigel nodded. He rubbed his back.

"Is it something my wife will jump all over?"

"Norris, if I do this right, we can enlist her help."

"You're out of your tree."

"And she won't even know it."

Morris's eyes widened. "You're gonna use the paper and use her and she won't know what's going on?" He waved his hands. "No, no, no. Don't tell me. I don't want to know. Oh, God, this is wonderful. When will it happen?"

"Soon. Perhaps tomorrow."

Morris laughed. "Every dog has his pony. And mine has come in."

Nigel laughed and turned to leave the office. "I'll let you know what's going on."

"Maybe not everything. Just the good stuff I can pass along."

Nigel opened the door. He paused and listened to a conversation outside the office.

"The major's wife is going to ride this case hard," Popcorn said. "She's going to go ballistic over these students."

"For once in your miserable life, you may be right," Dr. Mengele said. "She doesn't like police officers. And to her and to the public, these girls are pure victims."

"No such thing as a pure victim."

"You don't think the Emory students are pure victims?"

Maytag shook his head. "You know that about sixty percent of the women Sex Crimes deals with haven't really been raped. Maybe seventy percent. They're lying, guilty, pissed off at their boyfriends, or just vindictive little bitches."

Popcorn nodded in agreement. "Besides, you can't rape an Emory student. Rich little bitches. They were probably asking for it anyway. I haven't seen any toxicology reports. But I bet all of them were drunk."

"What about a woman who goes out to get cash from an ATM machine or goes down to the convenience store and is grabbed and raped?" Dr. Mengele said. "Is she a pure victim?"

Maytag shook his head. "She had no business being there. She should have been at home."

"What about a woman whose car breaks down and is picked up and raped?"

Maytag laughed. "I'll answer that. But first, do you know how women and parking spaces are alike?" He paused only a second before delivering the answer. "The good ones are taken and the others are handicapped."

Morris sighed. He avoided looking at Nigel. "Ah, shit," he whispered. He would have pushed open the door, but Nigel held him back.

Maytag was still talking. "She should take better care of her car. If she did, it wouldn't break down. It's her fault. She's not a pure victim."

"What do you consider a pure victim?" Dr. Mengele asked.

Maytag pointed his finger at Dr. Mengele. "Hey,

I'm a police officer. Not a fucking therapist. The *only* pure victim, the *only* one, is a police officer killed in the line of duty."

Dr. Mengele shook his head. "Sieg heil," he muttered.

Morris pushed past Nigel and stood in the door of his office glaring at his officers. Nigel stood behind him. For a moment no one said anything. Then, as Morris raised a finger toward Maytag, a uniformed officer rushed into the squad room carrying a dozen copies of *The Atlanta Journal*, the afternoon sister paper to *The Atlanta Constitution*. The officer handed a paper to Nigel and another to Morris, then passed out the remainder among the officers. Buchanan's story was on the front page.

He identified the victims as Kathleen Powers, eighteen, of Trenton, NJ, and Anne Justice, nineteen, of Scarsdale, NY, and said Powers was a freshman in premedical courses while Justice was a sophomore majoring in international business.

The detectives groaned when they read that the Emory connection was a major element of the investigation.

And when they read that Powers had died about two weeks prior to Justice and that Justice had been dead for about twenty-four hours when her body was found, Popcorn shook his head and said, "Somebody's been talking to Buchanan."

The detectives began putting on their coats and gathering personal materials. "Oh, shit," said Popcorn. "I'm on the road. Got investigations to conduct."

"You slow down a half second and you'll be behind me," Maytag said. "I'm outta here. Got to go be a policeman."

Dr. Mengele shook his head and sighed. "The chief is going to be calling every few minutes." He looked at Roach. "My friend, do us all a favor and find this person."

The detectives waved at Major Morris and began exiting the squad room.

"You bastards," Morris said. "I can't believe you guys are doing this after all the times I stuck my leg out for you."

Popcorn made the mistake of being the last officer to leave.

"Hey, you, Popcorn. You stay here and answer the phone. In fact, you got phone duty for the next week. You're grounded. Tell your buddy Maytag he's got night phone for the next week."

Popcorn gave Morris his kicked-puppy look. "Major, I got some good leads on some old cases. I need to be on the street."

Morris pointed at Popcorn's desk. "Park your skinny ass and keep it there. You got the duty. Anybody calls, from reporters to the chief, you deal with them. You don't know where I am. Got it? Good."

Popcorn plopped down in his chair and leaned back. His eyes were locked on the ceiling panel over his desk. As soon as the major went back to his office . . .

Morris was shaking his head like a wet dog. "Damn Buchanan. I'm going to jerk his police pass."

"You can't keep this stuff quiet forever," Nigel said.

"I hate these high-profile cases. And this one is queer as a two-dollar bill. Now all the Emory stuff is out. Somebody is going to drop a dime. Buchanan will find out about the other rapes sooner or later."

"Probably sooner."

Morris looked at Nigel. "The chief is going to be on my ass like a pound of bricks."

"Norris, I told you, we got two dead girls tossed on a hillside out there. And my theory about who he's targeting is wrong. I'm back at zero and he's ahead. So I'm going to try something. I don't know if it will work, but it's all I've got."

Norris looked at Nigel, then decided he didn't want to know what was about to happen. He shook his head.

Nigel put his hand on Morris's shoulder. "We've been down this road before, Major. We can ride it out. All we have to do is do our jobs."

"Yeah, yeah, yeah. Or vice versa." He paused. "Nigel, Maytag is a prick."

Nigel shrugged. "I used to work here." He limped toward the door. "I'm going to the GBI and then I'm going to make things start happening."

Morris stared at the closed door. He suddenly recalled something. Another reason for the Roach's nickname was that the deeper he immersed himself in a case, the more his physical problem manifested itself. The old back injury flared up. It began with Nigel frequently rubbing his back. Then he began limping. Finally, his back became so twisted and painful that when he walked he dragged one foot behind him. He walked sideways. He scurried ... like a roach.

12

The uniformed officer slowed his marked car behind the Carter Presidential Center, then pulled onto the manicured shoulder of the road. He turned on his caution lights, stepped outside, and looked around. He adjusted the Beretta 9mm on his right hip. He did not usually wear a weapon, and the weight was noticeable. He adjusted his hat over his closely cropped blond hair and slowly walked up the hill toward a clump of oak trees. He was tall and muscular, and his uniform was sharply creased and his leather sparkled. He looked like a recruiting poster picture of the ideal cop.

The officer paused halfway up the hill and looked over his shoulder. He did not want his car to be too close. Cops had sharp eyes. He looked along the treeline at the top of the hill and then over his shoulder toward the opposite side of the road.

Nothing.

But they were there.

He continued.

At the top of the hill, as he was about to enter the stand of oaks, a figure rose from a patch of kudzu. The man wore black fatigue pants, black boots, a black watch cap, and had camo paint streaked across his face. He held a shotgun by its pistol grip.

"We help you?" he said cautiously.

The uniformed officer smiled and waved. "Hey, just looking for you guys. Wanted to talk with you. You in command here?"

"Yeah. Sergeant Luke. Atlanta SWAT."

The young officer held out his hand. "Officer Brumley. From Emory." He paused and looked around. "You got other officers out here." It was not a question.

Sergeant Luke looked at Brumley with hooded eyes. "Yeah. My squad is back in the woods. We got others around." He looked down the hill at the marked car and at the young officer's shoulder patch. "Aren't you out of your jurisdiction?"

Officer Brumley smiled. It was a very disarming smile. "You got that right. But I'm worried about what's going on and just wanted to let you know that we're ready to help any way we can. Anything you need, you got it."

Sergeant Luke nodded. "We got this part under control."

This is where I brought them. These police officers are here because of me. There, right over there under those trees, is where I placed their bodies. I was very gentle and respectful of them. It's happening all over again. I can feel it beginning.

Brumley laughed and turned sideways away from the SWAT officer. "You guys could take on an army. The perp comes around here, you'll blow his ass away."

"Believe it." Luke paused. "Look, we don't know when the guy might come back. Maybe you—"

Brumley held up a hand and interrupted. "I know. I shouldn't be here. But I just wanted to let you know

Emory will cooperate however we can. Thank all of your officers for us."

"Okay."

The two men shook hands, and Brumley turned and walked toward his car. The sergeant watched him for a minute, shook his head, then walked toward his hiding place in the thick patch of kudzu.

"Hey, Sarge," came a voice from the trees. "Who the hell was that?"

"Stupid fucking rent-a-cop from Emory."

"What'd he want?"

The sergeant laughed. "To help." As the sergeant slid into the kudzu, he mumbled to himself, "Best way he can help is to keep his ass on campus and leave this to the pros."

As the young officer reached his car, he took off his hat. He opened the door and carefully placed the hat on the seat. He turned on the ignition, looked in the rearview mirror, and carefully eased onto the highway. A block away he stopped and removed the magnetic pad from his car door, the pad that was faced with the coat of arms of Emory University. After he crossed Ponce de Leon and headed toward Emory, Lucifer permitted himself a satisfied smile.

" 'We got this part under control.' Blah, blah, blah."

The police officers actually thought he might return. Silly men.

At Emory he knew of another girl who was looking for him. Any time he wanted, he could take her to the mountain top and show her his kingdom. He wanted to do it today. But those men in the kudzu needed to learn a lesson. Let that officious and arrogant SWAT sergeant and his men lie out in the kudzu waiting for him. Let them wait a few days. Then he would show them he was not coming back.

He would outsmart them again.

The air conditioner was broken in Nigel's car. He pushed the large box across the front seat, took off his coat and tossed it on the back seat, and then loosened his tie. He slid under the steering wheel and rolled down the windows.

A half hour later, he pulled into the parking lot of the Georgia Bureau of Investigation headquarters on Panthersville Road. The GBI head shed was disguised as a drab institutional pile of bricks. Inside was pretty much the same as outside. In the middle of the plain lobby was a circular seating arrangement. Against the rear wall was a display obviously put together by someone about to retire, someone whose brain had stopped working several decades earlier. Badges and awards were set behind glass in a display case that merited no more than a cursory glance even from the most curious of visitors. On the right of the lobby, sitting behind a low desk and staring at three small TV screens, was a uniformed security officer. He did not look up as Nigel entered. He had watched Nigel from the time he had parked and carried the heavy box across the parking lot and into the office. Nigel turned left, toward the forensics side of the building, where a woman sat behind a high desk. He put the box on the circular couch and showed the woman his ID. She nodded and picked up the phone. After a brief conversation, she handed him a visitor's badge. "Mr. Stone is on the way. He will be here shortly." She pointed across the hall, toward the administrative side of the building.

A few seconds later the locked door opened, and a
tall, lanky figure strode toward Nigel. The man had a
big smile on his face, and his hand was outstretched
in greeting. In the split second before the man spoke,
Nigel realized again that Ralph Stone would be an
easy man to underestimate. He did not cultivate the
gruff and standoffish exterior prized by so many police
officers. He was a warm and outgoing man, a gentle
man who truly liked people. Perhaps that was why he
was so good at what he did.

"Roach, how are you?" Ralph said. "I was tickled
to death to hear you were back and glad you called
me so soon. Come on back." The two men shook
hands. Ralph clapped Nigel on the shoulder. "You're
looking good for an old man."

"I'm doing okay, Ralph. Sorry to be back under
such circumstances but . . ."

"That's what keeps us in business," Ralph finished.

Nigel nodded. He reached for the cardboard box.

"Here, let me help you with that," Ralph said.

"No, I have it. If you'll take care of the door, I'll
follow you and dump all this on your desk."

Ralph laughed. He slid his ID card through the slot
on the side of the door, waited a second, then pulled
the door open. "Follow me," he said. "I'm back here
in this maze somewhere. Sometimes I think finding
my office is some sort of test."

For what seemed like several minutes the two men
wended their way through offices sliced up with half
partitions and around corners and down long halls
until they reached a spacious office.

"Put it on the desk," Ralph said. He started to
speak, but the look on Nigel's face stopped him. He
paused. "It's been a long time, Roach, and I'd like to

catch up. But I know you're overwhelmed and you want this stuff as quickly as you can."

Nigel nodded in gratitude. "Thanks, Ralph."

"Okay, guy. Go back down the hall to the break room and drink coffee for a while. By the time you find your way back, I'll have something for you." He reached for the box and opened it.

Two hours later, he sent a secretary to find Nigel.

Ralph looked up from his desk as Nigel entered. "You got a live one here, Roach."

The slender GBI agent stood up and began slowly to pace back and forth behind the paper-littered table. As he paced, he ran a hand through his white hair. He nodded toward the files, reports, and records covering his desk. "Your boy's about as rough as I've ever seen."

Nigel waited, trying not to be impatient. The coffee had made him tense and wired. He had been sitting in a corner of the coffee shop, back to the door, facing a wall, going over every detail of the case and wondering when he would be called to examine another victim. He needed a fresh perspective on the case. He needed to know what Ralph Stone knew. Ralph had spent a year at Quantico with the FBI's Behavioral Science Unit. In addition, he had a knack for profiling the perpetrators in unsolvable murder cases and in cases involving serial rapists.

"How's he picking his victims, Ralph? What have I overlooked?"

Ralph smiled. "You haven't overlooked anything. Don't worry about that. Let's walk through this and see what we got." Ralph waved at the papers on his desk. "Obviously, Emory is the key. That's his hunting ground. That's where he stalks them. So you have to look at the campus. Look at Emory personnel. All of them, but especially the faculty and staff and those who have dealings with students. Check for common elements among the victims. Have they all had a class with one professor, for instance."

"What about the similarities in coloring of the first four victims? All dark complexions with black hair."

Ralph smiled. "I wish I could give you a categorical answer. But I can't. I can give you two possibilities."

Nigel nodded.

"One would be to discount totally the complexion and hair. The only thing important is that the victims are women. Emory women. What does the university represent to the perpetrator? He is spending time where the victims are spending time. In this theory Emory is the key."

"And two?"

"Two would be that he is picking them by complexion and hair and that he picked the blond only to throw you off, to confuse you."

Nigel smiled. "Ralph, sometimes I understand why many police officers don't think much of this profiling business."

Ralph nodded. "You understand that we're dealing with human behavior here. This is not an exact science."

"But I need to know something hard here. He's still running around loose, and he's going to hit again."

Ralph nodded. "Let me tell you what comes to mind here. Those three survivors are important. You've got to talk to them. What they can tell you is crucial. They know the most about the offender."

Nigel shook his head. "I've tried. They don't want any part of this."

"Try again. It's crucial if you're going to catch this guy anytime soon."

"Okay."

Ralph picked up a legal pad and looked at his notes. "When you talk to the survivors, you need three things. First, you want verbal behavior. What did the offender say? What did he make the victims say? You want the exact language. The victims are young and embarrassed, and they will want to soften it or change the words. But you must get them to tell you *exactly* what he said. Second, you want his sexual behavior. What did he make the victims do? And in what order? If what he wanted was demeaning or degrading, how did he negotiate with them? What did he say? What threats did he use?"

"You think he's conning them or threatening them?"

"Could be both. What jumps out at me about this guy is how he's changing. He's unpredictable. Things he did with earlier victims aren't there with later victims. It's more than the fact earlier victims were not killed. That's only symptomatic of what's going on his mind. The increasing violence shows the nature of his fantasies. His fantasies may improve. But they won't change. They are offender-specific. The fantasies are for one reason: to give him psychosexual gratification. There is a direct link between his violent fantasies and the sex act."

Nigel started to speak, but Ralph held up a finger. "Consider this. The M.E. was not able to find semen in the two decedents. You need to know if he ejaculated when he had sex with the survivors."

"He used a condom."

"But did he ejaculate? He could have a sexual dysfunction. If so, it may be a result of great anger toward women. And make no mistake about it, this is one angry man."

Ralph looked at his notes again. "The third thing you need from the victims is this guy's physical behavior. How did he control them when he first approached them? We need to know both the nature and the level of his violence. His violence is increasing dramatically. His methods of control may change. But the more we know, the closer we can get to him."

Ralph paused. "The underlying and fundamental issue for him is control. He has no control over his life. He wants control. As a child he was told he would never amount to anything. He is a man not with low self-esteem but with no self-esteem. So he is reaching out for esteem. Whatever his plan or idea is, it is filled with grandiosity. That's how he shows he is in control. When his fantasy is working he is like God. He can take life whenever he chooses. That is the ultimate control. He is killing someone over and over, someone in his past, some female." Ralph looked at Nigel. "And the time is accelerating."

"How do we find what his fantasy is?"

"That is the key question. Because that is how he is picking his victims." Ralph shrugged. "Sometimes we never know until it's all over."

"What sort of man is he?"

"He spends a lot of time alone. He is quiet. Neat. Organized. Cares about his appearance. The condition of his body is important to him. He may try to inject himself into the case. If he thinks you are getting close to him, he will try to divert you by picking a victim who is not an Emory student. Do you have a profile of each of the victims?"

"Yes."

"He will know what you have, and he may pick a victim outside the profile to confuse you. That's why I said he may have picked the blonde to throw you off."

"Wait a minute. When you say *you*, you don't mean *me*, you mean any police officer?"

Ralph shook his head. "No. I mean *you*. I mean Nigel Trench. He knows who you are. He knows all about you."

Nigel looked away. Then he knows I have a special reason for wanting him, he thought.

"I saw the story in the morning paper," Ralph said. "He read the story. He's the kind who reads the newspaper rather than getting his news off television. So you have to maintain tight control over what is released to the press on this one."

Ralph raised a hand to stop Nigel's protest. "I know. With two fatalities sprawled in the kudzu at the Carter Center, no way you can keep it quiet. But if you taunt or insult or challenge this guy, he's going to react in a very powerful way. He will take you up on any challenge you issue. He will show you he is the boss, that he is in control. He may choose you or someone close to you as a victim. Don't try to fuck with his mind through the media. If you have to talk to the press, always hold something back, something that only the perpetrator knows. Because the loony tunes are going to begin confessing."

Nigel nodded. He had planned to plant a story with Buchanan taunting the offender, questioning his manhood, something that Marie Morris would have picked up and trumpeted about in several columns. He had known it would be a calculated risk, but he wanted to pull the offender out into the open. Now Ralph said that would be a big mistake. He trusted Ralph.

And he wondered if he was losing his touch. He wondered if concern for his wife and fear for his daughter were affecting his judgment.

"The offender is angry at some woman," Ralph said. "I don't know who. But he is getting back at someone. He can make things happen with these women. Whatever he wants, he gets. He is in control. When you get a suspect, look into his background for a controlling woman, someone who made his life miserable."

"That's his motive?"

"No." Ralph paused. "His motive is to be God."

"How long has he been like this?"

Nigel's thoughts went back to Rachel, and he wondered what bizarre twist of fate, what wrinkle in her karma, had placed her life in confluence with that of the offender.

Ralph paused. He was looking at the ceiling. "Roach, this is speculation. But I don't believe he started recently, or even three or four years ago. All the research the FBI has done indicates these guys don't pop up all at once as full-blown sexual predators. They go to work early. He may have a juvie record. There are many cases where the perp began killing when he was a child."

"You think . . . ?"

Ralph nodded.

"That far back?"

"You know how hard it is for civilians to understand that people like this walk among us. But, yes. It would have been someone vulnerable. She was paralyzed, bedridden, on crutches or in a wheelchair. She was handicapped in some fashion. She had to be vulnerable."

Nigel nodded.

"Chances are no one knew he did it. He got away with it. Everyone thought it was natural causes or whatever illness she had."

Nigel sighed and slowly shook his head.

"He probably ejaculated when he killed her. He had a spontaneous erection and ejaculated, and he enjoyed it. From that moment on he had no control. He might have controlled it occasionally if outsiders were a threat, but inside he was just waiting. Now he really knows. He's a juggernaut. And he's gaining momentum all the time."

Ralph paused and returned to his desk, where he thumbed through the papers. He did not look up when he said, "I see you have included an old case here, one that is not part of this series."

Nigel did not speak.

Ralph's voice was deliberately impassive and clinical. "I think that might have been a pivotal incident in many respects. It marked a clear border between the rape cases and those cases where he assaulted the women. Then he was gone for three years. Wherever he went or whatever he did in those three years, he learned a lot. Because when he came back he was a different person. Whatever control he might have had in the past, he had lost. The rapes became the prelude to the physical beatings. As you know, the M.O. in sexual cases is good for only two or three months. The offender changes either through education, maturity, or experience. This guy is changing as fast as anyone I've ever seen. The more he evolves, the closer we are to seeing who he really is. And it sure as hell ain't promising."

"That agrees with my assessment. Frankly, I was hoping you would prove me wrong."

"He felt remorse for the homicides. He felt shame. That's why he cleaned and washed the victims at the Carter Center. He's washing away the guilt. He's trying to undo what he's done. And then he puts the victims on display to show he has atoned. In his mind he is being a good boy when he does that."

"Until the next time."

Ralph did not speak for a moment. "The guilt and remorse will disappear. Probably already have. That's what you and I know, but what civilians don't understand, Roach. Some people out there are bad to the bone. This guy is like that. You could put him in jail for twenty years, and the day he gets out he will hunt for a woman. Even God would give up on this guy. He will never change. He will never be healed. He will never be rehabilitated. He will never stop. The only thing that will stop him is killing him."

13

Nigel hated this part of The Job.

He slowly put the telephone receiver back on the cradle. It took all of his willpower not to slam the phone down. The parents of the first two assault victims had refused to allow their daughters to talk to the Atlanta officer. "We told you before, this is behind us and we don't want to bring it up again," one of the mothers had urgently whispered.

He understood why they did not want to talk. But they did not understand why they had to talk.

"My daughter was released from the hospital yesterday," the father of the second victim said. "Don't you people in Georgia have any feelings at all? I'm telling you not to call us again." The receiver clicked.

Nigel rubbed his eyes. This case was not going well. He could not talk to the first two victims. He had almost committed a serious mistake with his plan to taunt the offender by leaking information to Buchanan. He did not know how the offender was picking his victims. And the offender had graduated from rape to murder and soon would strike again.

Nigel tried to think of him clinically as "the offender." That way he could keep a certain dispassionate distance from the man. That way he could depersonalize what the man had done. That way he could control the anger and rage bubbling in his soul.

Every honest cop, every cop who has ever put his life on the line, every cop who has ever had a dirtbag take a shot at him, has at one time or another asked himself, "Don't I deserve more?" He has asked himself the question "How can I rip off a bad guy and not fuck society?" He might find a stash of dope money, enough for his retirement, and wonder about making one big score. But Nigel's thoughts, when they roamed in that seductive and forbidden wilderness, were not of taking money for his retirement. He thought of killing rapists. He wondered what it would be like to apprehend this offender when no one else was around, to handcuff him to a tree, and then to devise a special method of dealing with him. He fantasized about the different ways of exacting revenge. Shooting was too easy and too quick. Except for maybe a shot in each kneecap. Knives were not his thing. He never felt the need to take the classic revenge of cutting off the man's testicles and stuffing them in his mouth. He wanted to do something up close. He wanted to see the fear and terror and pain on the face of the man who had caused so much fear and terror and pain among so many innocent people. He had thought of choking. But he could not do that. In fact, he had never really come up with a way that was acceptable. At bottom he had a Manichaean view of law enforcement. He was a cop. Cops uphold the law.

Nigel sighed and came back to the business at hand. The two homicides had taken the case public, and it was only a matter of time before Buchanan tied the first rape to those of the other two Emory students who had dropped out of school. When he tied those first three rapes to the two homicides and the words *serial rapist* or *serial killer* began appearing in the media, the mayor would go nuclear. Nigel almost smiled. If the case went public, at least the students would know the danger they faced. Their parents would know. It was important to Nigel that both the students and their parents knew about the case, because he had not yet figured out the most basic and most crucial part of the investigation: how the offender was picking his victims. It had to be more than age and availability. There was some plan at work here. But what was it?

Nigel looked at the phone number and name of the third victim. He rubbed his eyes again. He stood up, paused, and put both hands, fingers down, on the small of his back and rubbed, kneading his spinal column and moving his torso slowly from side to side. He wondered if he had made a mistake by taking on this case. All he wanted was to take care of his wife and daughter and tend to his flowers. But his wife and daughter were the reasons he was here. He had no choice; he had to be here.

He opened the folder for Monaco Jackson and stared at her picture. God, she looked like Sarah. She had been flown back to New York on a special jet charter flight and was in a hospital with a broken leg and three cracked ribs. And Norman Jackson and Cynthia Jackson, the girl's parents, were doubtless hovering over her. Nigel knew they were as resentful of Atlanta police officers as the other parents. He would be.

Nigel made up his mind. He picked up the telephone and quickly punched in the numbers.

A male voice answered. Nigel took the plunge.

"Mr. Jackson?"

"Yes." The voice was guarded, as if trying to remember the identity of the caller.

"Mr. Jackson, this is detective Nigel Trench with the Atlanta Police Department. We've talked before. I want you to listen to me for a moment. You are going through a period of great pain and great anger, and I understand that—"

"You can't understand," the voice sputtered. "You don't know. Why are you calling? I specifically asked you not to call again."

Nigel closed his eyes. His voice was low and intense. But underneath it simmered. "Mr. Jackson, my wife was raped three years ago. She was raped and brutally beaten. She underwent months of therapy, but today she requires the constant care of a doctor. She is hospitalized most of the time. She will never again be the wife I once had, Mr. Jackson. Do you understand that? Can you understand that?"

For a moment there was no answer. "I didn't know. I'm sorry. But even so . . ."

"Mr. Jackson, the individual who did it was never caught. We believe he has returned to Atlanta and that he is the man who attacked your daughter. We believe he may have attacked two other Emory students. And if you've read the paper in the last few days, you've seen the story of the two students whose bodies—"

"The ones at the Carter Center?"

"Yes, Mr. Jackson. The same man did all of that. This will be difficult for you to understand right now. But your daughter is fortunate. She was assaulted and she is in the hospital, but she is alive. She is alive. She is young and one day, God willing, she will be okay. The two most recent victims are dead. They will never be okay. I need your help, Mr. Jackson. I need your help very badly."

"I saw that on CNN." Jackson's voice was incredulous. "One of the girls was from Scarsdale, and the other was from up in Jersey."

"Mr. Jackson. I have one child; a daughter. She is a student at Emory. She bears a striking resemblance to your daughter. In fact, we are wondering if the students are targeted because of their physical appearance. If we are right, my daughter could well be a target of the same man who attacked your daughter. Am I getting through to you, Mr. Jackson? Do you understand the level of my interest in this case?"

There was no answer. Nigel plunged ahead.

"You're correct about the two girls who were killed. They're both from up your way. Now, as I said, we believe the same man may have committed all these crimes. I know you are angry about your daughter, and I know you are angry about what happened to the other students at Emory. I would be. I am. I've never admitted this to anyone before, Mr. Jackson, but I have more anger than you can imagine about what happened to my wife three years ago. That's the reason I am here today. I'm offering you a unique opportunity, Mr. Jackson, an opportunity to help catch this man. He will be caught. And when he is, you can take great consolation in the fact you were instrumental in helping catch the man who harmed your daughter. I know you want to see him punished."

"Punished? Punished? I want to see the—"

"I know you do, Mr. Jackson. The first step is letting your daughter talk to me. She is crucial to our identifying this man and catching him. You can be a big help to us, and you can feel better knowing you had a part in this."

For a long moment there was no answer. Nigel was about to speak when Jackson said, "I don't know." He paused again. "Who would be there?"

"Just your daughter and me, Mr. Jackson. You and your wife don't have to be there. Your daughter and I must talk about what happened, and I don't think you would want to be there. But you can be close by, just outside the room."

"It bothers me to think of her talking about it, reliving it."

"It will be painful for her. You are right. But she must confront this and deal with it and then put it behind her and move on."

"I don't know. My wife ..."

"She doesn't feel the same need to punish this man that you do? Is that what you are saying?"

"Yes. She ... well, she just wants to take care of Monaco ... of our daughter. She wants to forget it. She is trying to pretend—"

"It never happened," Nigel finished. "We are different from women in that respect, Mr. Jackson. You and I want vengeance. We want that man to feel pain. We want to see him punished, don't we?"

Jackson exploded. "I want to see the son of a bitch burn in hell. I want to kill him myself. I want to hurt him. That's all I think of. I just can't get it out of my mind. I want to hold him down and—"

Nigel squeezed his eyes tighter together. "I know," he whispered. "Let me talk to your daughter, Mr. Jackson. It will be a first step for both of us in catching this man."

Another long pause.

"When?"

Nigel thought rapidly. Delta had an early flight to LaGuardia. "I can be there by eight A.M. tomorrow."

"Make it ten. Monaco has a difficult time with that broken leg in the mornings. And by ten the doctor will have made his rounds. I'll talk to my wife and daughter. But it will be okay. She's at Metropolitan Hospital." Jackson gave him the address of the hospital on the upper East Side of Manhattan.

"Thank you, Mr. Jackson."

"One more thing, Officer . . . what did you say your name was?"

"Trench. Nigel Trench."

"One more thing, Officer Trench."

"Yes?"

"When you catch this son of a bitch, I want you to call and tell me."

"I will, Mr. Jackson."

"Have me paged when you get to the hospital. I'll come down and get you."

"Ten o'clock."

"Good-bye."

"Good-bye, Mr. Jackson."

Nigel looked at his watch. If he hurried he could reach the hospital and spend an hour with Rachel before they fed her.

"Norris, I want you to do something for me. Something personal."

Major Morris looked at Nigel in surprise. Nigel was staring at the wall, deep in thought. Morris waited.

"I want you to ride out to the hospital with me."

Morris cleared his throat. He knew which hospital. "Okay."

"I'm not quite sure how to handle this," Nigel said. "But I've thought about it, and this is the way I want to do this."

"Do what?"

"Norris, she mustn't find out what I'm doing. Under no circumstances can she know." Nigel paused. He shrugged and turned to face Morris. "I'm talking to you as a friend. The doctors say she can't handle stress."

He looked away. "If she knew . . . if she knew *he* was back in town . . . well, I don't think she could deal with it."

"What do you want me to do?" Morris was uncomfortable. Nigel had talked about all this before.

"I haven't seen you in several years. She knows that. I want her to think you called and that we got together at Manuel's for a beer. For old time's sake. And that we decided to go to lunch one day soon."

"And I asked about her and you brought me out to say hello," Morris added. "As an old friend. Like two peas in a jar."

Nigel nodded his thanks.

"This is insurance. Just in case she somehow finds out. I don't want anyone calling or paging me at the hospital or at home unless it's an absolute emergency. If she's at home, I can't talk on the phone. I hope this situation doesn't arise. But if it does, you'll have to get someone else to handle it until she goes back to the hospital. She only comes home for a day or so every few weeks, so it shouldn't be a problem. But if it happens, I want you to know she comes first."

Morris nodded. "I've always known that."

"If I am at the hospital, I'll let you know in advance. No one is ever to call or page me there. No matter what the emergency."

"Want me to wear civilian clothes?"

"Yes. Let's ease her into this. I'm not sure she could deal with the sight of a uniform right now."

"When you want to do this?"

"You're wearing civilian clothes today." Nigel paused. "In fact, that's a very nice-looking suit."

Norris held his arms out and examined his sleeves. "Yeah. Vietnamese tailor over on Cheshire Bridge Road fixed it for me. He does good altercations."

"Lots of experience."

"Yeah, I guess so." Norris looked at Nigel. "You want to go now?"

"Yes."

Morris stood up. "Now is fine. Or vice versa." He paused. "Funny how things work out. You really care about your wife. You had a great marriage. About the only cop I know who did."

"We had our rough spots."

"Yeah? But you had a good marriage. Look at me and my wife. She thinks I'm an idiot. I know she is. I got a marriage from hell."

"Why don't you get out?"

"I don't know. Pain gets comfortable, I guess."

Neither man spoke for a moment.

"One more thing," Nigel said. "When we get there, let's keep it light. Just chitchat. Nothing about The Job."

"Okay." Morris smiled in agreement. "We can talk in semaphores."

"Or vice versa."

"You got it."

*   *   *

Nigel had a window seat on the return flight to Atlanta. He sat there, coat on and tie snugged tight, staring down at billowing, dark thunderclouds, towering cumulonimbus reaching up for him in the high, calm air, and replayed the interview with Monaco Jackson.

She had been so traumatized by the event that she remembered few details of what had happened. She recalled that the offender had gained entry by pretending to be an apartment maintenance man. The lights, the television, everything electrical in Miss Jackson's apartment had suddenly stopped working. Two or three minutes later, as she was about to call the apartment manager, the telephone rang. A man's voice on the other end explained that some repair work was being done in the downstairs laundry room. It was being done at night in order not to inconvenience the tenants. Several wires from one of the fuse boxes had been accidentally cut. Was her apartment affected?

When she said yes, the man apologized and said a repairman would be at her door in about two minutes to fix the problem.

Nigel shook his head ruefully at the lack of knowledge among young women about things electrical. If the problem were in the laundry room, why did someone need to come to her apartment? And why didn't she verify all this with the apartment manager? But she readily agreed. Nigel made a note to check for the location of the nearest pay phone to the apartment. If there were no pay phone nearby, that meant the offender used a cellular phone. He made another mental note to call the telephone company and see if records were kept on the numbers called and from what numbers. He might be able to locate the cellular phone that had called her.

Several minutes after the phone call, there was a knock on Monaco Jackson's door. She looked through the peephole, but the outside light was also off and all she saw was a silhouette of a man wearing a hat.

"Maintenance," said a soft voice.

She opened the door.

Miss Jackson's account of her attack did not add substantially to what was already known about how the offender worked. He played music that she recognized as Wagner. he talked about God and heaven and hell. He had pale eyes. He wore an expensive cologne. The sex act had lasted a long time, almost an hour. She did not believe he had ejaculated, which might be important in his psychological profile, but would be of little help in identifying him. But the offender had said one thing to Monaco Jackson that bewildered Nigel. It was important, but he did not know how. It was after the offender had raped her and was beginning to beat her. Hanging onto consciousness, in surprise and astonishment, she asked, "Why? Why are you hurting me?"

"Because," the man answered. "Because I am the Son of the . . ."

She fell unconscious and did not hear the remainder.

Son of the . . . son of the . . . Nigel shook his head. Somewhere in the past, perhaps from something he had read, a faint bell was ringing.

Son of the . . . son of the . . .

It was gone.

*   *   *

Maytag walked into the squad room, swung the door wide, and stopped. "Major in?" he asked the room at large.

Dr. Mengele did not look up.

The Undertaker peered around the urn atop his desk but said nothing.

Maytag pulled a copy of *The Atlanta Constitution* from his pocket and waved it overhead. "Anyone see what the major's wife wrote today?"

No one answered.

Maytag waved the paper again. "You won't believe this crap. When the chief reads this, she will miss a period and go into PMS overload." Maytag began leafing through the paper.

"You guys got to hear this." Maytag laughed in derision. "She's back on that interpersonal violence kick."

"Not again," Maggot moaned. "Next thing you know she'll be writing again about taking rape victims out of the emergency rooms and letting specially trained nurses treat them."

"We can all read," Dr. Mengele said.

Maytag ignored him. "She's only written about it fifteen times." He folded the paper, looked around the room, and said, "Okay. Here goes."

" 'The tragic inability of the Atlanta police to identify and locate and apprehend the fiend who is attacking Emory students reminds me again of a serious flaw in the way the police department is constituted.' "

Maggot nodded in mock seriousness. "We have a serious flaw."

" 'The antediluvian label of "sex crimes" is still applied to the squad that investigates crimes of interpersonal violence. And sex crimes are all too often considered a perverse sideshow for police officers.' "

Maytag paused. He looked up. "What the fuck is antediuvian?"

Maggot waved her hand. "Who cares? We're a perverse sideshow. I like that."

" 'The inherent problem is that, for most people, the word *sex* evokes a specific set of emotions: love, pleasure, joy, warmth, sharing. On the other hand, the word crime is associated with an entirely antithetical set of emotions: violence, brutality, fear. The words do not match.' "

Maytag grinned. "Can't have words that don't match."

" 'This is neither a trivial nor an insignificant distinction. We must never underestimate the power of words. Because these two disparate words are placed together, the people who work in the so called "sex crimes squad" all too often see their work as a sideshow. They spend too much time trying to convince other officers of their legitimacy, that they are not out chasing "wciner waggers" and "booty bandits." This is abundantly manifest in their profanity, inappropriate jokes, and sexual remarks.' "

"Hey, Maytag," Maggot interrupted. "Convince me you are legitimate."

"Hold on. The good stuff is ahead.

" 'The insensitivity and insecurity of these officers, were the consequences not so serious, could be dismissed. However, one must always keep in the forefront of thought exactly who are the victims of these officers. The victims of sexual assault are double victims. Not only are they victims of their assailants, but they become victims of the very people whose job it is to help them. They become victims of the system. The victim is experiencing fear, anger, guilt, and humiliation. The officer who works with her will be dealing with these very powerful emotions. The problem comes when the officer is unable to control his or her emotions. Some officers have hidden agendas. Some ask victims to repeat details an unreasonable number of times.' "

Maytag stopped reading and looked at his trousers. "Stay in there, you hidden agenda."

Maggot laughed.

"We can all read," Dr. Mengele said. "Take a rest."

"Listen to this. 'Everyone who works on these crimes of interpersonal violence should be a volunteer. Officers should not be sent to this squad as punishment. If assignment to this group is a punishment or is used as discipline, then only mediocre officers or mediocre performers will represent Atlanta in dealing with victims of this most tragic of crimes.' "

Maytag looked up. "Am I a mediocre officer?"

"That would be a promotion," Dr. Mengele said.

Maytag returned to his reading: " 'Observers can tell a great deal about the attitude of a police department toward sexual offenders by those who are selected to investigate these crimes. In fact, the people chosen to work these crimes of interpersonal violence send a much louder signal to the world than does all the hoopla about the Olympics.' "

"Ooooooohhh," Maggot said. "Low one."

" 'The homicide squad is usually considered the most elite investigative group within a police department. Year-end statistics always boast of homicides solved. But how often does Atlanta boast of sexual offenses solved?

" 'Why is the solution rate for homicides always greater than that for sexual crimes? This is particularly significant when one considers that homicide victims are deceased and can't provide help to the police officer. But rape victims usually survive to help the investigator.' "

"How long does this go on?" Dr. Mengele asked.

"One more paragraph. She saved the best for last.

" 'Beverly Harvard had the chance to become a great chief of police. She was the first black woman to head the police department in a major city. She had the chance to respond to the overwhelming need of more than half the population of this city by setting up an entirely new investigative group, calling it the "Interpersonal Violence Squad" rather than "Sex Crimes" and by making it the premier investigative group within the department and arming it with the full weight of her office.

" 'Instead, her focus has been on the Olympics. The Olympics will be gone in several weeks. But the women of Atlanta—more often than not, the young women of Atlanta, those who are the most precious resources of society—will continue to be raped.' "

Maytag folded the newspaper and looked around. "Is the woman a missionary or what?" He waved the paper toward Dr. Mengele. "What would your friend the Roach man say about this?"

Dr. Mengele looked at Maytag and smiled. "He would agree with every word."

It was ten p.m. Saturday when Virginia Blair yawned and pushed aside the papers from her journalism class. She checked the chain and dead bolt on the door of her second-story apartment, turned off the lights, and opened the rear windows. For a moment she enjoyed the slight breeze. Then she knelt by her bed as she had done every night since she was a child, prayed for several minutes, and crawled into bed.

A half hour later, the insistent chimes awakened her. They sounded almost like church bells. For a moment she lay still. Then she realized someone was at the door.

She threw on a cotton bathrobe and walked down the hall. Several steps before she reached the door, she stopped in surprise. Her feet were sopping wet. She turned on the light, looked down, and saw that the carpet was soaked. The door bells chimed again.

"Who is it?" she asked, wondering in dismay why her carpet was wet.

"Maintenance. We've got some broken pipes. Is your apartment okay?"

"No, it's not. I'm up to my ankles in water." She waded closer to the door and looked through the peep hole. Her eyes had not yet adjusted to the light. She saw a man holding up what appeared to be a plumber's bag.

She opened the door.

14

Nigel closed the door after entering Ed Medlin's office.

"Ed, I need your help."

"Name it," the tall, bearded director of the Emory Police Department said.

"What sort of background information do you have on the faculty and staff?"

Ed laughed. "You get right to the point."

"Sorry, Ed. Things are moving fast."

"Think the perpetrator is someone on campus?" As Ed spoke, he reached for a stack of folders on the credenza behind his desk.

"I'm almost certain."

Ed slid the stack of folders across the top of his desk and pointed at them. "Computer printouts of the names of every staff member on campus. My staff is included, all of my officers are in there. I'm sure you'll want to dig deeper on some of those names, so the DOB and Social Security number of every person is included."

"How many people are we talking about?"

"I didn't include the Emory Clinic. It's a separate payroll." He tapped the printouts. "We have about eighty-five hundred people on the payroll."

Nigel looked at Ed. He chuckled. "How'd you know?"

Ed shrugged. "It crossed my mind the other day you might want this, so I ordered it done."

Nigel looked at the stack of records. "Eighty-five hundred people." He shook his head. "I'm going to have to bring in several dozen officers to go through this stuff."

"The good news is, this is not as bad as it would appear at first glance."

"What do you mean?"

"We know the perp is white, right?"

Nigel nodded.

"I don't know the exact numbers. Some job categories are ninety-nine percent white and some are ninety-nine percent black. But overall, I estimate sixty percent of the staff is white and about thirty percent of that number is male. So right away the universe is narrowed down to about twenty-five hundred people."

Nigel nodded. "You said that was the good news?"

"The bad news is that those names are only part of the records."

"Part . . . ?"

"The faculty is not included. We don't do background checks on faculty members."

"Why?"

Ed shrugged. "Because they are the faculty." He paused. "Truth is, we have very few problems of that sort with the faculty. *The Wheel,* the student newspaper, did a piece a year or so ago about one faculty member who was masturbating in Woodruff Library. We investigated. He had several priors. But that is unusual."

"No other faculty members with questionable backgrounds? No sexual offenders? No one with record of assault? These are all saintly beings?"

Ed laughed. "Didn't say that."

"Do you have any records at all on the faculty members?"

"The official response to that question is that if you develop a profile of what you are looking for and give it to me, I will pass it along to the human resources people. They will run it through their computers."

Nigel nodded. Slim shot. But worth it.

"Can they do it quickly?"

"In this instance, yes."

"What else can we do?"

"I can give you a list of all faculty members, and you can run the list through the GCIC computers or NCIC or whatever other databases you choose."

"Don't tell me. You have such a list."

Ed pointed toward the top-most folder.

Nigel stared at him. "You read minds in your spare time?"

"I sat down with some of my people, and we worked this out. I just got those printouts. If you hadn't called today, I was going to call you and ask if you wanted them."

"Find anything interesting?"

Ed shrugged again. "Counting faculty and staff, we have about ten thousand people working here. Add in the students, part-time workers, visitors, and we have about twenty-five thousand people on the campus every day. In fact, during the day we are the largest city in the county. But going back just to the faculty, any group that large always contains a few who make you wonder." He pointed toward the folders. "Their names are flagged. I assumed you wanted to narrow the search by age also, so I flagged the folders of those under forty. That's a bit old, but it gives us a margin."

Nigel nodded in agreement. "What else can I get on the faculty? Can't you give me anything other than their names and where they got their Ph.D.s?"

"The equal opportunity office has all this broken down racially and by gender. I don't think that will be of much help here." Ed pursed his lips and tapped the folders.

Nigel sensed there was more. He waited.

"You ever been around faculty members at a university?"

Nigel shrugged. "Not since college."

"We off the record here? Officer to officer?"

"Always."

Ed tugged at his beard. A half smile was on his lips. "The combination of a Ph.D., tenure, the campus environment, bright young people who are in virtual awe of the professors, all breeds a strange creature. The natural habitat of these professors is Mount Olympus. They all fell to earth from heaven, you know. They don't make much money. Well, more than most people think, especially if they have a chair or a grant, but still, not much by real world standards. So they cling to their little perks, to things that don't matter much to the rest of us. And they wrap these little inconsequential perks in bands of steel."

"I'm not sure I'm following you."

"The fact they have a Ph.D. and tenure is all we need to know about them."

Nigel stared at Ed. "You can't go beyond that?"

Ed nodded. "Not supposed to."

"But?"

"But we have to consider the frailties of human nature, the realities of the world, our mandate to anticipate problems before they become problems, to protect the Emory community, the Emory name."

"Which means there are sexual offenders on the Emory faculty?"

"You better believe it."

"The stories you could tell."

"The stories I could tell."

Nigel glanced at the folders. His eyebrows climbed. Ed shook his head.

Nigel looked over Ed's shoulder and pointed at the computer.

Ed shook his head again and pointed toward the rear wall of the office.

Nigel's eyebrows climbed.

"In the safe. Hidden in the wall behind that file cabinet. Only one copy of those records, and you'll have to read them here."

"How long will it take?"

"Two hours. Maybe three."

"Lots of sexual offenders?"

"Lots of professors with . . . shall we say . . . interesting backgrounds."

"Any of them in particular get your attention?"

"The race factor excludes many of the staff. And the age factor excludes many of the faculty. I can narrow the search a bit if you tell me how far you want to go back."

Nigel looked at Ed and realized he knew. "The offender first surfaced a little over three years ago. But he was active before that. So let's go back five years to be sure. He disappeared a little over three years ago, at the time we targeted him, and I don't believe he has been here during those three years. He went somewhere—maybe to jail—and came back."

"You don't think he could have been dormant?"

For a long time Nigel did not answer. "I don't think so. I know him. He has to be doing what he does. But I could be wrong. I don't want to overlook anything. So let's assume he might have been here and was doing his thing somewhere else."

"Same age group as with the staff?"

"Yes. Make it under forty."

"If we look at male faculty and staff members under forty, people who were here five years ago or who came here in the last five years. Let's see. We hire about thirty-five people per week on campus. That's about fifteen hundred a year. We have about a fifty percent turnover on the staff side." He looked at Nigel. "You want to include the medical school, the faculty, and staff at Yerkes, the Grady and Crawford Long hospital staffs? They're all connected to Emory."

"I want every white male under forty who has been even remotely connected to Emory during the past five years."

"A computer search utilizing the date of entry will do that." Ed looked at his watch. "Got something to do for an hour? Want to go over to the cafeteria and get some coffee? Or do you want to sit there and watch me narrow down the universe?"

"No." Nigel paused. "Would you know how to find a student at any particular time of day?"

"Your daughter?"

Nigel laughed. "Yes. I want to see her and then I'll come back here."

Ed remembered Sarah's schedule, but he went

through the motions. He picked up the telephone, called his secretary and, as she talked, he wrote on a legal pad. He hung up and looked at the pad. "She's got a Yeats class in an hour. If she is anything like the other students, my guess is you will find her either in her room or over at the DUC in the Coca-Cola Commons. Probably the DUC. Students gather there this time of day."

Nigel stood up and shook hands with Ed. "See you in an hour."

"It will be ready. By the way, don't stumble over the U.C. people. They're all over campus."

"Noticeable?"

Ed shrugged. "To me they are. But I haven't heard any comments from the students. Maybe they haven't noticed." Ed paused. "You'll be interested in this. We are installing on an emergency basis a campus alarm system to protect the students."

"How does it work?" Nigel knew most alarm systems catch only the inept. Most alarm systems are easily circumvented. That meant Emory was installing the system for public relations reasons.

"Simple. Every student will be given a small electronic device. A security device. So small it will fit on a key chain. The student presses a button on the device, and it emits a signal that immediately lets us know the location. That location is displayed on a computer screen in the dispatcher's office. In addition, a siren and a blue light affixed to a pole—the one nearest the student—are activated."

"Are the devices unique to each student?"

"Yes. We get an emergency signal, the computer screen shows not only her location on campus, but her name, address, and telephone number."

"What is your estimated response time? The longest time?"

"Three minutes max. Usually less."

"The system cover the entire campus?"

"We have a problem there."

"Oh."

"As I said, we're installing this on an emergency basis. The main campus will be covered by noon tomorrow."

"The main campus?"

"Lullwater Park won't be covered for another week. Same for one or two of the remote parking decks and a few odd corners of the campus. But we'll be ninety percent covered."

"The sirens and blue lights. They will be all around the campus?"

"Another problem. The board thinks the blue lights and sirens mounted on chrome poles—they're about six or eight feet tall—gives us too much of an institutional look and detracts from the landscaping and campus esthetics. We're not going to get the coverage there we think is necessary."

"How many poles?"

Ed shrugged. "A half dozen. Maybe."

"How many did you want?"

"More than a hundred."

Nigel nodded. The Atlanta syndrome was part and parcel of Emory. Atlanta, like Nineveh, thought of itself as a great city on a hill, far better than other cities. But rather than being a shining city on a hill, Atlanta was more like a disease-ridden prostitute, one in expensive custom-tailored dresses and wearing lots of makeup and expensive jewelry. Her body was covered with chancres and her mind was paretic. Nevertheless, the smiles and makeup and pretension kept her on the stroll.

Emory, like Atlanta, was in love with its image. It ignored the bleeding sores. Students were dying. More might die, solely because they were Emory students and the school would allow no more than a token security system because it detracted from the landscaping.

Nigel walked slowly down the left side of the quadrangle. The Emory campus was always lush and beautiful, and the grass was always green. Flowers of one sort or another bloomed year round, both in carefully maintained beds and in enormous pots scattered about the campus. The big oaks in the middle of the quad were full and green, and under their umbrageous coolness students gathered, sprawled out on the grass or thumbing in a desultory fashion through their books. The girls and boys wore shorts and T-shirts, and many had kicked off their shoes. It was an idyllic picture. Emory was obviously the home of the gifted and the privileged.

Nigel passed the cool marble exterior of the Pitts Theology Library and the Physics Building, then angled to the left of the Candler Library—named for the family that once owned Coca-Cola—and down the hill toward Asbury Circle. He crossed the road and walked slowly up the hill toward the DUC. He met an occasional student who looked at him curiously. Nigel was puzzled. He thought he would be mistaken for a faculty member, and then, after he saw an occasional older person whom he took to be a faculty member, he understood why students stared at him. Faculty members dressed like homeless people. Their hair was long and disheveled. They wore tennis shoes or desert boots. They ambled or shuffled rather than walked. And all of them appeared to be preoccupied. He wore a suit, his hair was closely cropped, his black wing tips glistened, his shoulders were back, and he walked with purpose.

A few moments later Nigel walked through the door of the DUC and out into a broad, spacious room known as the Coca-Cola Commons. he stood in the door, looking around, eyes raking over every student at every table. He immediately picked out a half-dozen U.C. people. He could always identify another cop, even a young cop. It's in the eyes and in the demeanor. Nigel was not aware of his own demeanor. he stood there looking around as if he owned the campus. Students stopped talking and looked at him curiously. He obviously was not faculty or staff. He was a visitor. Was he a father? Who was he?

Nigel's expression softened when he saw his daughter walking toward him. She was wearing cutoff shorts. Entirely too short. And her top was too tight. The girl she was with was dressed far more conservatively.

He tried to catch himself, but it was too late. Sarah recognized the expression on his face, and her smile of welcome faded.

"Hi, Daddy," she said in a neutral tone of voice. She turned to her companion. "This is my father. Daddy, this is my friend Shari Kaufman." She smiled and added, "Shari is editor of *The Wheel*. She's from Atlanta."

Nigel smiled and nodded. The girl was shorter than Sarah and a bit on the plump side. She wore glasses. Behind the glasses her eyes glistened with intelligence. Her face could only be described as sweet. The combination of penetrating eyes and cherubic face was intriguing. It was a face found in old paintings.

"A double distinction," Nigel said to her. "Being editor of the college newspaper ranks right up there with being an Atlanta native."

The girl laughed. "There are not many of us," she said. She shook hands and said, "Hello, Mr. Trench." By the way Shari looked at him, Nigel knew Sarah had told her of Nigel's work and how he was investigating the cases involving Emory students. He had seen the look before.

The girl looked at Nigel and looked at Sarah and stepped away. "Sarah, I just remembered I have to pick up something in my dorm. See you in class." She looked at Nigel. "Nice to meet you, Mr. Trench."

Nigel nodded.

"What brings you back?" Sarah asked. "You're getting to be a regular visitor."

Nigel shrugged. "I had a meeting on campus and just thought I'd say hello. You okay?"

"I'm fine. I was just going over to let Pepsi out for a minute before I went to class. Want to walk with me?"

"Yes, I'd like that."

"How's Mom?"

"She's fine. Saw her yesterday."

"I'm going over later today. Will she ... will she recognize me this time?"

"I don't know, Sarah. In her good moments she asks about you. She worries about you."

Sarah looked at the ground. "I know. It's so sad. I don't think she will ever ..."

"Don't say that, Sarah. One day she may be okay again."

Sarah shook her head. "I'm grown, Daddy. I've taken enough psychology courses and talked to enough of my psychology professors about her to know that is not likely."

"They don't know your mother's case."

"They know enough."

"Sarah, have you given any more thought to—"

"I'm going to a concert Friday night, Daddy."

Nigel had interviewed enough people not to be diverted by a sudden change of topic. But he was making a conscious effort not to be a cop when he talked to his daughter. So he went along.

"What sort of concert?"

"Rock concert. It's here on campus. Outdoors under the stars. It's wonderful. They don't usually have them in the summer, but this band was not expensive.'"

"Got a date?"

She laughed. "No. Shari and I are going."

"You seeing anyone regularly?"

She looked at him, wondering if the cop was talking or if it was an honest inquiry. She saw nothing in his face to indicate he was being a cop. She shrugged. "No. I date a lot of guys. But nobody regularly." She smiled and put her arm through his elbow. "I'm checking out the field, Daddy."

"Ummmmmm. You need any money for the concert?"

"No, I'm okay. All it takes to get in is my student ID."

"They don't charge you?"

"No. Emory pays the band. They just want to make sure that everyone attending is a student. We show our ID cards and the security guard waves us in."

"You take Pepsi with you?"

"Yes. He is inside too much. He needs to get out."

"Sarah . . ."

"Daddy, please." She withdrew her arm. "Don't start that again. I'm staying on campus. Don't worry about me."

"Sarah, this fellow—"

"Daddy, I don't want to hear it. I don't want to know about all that paranoid police stuff. I've talked to other students about this. It's your job to catch him. That's what you are paid to do. But I don't want to be a part of it."

"I was hoping you might come home for a few days. I'm asking if you will."

"Why? None of the other students are going home. They're scared. The whole campus is scared. We read the paper. I knew Kathleen Powers. And word is getting around about the two girls who were attacked and who left school. But we're all more careful." She paused. "And we are expecting you to do your job."

"I'm doing all I can." Nigel, for the first time in his life, felt defensive in talking with his daughter.

"They're giving all the students little beepers tomorrow. A new security system on campus. You know about that?"

"Yes. But—"

"I'm not a child anymore, Daddy. I have my own life."

Nigel sighed.

"Daddy, I'm uncomfortable with this. I'd rather you didn't walk with me over to the dorm. I'll call you after I see Mom."

Nigel stopped and stared at his daughter for a long moment. "Okay, Sarah." He paused and looked longingly at her for a long moment. "You are the only child I will ever have."

Sarah's heart softened and she took a step toward him. "I know."

"Go on to the dorm and take Pepsi for a walk. I'll go back inside and have something to drink. They do let dinosaurs like me in there?"

"Daddy, if you're a dinosaur, you are tyrranosaurus rex. You rule the jungle."

Nigel laughed. "Some jungle. I can't even tell my daughter what to do." He shook his head and pulled Sarah to him and hugged her. "Enjoy the concert."

"I will, Daddy."

"I like your friend Shari."

Sarah's face broke into a wide smile. "Thanks. She's nice."

Nigel watched her walking away. He sighed and turned around and walked back up the hill toward the DUC. Once inside he walked up to the counter.

"Yes, sir," said the student who waited on him. "What can I get for you?"

"What do you have?"

"How about a Coke?"

"That it?"

"This is Emory."

"I think I'll have a Coke."

15

It was 12:45 A.M. when the ambulance raced up to the emergency ramp of Grady Hospital, swung forward, ground into reverse, and backed up under the overhead covering. The rear doors of the red EMT truck swung wide, and three black-clad EMTs, trousers bloused over lace-up boots, jumped to the ground and pulled out a gurney all in one smooth, uninterrupted motion.

"That the fifty-one forty-nine?" Maytag asked. He had just arrived. His police car was parked, door open, in the emergency zone.

An EMT nodded, and Maytag joined the group. His shield was on his coat pocket, and he carried a radio in his hand.

The gurney was pushed rapidly past the security guard and swung into a hard right turn. The triage coordinator was waiting.

"We got a fifty-one forty-nine," Maytag said. "Let's do it, people. Let's move it."

The white-haired triage nurse slapped a stat pack on the gurney, which never slowed as the EMTs turned left.

"Red zone," the triage nurse said, pointing toward two large double doors. She glared at Maytag. As the gurney disappeared through the doors, crossed the hall, and entered the red zone, the triage nurse turned to a paramedic and shook her head. "That son of a bitch," she muttered. She picked up the telephone. "Rape crisis, please."

The paramedic was surprised. Nothing ruffled Sally Sears. She had been on the job almost thirty years. She even ordered residents around.

"The policeman?" the paramedic asked.

The nurse hung up the telephone. "No answer. Yes. I met him when he worked Vice. Now he is on some sort of task force. A really unpleasant man. I wish he'd be a patient one night when I was on. I'd use a hooter tube big as a garden hose on him."

The paramedic winced at the thought of such a large catheter. His eyes went to the swinging doors through which the policeman had passed.

The red zone, as usual at this hour, was chaos. Doctors and nurses rushed to and fro. Lights were blinking over the door of every trauma room, indicating the rooms were occupied by a host of medical experts and a patient in serious trouble. The walls were lined with gurneys on which patients awaited treatment. The gurney containing the 51–49—a woman who had sustained cutting injuries as well as being raped—was pushed against a wall, and the EMTs turned to leave.

"Wait a minute," Maytag said. "Tell me what you got."

The crew chief looked at her clipboard. "Virginia Blair. Twenty-one. Deep lacerations on the back of her neck. Rape."

Maytag looked at the young woman on the gurney. She had a tight, fixed smile.

All task force members were to call Trench on any reported rape. But it wouldn't hurt to wait a little while. He could solve this thing before the famous Roach got his ass out of bed and got down here.

"She tell you what happened?"

"Short version is somebody knocked on the door. She opened it. She was raped, beaten up, and cut."

"She been drinking?"

"No indication of that. Said she had been studying all evening."

"Studying? Studying what?"

"I don't know. Said she was an Emory student."

Maytag's eyes widened. Another victim in the high-visibility case. He was more determined than ever to use the case as a chance to show his investigative skills and redeem himself in the eyes of the major. He had the morning watch as a punishment detail, and look what had fallen into his lap. He was going to turn chicken shit into chicken salad. This kid from Emory was a meal ticket. But he had to move fast.

He pushed a nearby gurney farther down the wall to make enough room for him to squeeze in near the head of the Emory student. The gurney had a patient who wore a thick layer of gauze around his head and covering his eyes. Over the gauze was a pair of sunglasses with bright yellow lenses. The lenses, made all the more bright and all the more yellow by the white gauze and the bright lights, were like two yellow spotlights.

Maytag did not notice that across the hall from the Emory student was a man who was handcuffed to the gurney. He was staring at the ceiling with the patience of a caged animal. He rolled his head to the side, and his eyes met those of Virginia Blair's. He smiled, an evil, leering smile, and his long tongue came out and swept around the edges of his mouth.

Virginia Blair turned her head away. Now she was staring at the hooks on the wall, used to contain bags of IV fluids. And there was a sign in bold red letters giving a hotline number to call in the event of a needle stick. Until that moment she had not thought of AIDS. Her smile became even more fixed.

Maytag grimaced at all the furor and motioned for the crew chief to come closer.

"Is this a for-sure deal?"

The crew chief looked at him. "What do you mean?"

"I mean, those Emory kids fuck like rabbits, for Christ's sake. She's lying over there grinning. Was she really raped? Or did she fuck her boyfriend and then scream rape just to stay straight with Mama and Daddy?"

The crew chief backed up a step. "I found her in the shower bleeding. In addition to the deep wounds on her neck, which could not be self-administered, she was bleeding from the vaginal area and from the anus. She said she was a virgin, and all the circumstances bear that out. Yeah, I'd say this is what you call a for-sure deal."

"What was she wearing?"

"Nothing. She was in the shower."

"What had she been wearing? A nightgown? Something that would have teased a guy?"

"I don't know. We found a robe and a nightgown on the floor in the bedroom."

"I thought so." Maytag wrinkled his nose. He

looked around. The foot of the man on the gurney next to him was covered with a blob of feces.

"Oh, for Christ's sake," Maytag said, glaring at the unconscious patient.

He turned back to the crew chief. "She say she had been out anywhere tonight?"

"No. As I said, she told us she had been in her apartment all evening studying."

"She say she had gone for a walk and that this guy might have followed her?"

The crew chief shook her head.

"Okay, okay. Get out of here. I'll talk to her."

The crew chief motioned for her assistants and strode rapidly from the red zone.

As they were leaving, another group of EMTs entered. With them was a middle-aged man waving his arms and emitting guttural sounds. His mouth was filled with a shiny white object. An intern slowed, his face a question mark.

"Cue ball, Doc," said one of the EMTs.

"Cue ball?"

"Yeah, he was in a bar drinking and bet one of his buddies he could put a cue ball in his mouth. He could. He won the bet. But now he can't get it out."

"We have a special tool for that," said a resident. He pointed of the desk down the hall. "Time for you to get some experience. You do it."

Maytag stepped closer to the gurney containing the Emory student. He looked around. Then he looked at the student. She had black hair and dark eyes. "This ain't the red zone," he said. "This is the goddamn twilight zone." He laughed.

The young woman smiled. "I need a doctor," she said. Her voice was strong.

"Sweety, I'm afraid it's gonna be a while. Lots of customers tonight. But I'm gonna stay with you. I need to ask you a few questions while we're waiting on the doctor."

"I want something for the pain. I hurt so bad." She smiled at him.

"Yeah, if we can get somebody over here." Maytag made no effort to attract a doctor's attention. "Tell me what happened."

"I told the policeman what happened. I told the medical people who brought me here what happened. Do I have to do it again?"

"Yes, you do. Start at the beginning and tell me what happened."

Maytag put his hand on Virginia's shoulder. He did not notice how she recoiled. "Never mind. Hold that thought. I have to hit the head." He turned and disappeared down the hall. It was twenty minutes before he returned.

"Now, where were we?" he asked.

"I'm in a lot of pain. Can't you talk to those other people and ask them to tell you what I said earlier?"

"We've been though that," Maytag snapped. "If you want me to catch this guy, start talking."

"I was in my apartment and—"

"Do you live alone?"

"Yes. And—"

"You ever have boys there?"

"Yes. but—"

"When's the last time you had sex?"

The young woman's eyes sliced toward the detective. Tears welled up and flowed down her cheeks. "I never have."

"You're twenty-one, a student at Emory and . . ."

The interview went on for about forty-five minutes. Maytag asked the same questions over and over. The interview was interrupted when a nurse across the hall shouted, "We have an arterial bleeder coming in." Nurses and doctors began snapping on rubber gloves.

A nurse listening to a radio raised her head and announced, "He's on the ramp. He's on the ramp."

"Oh, shit," Maytag said. He moved against the wall just as a gurney flanked by EMTs pushed through the door into the red zone. One of the EMTs held a pressure bandage to the patient's arm. The patient, a young pasty-faced man, was impassive. The gurney was followed by a uniformed officer.

Maytag stopped the officer. "You got charges on this mutt?"

The young officer grinned. "Sure do. The son of a bitch got into a fight with his wife. He pushed her through a window. She grabbed a piece of glass and came back inside and caught him across the inside of the elbow. Cut the shit out of him. We got there and there was blood everywhere. I mean everywhere. All across the ceiling. God damn, what a mess."

"Looks like he's on the launching pad," Maytag said. He grinned.

"Launching pad?" Virginia said in a bewildered voice.

Maytag put his hand on her shoulder. "Relax, little darling. Means he's about to leave this world."

"What sort of place is this? Where am I?"

The door to one of the trauma rooms burst open,

and a gurney pushed by men and women in green scrubs and blue scrubs rushed through. One of the doctors wore a clear plastic shield across his eyes. He tilted it up and shouted "Tell surgery we got one coming."

The gurney and its outriders disappeared down the hall toward an elevator.

As Maytag looked around, he noticed a woman trying to climb atop a gurney with a man. She was pulling at the sheet. The man was looking around for help. He saw a doctor and waved frantically. As he waved, the woman pulled the sheet away and exposed his erection. She redoubled her efforts to climb aboard the gurney. The man grabbed the arm of a passing doctor. "Doc, I got enough problems. Can't you get her away?" The doctor pulled at the woman's arms. "Come on, Janie. Leave him alone." He motioned for a nurse.

As the doctor passed, Maytag pulled at his arm. "Hey, Doc. What was that all about?"

"He has sickle cell anemia. One of the symptoms of an advanced case is priapism."

The doctor saw Maytag's bewildered expression. "He has a constant erection. And Janie over there, who drinks too much and who is a frequent guest of ours, thought that was interesting." The doctor moved on.

Maytag shook his head.

Suddenly a nurse appeared. She motioned for an orderly to help her with the gurney. "Okay, honey," the nurse said. "We're gonna put you in a room and take a look at you."

"Christ," Maytag muttered. "When do I get to finish my interview?"

"You know the rules, Officer. Wait here in the hall," the nurse said.

Virginia Blair had been in the room no more than thirty seconds, just long enough for a resident to begin to peel away the bandages around her neck, when the charge nurse suddenly appeared. "We got a gunshot wound on the ramp. Move this patient out in the hall. Stat!"

Seconds later Virginia Blair was back against the wall, her eyes wide in fear and disorientation. "Somebody please help me," she cried.

A gurney carrying an eight-year-old boy was pushed past her at high speed. His skin was ashen and there was a blood-soaked bandage on his stomach. The gurney was followed by a half-dozen people wearing green or blue scrubs. One man, obviously in charge, wore a clear plastic shield over his face.

"Stops spewing blood from getting into his eyes," Maytag said. "Keeps the doctor from getting AIDS or hepatitis." He shook his head. "Now, that puppy is really on the launching pad. He'll go out the back door."

He watched for a moment, then turned back to Virginia. "You had a short trip to the treatment room," he said. "Now, where were we? Oh, yes. Did you have an orgasm?"

Virginia Blair stared at Maytag.

"What? What?"

"Did you have an orgasm?"

"Are you supposed to ask me that?" Virginia Blair began crying. "You have no right to ask me that."

A young black woman who was talking to a patient down the hall heard Virginia's voice. She looked up, saw the badge on Maytag's pocket and the radio in

his hand, and whispered something to the patient.
Then she hurried down the hall.

"Officer. Officer," she said loudly.

Maytag looked up. "Oh, shit," he mumbled. "One
of the dikes from rape crisis. Who called her?"

"Is this a forty-nine?" the brisk young woman
asked.

"Yes."

"What did you say to her?"

"I'm interviewing a victim, lady. Do you mind?"

The young woman reached for Virginia's hand.
"My name is Terri," she whispered. "I'm here to
help you. I'm here for you. How long have you
been here?"

"I don't know. An hour. Maybe more. It seems like
forever." She looked at Maytag and back to Terri.
"Please help me."

The counselor from rape crisis looked at Maytag.
He shrugged.

Terri turned around. "Charge nurse. Charge nurse,"
she shouted.

A middle-aged woman came forward. "Yes."

"Nurse, why is someone not seeing this patient? We
need a pelvic on her now. Why is she still in the hall?"

The nurse waved her arms. "Look around. We'll
get to her when we can."

"Can we take her to G-Y-N and then bring her
back here?"

The charge nurse looked at the stat pack on the
gurney and shook her head. "She needs medical first
to take care of the lacerations. The doctors don't like
for them to go to G-Y-N first."

"What about X-ray? Can you take her to X-ray
while we're waiting on medical?"

"No. She has to be treated for the lacerations first."

"What ever happened to the thirty-minute rule?"

"That's up in G-Y-N. Not here."

Terri muttered something.

She turned to Virginia Blair. "You okay, honey? I would have been here sooner, but I have two other patients down the hall. I must have missed the phone call about you. But now I'm here to be with you on your terms. You tell me what you need."

Virginia motioned for Terri to come closer. "He asked me if I was a virgin," Virginia said, mouth trembling. "He asked me if I had an orgasm."

Terri glared at Maytag. She seized his elbow and pulled him several steps down the hall. "You have no right to ask those questions," she hissed. "You know that."

"It didn't bother her. She came in here smiling."

"You haven't worked with rape victims before."

Maytag shrugged. "So what?"

"It is not uncommon for rape victims to come in here smiling." She stepped closer to Maytag, still pulling on his elbow. "Do you know why they're smiling, Officer?" She did not wait for an answer. "They're smiling because the man who raped them threatened to kill them. He might have even tried to kill them. They are smiling because they are glad they are not dead."

Maytag jerked his elbow away. "Don't tell me how to do my job, lady."

"Somebody has to tell you because obviously you don't know your job. You are not here to make judgments. You job is to get information and see if there is sufficient evidence to charge a man with rape. It is not your job to be an inquisitor. We are both here to

provide a service, to provide sympathy, not to decide
who is telling the truth."

"Who died and made you the hall monitor?"

Terri stepped closer to Maytag. "If you find later
on that what she says is not true, then that's okay.
But for now, stick by her."

"I'm not some goddamn support group, lady. I'm
a cop."

Terri stuck her finger under Maytag's nose and was
about to speak when suddenly there was a great furor
in the hall. Shouts and angry screams could be heard.
Dozens of screaming and shouting people suddenly
filled the hall and were banging at the door and kicking the walls. They were pushing at the nurses and
doctors and shouting profanity and trying to force
their way into the red zone.

They all wanted to see their friend, the man whose
wife had cut him with a piece of glass. The young
security guard from the emergency door, who was
talking frantically into his radio, was pushed back farther and farther, overwhelmed by the mob trying to
break into the red zone. When he looked over his
shoulder and saw Maytag, an expression of relief flitted cross his face.

"Hey, man. Call the cops. I got to have help here."

Maytag turned around and was immediately was on
the radio issuing a 63—an officer in need of help. He
knew the call would galvanize every cop on Zone 5, in
downtown Atlanta. In addition, security guards from
Georgia State University, two blocks away, would
come running.

Maytag finished the radio call and turned to help
the security guard. "Cavalry's coming," he shouted.
He found himself facing one of the angry men who

had pushed through triage into the hall. The man took one look at him and instantly disliked him. "You little fuck," the man said as he swung an uppercut. The blow caught Maytag under the chin, lifted him off his feet, and sent him skidding across the floor. He was still there several minutes later when additional hospital security officers along with a flying squad of Atlanta police officers pushed through the door and took swift control of the angry crowd, pushing them back out the door.

In the lull, Sally Sears saw Maytag on the floor, his head twisted to the side where he had been jammed against the wall.

"Oh, my," she said in mock distress. "The nice officer needs help. Put him on a gurney," she whispered to an aide, who dashed down the hall. She snapped on a pair of rubber gloves.

Maytag awakened a few minutes later. He shook his head. The last thing he remembered was some guy poking him. He was going to get up and knock hell out of that guy, but then something hit him in the head and all went black. He shook his head. He lay still for a moment. Nothing seemed to be broken. He opened his eyes but closed them quickly. Too many bright lights. He peeped through narrowed eyes and saw shadowy figures leaning over him. He felt strong hands holding his shoulders. What was going on here? He grunted and tried to sit up. Then he heard the voice of the head triage nurse. She was leaning over him, wearing a mask.

"Officer, you may have sustained head injuries. I'm going to have to catheterize you before you are treated."

Maytag groaned. "Bullshit. Let me outta here."

The hands on his shoulders held him securely.

"Don't worry, Officer," the nurse said. Her eyes were smiling when she waved an enormous tube before his face.

"This is for your own good."

16

It was almost three a.m. when the telephone in Nigel's apartment rang. Dr. Mengele was calling. His police radio had been on, and he snapped awake when he heard the help call from Maytag. "About a half hour ago we got a sixty-three from Maytag. He was down at Grady when it hit the fan. Got himself decked."

"What was he doing at Grady?"

"Roach, you not gonna like this. But there was a forty-nine. Emory student. Name is Virginia Blair. The uniformed people called the task force. Maytag answered and took it upon himself to respond rather than to call you as we have all been instructed to do. Everybody thought he had called you. We wouldn't have known he was handling it if that mob hadn't tried to break into the red zone."

"The victim alive?"

Dr. Mengele paused. Why did the Roach ask that? "Yes. She's going to be okay."

"Has she been treated?"

Dr. Mengele laughed. "Roach, there are some things in this world that don't change. One of them is that a forty-nine can wait at Grady for three or four hours before being treated. She's still on a gurney in the red zone."

"Oh, God. Is someone from rape crisis with her?"

"Yes, but she's got two other customers down there. So ..."

"Wait a minute. Two others?"

"Yeah, but they are older black women. Don't fit the profile of the female your guy is targeting. So you weren't notified."

"Crime scene sealed off?"

"They did that part right. Uniform is there. No one allowed in until you say so."

"Did Maytag call for an ID tech?"

"Not that I know of."

"Have one meet me in the red zone." Nigel looked at his watch. "Fifteen minutes."

"You got it."

"I'm on the way. Thanks, Dr. Mengele."

"Sieg heil. And, oh, by the way ..."

"Yes."

"The triage nurse on duty is Sally Sears."

Nigel paused. He rubbed a hand across his eyes. "Thanks." He hung up the phone.

Because Atlanta cannot afford to pay its bills, several years ago the city fell behind on its payments to Georgia Power. The power company, as it would do with any deadbeat client, began cutting off entire grids of city lights. As a result, Atlanta is one of the darkest cities in the nation. Streets are dark. Miles of expressway are dark. This provides a happy hunting ground for criminals. Like predatory wolves, they prowl Atlanta's streets after dark, knowing they can commit their crime of choice and easily become lost in the darkness.

Nigel sped through the dark streets, eyes alert at

every traffic light, barely slowing as he checked for traffic, then sped on.

His coat was streaming behind him when he limped through the big glass doors of the emergency entrance to Grady and swung into the triage area. He smiled when he saw Sally. She saw him at the same moment and reached out both arms. "Nigel, I heard you were back. Are you okay? Come here and hug my neck."

"Sally, how you?" Nigel said, hugging the wiry white-haired nurse. "You still have triage under control, I see."

"You better believe it." She looked up quizzically. "Nigel, are you doing okay?"

"Sure, Sally. I'm fine."

"And Rachel?" she said softly. "How's Rachel?"

Nigel shook his head. "No change, Sally. Not since the day you looked after her. I don't know if she will ever improve."

"You never know, Nigel. You never know. I've seen enough miracles here to know that we medical professionals are not always in charge. You tell her I'm praying for her."

"Thanks, Sally. Let's talk later. I'm working and I—"

"You got a forty-nine?"

"Yes, a young woman brought in about three hours ago. Her name is Virginia Blair. Can you help me find her?"

She looked at him and shook her head. "Nigel, I don't see how you do it." She paused. "Come with me." She took his hand and pulled him through the double doors and across the hall into the red zone.

She chatted briefly with the charge nurse and then pointed at a gurney halfway down the hall. The ID tech was already there, hovering nearby with two cameras around her neck.

Nigel arrived at the gurney at the same time as the counselor from rape crisis.

"Hello. I'm Nigel Trench, A.P.D."

"Terri," said the confident young woman.

Nigel turned to Virginia Blair. He swallowed. She had dark hair, long dark hair, and was about the same size as Sarah.

She fit the profile.

"Miss Blair, my name is Nigel Trench. I'm a police officer, and my job right now is to get you treated as quickly as possible. Your treatment and your safety are my only concerns right now. I know you have been through a frightening experience. It's only natural that you are scared. It's okay if you want to cry. You are someone special to all of us. And I am here to protect you. From anything and from anyone. You are safe."

Virginia looked at him, mouth trembling, then broke into racking sobs. "Oh, thank you. He was going to kill me. He said he was going to kill me. I want to go home. I want my mother."

"Who's the charge nurse?" Nigel asked Terri.

She looked down the hall and pointed.

Seconds later Nigel was in an earnest conversation with the nurse. And almost immediately Virginia Blair was wheeled into a private room to have the slashes on the back of her neck treated.

"I need photographs, Doctor," Nigel said to the head resident. He pointed at the ID tech and motioned for her to go inside the treatment room. "Shots of where she was cut," he said.

"That's all. Nothing else," the resident said. He

waved at the ID tech. "And stay out of our way."
He mumbled something about "overbearing cops"
and was walking off when Nigel grabbed his arm.

"Listen to me," he said. "We have a serial killer
loose in this town. For some reason, I don't know
why, he let this girl go. I want shots of her. I want
good shots of her. I decide, goddammit, what I shoot
and how many and when. I decide when there is
enough. You give me any shit, mister, I'll put your
ass in jail for obstructing justice." Nigel poked the
doctor in the chest with his finger. Hard. "You got
that?"

The doctor stared at Nigel for a moment, his olym-
pian facade crushed, opened his lips a few times like
a beached guppy, then turned and followed the ID
tech into the treatment room. He now had a better
understanding of just where young doctors fit into the
overall scheme of a homicide investigation.

Very quickly Virginia Blair's neck injuries were
photographed and treated. She was wheeled into X-
ray, and then her gurney was rolled onto an elevator
for 4-K, the OB-GYN floor. Nigel was with her every
step of the way, always whispering that he was there
to help her and that his sole concern was to move her
through the hospital rapidly.

"The doctor said you should be hospitalized for a
day or so because of the injuries to your neck," Nigel
said. "Do you want to stay here, or can I make arrangements for you at a private hospital?"

"A private hospital. I don't want to stay here."

"Okay, I'll make the arrangements for you to be
transferred as soon as you are through here. And I'll
put a police officer there to guard your door."

In the elevator going up to 4-K, while a nurse fussed

over Virginia and made her more comfortable, Terri
turned to Nigel. "You seem better than the last one.
But then, anyone would have been an improvement
after him."

"He has a lot to learn," Nigel said.

"He shouldn't be learning at the expense of
victims."

Nigel said nothing.

Terri waited a moment. "Did I hear you say your
last name is Trench?"

"Yes."

"Are you the one they call the Roach?"

"Yes."

Terri said nothing. But for a moment her eyes widened. And Nigel knew that she knew.

"I like the way you work, Nigel Trench." She nodded toward Virginia. "You guys don't usually hang
around so long. Special case?"

"Very." He paused. "I'm going to need your help
later on in talking with her."

"You know she talked to the EMT and to that other
police officer?"

"I'm sorry."

Terri looked at him for a long moment. "I read the
papers, Officer. In addition, I work in rape crisis. I
know what's going on. Let me know what you want
me to do."

The elevator doors opened, and a resident was waiting. "What we got here?" he asked abruptly.

"A forty-nine," Terri said.

"A forty-nine? What's that?" The resident's face
was blank.

The nurse whispered to him.

"Oh." He looked at the badge on Nigel's coat. He

backed up a step and looked around the ward as if seeking help. "Look, I got a half-dozen C-sections going. It's a busy night. Does treating her mean I'm going to have to show up in court?"

Nigel seized the doctor's elbow and pulled him several steps away. He had had enough of young doctors for one night. "Let me tell you something. You may be God in this little ward. But I'm God out in the real world. You treat this patient *now,* or I'm going to put you in jail. And as young as you are, it will take about an hour to find out from personal experience what it is like to be a rape victim."

The resident paled. "Yes, sir," he said.

Terri smiled at Nigel and turned to the resident. "Doctor, I can tell you haven't handled a forty-nine before, so I'm going to stay with you and help you through this."

He looked at her name tag. The color and the codes revealed she had the authority to stay with the patient. He looked down at Virginia Blair. "That okay with you?"

Virginia motioned for Terri to come closer. As the counselor leaned down, Virginia whispered, "Is there a woman doctor who can do this? I don't want a man doing that right now."

Terri held her hand. "I hear you. And I know this is difficult for you. But he is a doctor and this is a hospital."

Virginia's eyes dropped as she answered the doctor. "Yes. I want her to stay." She looked at the nurse. "The nurse, too."

The doctor nodded. "Let's go."

Virginia Blair was wheeled into a private treatment room. Nigel looked for a telephone. He called

Major Morris at home and asked that a uniformed officer be detailed to Piedmont Hospital to wait for Virginia Blair. He called Piedmont, made arrangements for Virginia to be transferred, and told them a uniformed police officer would accompany her. Then he waited.

Inside the small treatment room the resident turned to Terri. "Where's that list of questions?" he asked. "I heard someone talking about it the other day."

Terri pulled a sheet of paper from a drawer in a small table and handed it to the doctor. At the top was typed "Questions for 49 During Exam." The doctor scanned the list. He had never seen it before. "Let's see," he mumbled. He began reading rapidly. "Name, age, parity, PHH, LMP, current contraception, last consensual intercourse, was condom used, time of assault, da dah da dah, vaginal or rectal or oral intercourse, douched since assaulted, patient's emotional condition, da dah da dah. Okay." He placed the list on the gurney near Virginia so he could refer to it, smiled at Virginia, and said, "Let's do it."

A half hour later, the form completed, he patted Virginia's shoulder. "You're doing fine," he said. "Let's do the exam." He turned to Terri. "Isn't there a kit of some kind I'm supposed to use?"

She pulled a white 7½" × 10½" envelope from a drawer. Across the top was written in bold letters: SEXUAL ASSAULT EVIDENCE COLLECTION KIT. The doctor turned the envelope over, broke the seal, and pulled out a handful of material.

The nurse bent closer to Virginia. "We need for you to take off your clothes and put this robe on."

Virginia was helped from the gurney. Head down, she walked slowly into the adjacent bathroom. She looked longingly at the shower. "You can go in there for as long as you want as soon as he is through," the nurse said.

Virginia returned to the gurney.

"First we have to examine your body for encrusted semen," the doctor said. "Did he ejaculate anywhere on your body?"

Virginia shook her head.

The doctor examined her closely for redness, injury, and foreign matter.

He picked up her hands and looked at her nails. "Did you scratch him? We need to clip your nails if you did."

Again, Virginia shook her head.

She cried when the doctor combed her pubic hair.

Terri leaned closer to Virginia. "Just so you understand what the doctor is doing, this is divided into two parts. We want whatever evidence we can find. And second, we want to offer you various medications."

"Medications? For what?"

Terri held Virginia's hand. Her voice was very soft. "For gonorrhea and syphilis. We also give you a pregnancy test. The doctor will also prescribe what we call a 'morning after' pill that will prevent you from becoming pregnant."

Virginia's lips twitched as she tried not to cry.

The doctor used cervical and vaginal swabs. He took a G.C. culture and a pap smear and did a bimanual exam. With a syringe he administered a vaginal wash of saline solution.

"Did he force you to have oral or anal sex?" the doctor asked.

Virginia nodded. Her eyes glistened with tears.

"Okay, we have to do those exams. First the oral."

He gave her a clean cotton cloth. "Blow your nose for me. Hard."

She did. With forceps he picked up the cotton cloth and placed it inside a sterile container.

"I could use a swab for the next part, but I think I'll use distilled water," he mumbled. He handed her a glass of water.

"Slosh this around in your mouth. Thoroughly. Then spit into this sterile container."

She did.

"Okay, now the anal exam."

Again she cried.

Finally it was over. The doctor gave Virginia an injection of five hundred milligrams of Cefizox to fight any possible STD and wrote a prescription for doxycycline and terazol cream. He gave her Benadryl to help her sleep.

"Okay, young lady. I'm dismissing you from Grady," he said. He nodded toward Terri.

"I'll take care of her from here on, Doctor," Terri said. "Thank you for your help."

The doctor hurried from the room.

"I want to take a shower," Virginia said.

"Be careful of the bandages on the back of your neck. I'll have some clean clothes for you when you get out."

It was almost an hour later when Terri and Virginia walked from the treatment room. Virginia looked small and vulnerable in the old clothes given to her by the rape crisis counselor, and her eyes were dulled with fatigue and pain. But still there

was something in her carriage that showed resolve
and determination.

Terri looked at Virginia and then at Nigel. "Officer,
Virginia is ready to talk to you. She will answer any
questions you have."

17

It was almost noon when Nigel pulled the last page from the printer, stacked the pages neatly on his desk, and sat down. He winced from the sharp pain in his back. Sitting had become painful, and he had been sitting in front of a computer terminal since he left Virginia Blair's apartment at sunrise. He had interviewed the victim at length and spent several hours at a fresh crime scene. From this victim and this crime scene he had learned much.

Most crime scenes are studied from the standpoint of the victim. But Nigel believed in also studying them also from the view of the offender. One way to know the offender was to become the offender.

The stack of papers on the desk was the result of his labors.

He picked up the report and leaned back in the chair. He shifted to and fro for a moment as he sought a comfortable position. Then he began reading.

Victimology: The victim, Virginia, is a white female, 21. She lives alone in an apartment. She is a junior at Emory University and is active in the Glenn Memorial United Methodist Church. She is bright, articulate, and poised—a "take-charge" personality. She drives a secondhand Chevrolet, a gift from her parents. Her father is a Methodist minister in Decatur, AL. Her personal life is more ordered than that of many college students. She has several "casual" boyfriends but is serious about none of them. She is an A student and spends much of her spare time involved in church activities. She rarely eats out. She has regular habits and is careful to lock her doors and close her blinds at night. She believes she may have met her assailant or heard his voice. Something about him seemed familiar to her.

Attack Environment: Virginia resides in a medium-sized (four buildings) apartment complex about two miles from the campus. The apartments are in a middle-class and long-established area of Atlanta near the Toco Hill Shopping Center. Virginia's apartment is on the second floor and overlooks a buffer zone of trees that separate the apartments from nearby homes. Windows of her apartment face the wooded area.

Assault: On the evening of Saturday, June 22, 1996, Virginia studied until about 10:00 p.m. and went to bed. The evening was hot, but her air conditioning was off and the windows were open. She wore a cotton nightgown to bed. About 10:30 p.m. her doorbell rang. She put on a bathrobe and went to the door. The carpet in the hallway leading to the door was sopping wet. When she asked who was at the door, a voice said, "Maintenance," and then told her a water pipe had broken and he wanted to make sure her apartment was okay. She looked through the peephole and saw a man wearing a hat and holding up a bag which she thought was some sort of bag a plumber would carry. "My apartment is flooded," she said, and opened the door.

The individual lowered the bag, and she saw he was wearing a ski mask. When he grabbed her mouth, she realized he was wearing latex gloves. He pressed a knife

to her throat and said, "If you do as I say, I will not
hurt you."

"What about my carpet?" she asked. The man
laughed and said he had poured five gallons of water
in front of her door and let it seep into her carpet
before he rang the doorbell. The man checked the lock
on the front door and turned off the apartment lights.
He closed the windows and turned the air conditioner
to the lowest setting. He forced the victim to return to
her bedroom, where he again said, "If you do as I say,
I won't hurt you." He unplugged her telephone. His
voice was soft, educated, and the tone was more ad-
monitory than threatening. "Take off the robe," he
said. Then he told her to take off her nightgown. "You
have beautiful breasts," he said. "We're going to
make love."

"No. I'm a Christian. I've never done that," she said.

"It's okay." he replied. He used his knife to slice
away her nightgown. He was careful not to allow the
blade to touch her body.

He held the victim's arms and forced her down on
her bed, where he kissed her and caressed her breasts.
"Kiss me like you mean it," he told her. "Tell me you
love me," he insisted. She refused to do either. "I want
you to leave my apartment," she said.

The individual kissed her breasts, inserted his fingers
into her vagina, and then performed cunnilingus for a
period the victim estimates at twenty minutes.

Afterward she heard noise and asked what it was.
"I'm putting on a condom," he said. He then said,
"Open your legs." When she cried and refused to do
so, he again pressed the knife to her throat. When he
attempted to insert his penis into her vagina, she moved
away. When he entered her and she cried out, he

quickly put a hand to her throat and told her, "Be quiet. The only thing I want to hear from you is 'I love you.' " However, he tried not to hurt her.

"Move your ass for me," he told her.

Afterward, he put a pillow case over her head and walked her out onto the deck of her apartment overlooking the wooded area. They stood nude on the deck, and he ran his fingers up under the pillow case and through her hair and massaged her scalp. He said he had noticed she did not have dandruff. She replied with anger that she did not have dandruff because she kept her hair clean. She said he was then silent for a long moment before saying that being on the deck reminded him of being in a florida room.

He asked her, "Was I a good boy?" She did not reply but nodded, which seemed to please him.

She asked if she could take a shower and put on some clothes. Instead he took her back to bed. He made her wear the pillow case. She heard him moving furniture around and sensed he had turned on a small lamp. She heard him rummaging in his bag, and then he turned on a tape recorder and played a song she recognized as "Ride of the Valkyries." Again he inserted his penis into her vagina. She did not know if he wore a condom. After a few minutes he withdrew and turned her over. "I'm going to fuck you in the ass," he said.

"No, please. That's wrong." When she cried out, he pressed the knife to her throat, this time hard enough to break the skin. She was terrified when she felt blood on her neck. "I'll cut your goddamn head off," he said.

"You are my lord and master. Say it," he ordered.

"Say what?"

"Say, 'You are my lord and master.' "

"You are my lord and master."

"You are ruler of heaven and earth. You reign over all."

"You are ruler of heaven and earth. You reign over all."

After five minutes of anal sex he forced her to perform fellatio.

He tied a string around his penis and had her tug on the string.

"Say, 'You little turd.' "

"You little turd."

"Not like that. Sound as if you are mad at me."

She took a deep breath. "You little turd."

"Pull harder."

She did.

"Say, 'This will make you grow.' "

"This will make you grow."

Then he pulled her from the bed and forced here into the bathroom. He was carrying the bag he had brought into the apartment. He shut the door and turned on the light. She heard him rummaging in his bag; there was a rustling noise, and when he removed the pillow case from her head he was wearing only a ski mask. He was about six feet tall, very muscular, and had fair skin. She saw blond eyebrows under the ski mask and believes him to have blond hair. She said he was very clean and smelled of soap and cologne. Upon entering the bathroom, he sat on the toilet and urinated while holding the victim's hand.

He asked her where her douche bag was located. She said she did not have one. He pulled one from his bag and used it himself, demonstrating some experience. He pushed her into the shower, where he washed her hair, scrubbed her body, and then, using a comb he took from his bag, combed her pubic hair. The combings he flushed down the toilet. He also flushed the condom. The towel was placed in the bag.

He dried her body carefully. "What are you going to do when I leave?" he asked.

"I'm going to get dressed and call my mother," she said.

"Will you cry?"

She began crying and could not answer.

"Will you call the police?" he asked.

"I don't know," she said.

He laughed and said it did not matter, that the police would never catch him because he knew every step they made. he said he knew what the police were going to do before they did it.

"Will you leave here tonight?" he asked.

"I don't know. I don't know," she said.

"That old vehicle parked in space C6 won't transport you very far, and it won't take you very fast," he said.

She stared at him. She noticed then his eyes were pale with what appeared to be a yellowish cast.

"The Chevrolet," he said with a smile. "The green Chevrolet."

"How do you know about my car? Are you going to hurt my car, too?"

"I haven't hurt you, have I?" he said. "I don't hurt women. I have great respect for women."

She said she was afraid to answer.

He took her into the hall and held her hand while he defecated on the floor. Then he pulled her into the bathroom.

"I want to get dressed," she said. "You got what you came for. Now I want you to leave."

"I'm not leaving," he said. "We are going to have

*an adventure. I'm going to take you to the mountaintop
and show you my kingdom."*

She asked why and he answered by picking up a
small lamp on the dressing table and moving it, smiling
enigmatically. He pulled a tape recorder from his bag,
placed it on the floor, and turned it on. The victim
recognized the music as Wagner's "Entrance of the
Gods into Valhalla." Then the offender took another
tape recorder from his bag and pressed the record
button.

He pressed her against the wall and began beating
her with his fists, hitting her in the stomach and breasts
and face until she was semi-conscious.

She sensed that he was taking something from his
bag, and then she felt him taping her mouth. She tried
to move but fell over on her face. He apparently
thought she was unconscious and dragged her by her
hair into the shower stall and dropped her face down.

She felt a sharp pain across the back of her neck
and realized he had cut her. Blood gushed from her
neck and across one hand. The pain forced her wide
awake. She thought she was about to die. With her right
hand she wrote "God" in her own blood on the shower
wall. He was astride her back but absolutely still, and
she sensed he was watching what she was doing.

Again she felt the knife cut across the back of her
neck. He groaned.

Then she wrote "I" in blood.

He reached over and jerked the tape from her mouth.
"What are you doing? What are you trying to say?"
he whispered. She said his voice was very intense.

She did not answer but instead continued to write.
When she was finished, there in blood on the shower
wall was "I God's Child."

"What do you mean? What do you mean?" he said.

"I am the child of God. I am His perfect child," she groaned. "Nothing you can do will really hurt me."

He moaned and she heard him say what sounded like "Phony." He repeated it several times.

He quoted the Bible for several minutes. She does not remember any of the quotes. He put a towel on her neck and told her not to move. He was gone for several minutes, and when he returned he was dressed. He wore blue pants and a blue shirt. He had on the ski mask and was stuffing a towel and sheet into the bag. He also put the towel he had dried off with into the bag. He looked at her and left. A moment later he returned again, this time carrying a telephone. He put the phone on the floor and said, "I'm going to dial nine-one-one for you, but you will have to talk with them. Can you do that?"

"Yes," she whispered.

He dialed and stretched the phone line for her to reach. He placed the phone against her ear and quickly turned and left.

The door was unlocked when police arrived.

Nigel turned over the last page of the report, stood up, and rubbed his lower back. He paced about the small office for a moment, then returned to his chair. In addition to the report, he had put together an analysis of the attack on Virginia Blair.

Virginia was a low-risk victim. The assailant obviously sought her out.

The M.O. here bears a striking resemblance to that in the other attacks on Emory students. It should be remembered here the three purposes of an offender's M.O.: to insure success, protect the identity, and facilitate escape.

He used a "con" approach. He had every reason to believe she would be unprepared for an attack. He knew the car she drove and knew it was parked in the parking lot. There is no doubt she was targeted in advance. He did not ask if anyone else was in the apartment or was expected. This indicates he was familiar with Virginia's routine and was aware she lived alone.

Although he had a knife, he relied in the beginning on threats to control her. His language in the beginning did not indicate hostility or anger. He brought a bag containing tape, apparently a knife, a condom, a douche bag, and other items. Carrying a "rape kit" indicates prior planning.

The offender had several instances to rationalize use of physical force against the victim but did not actually strike (cut) her until after the first assault. The force used consisted of (1) placing a knife against her throat, (2) pushing her down on the bed. Of behavioral interest is the fact that when he hurt her and she told him so, he did not hurt her again. His threats were more stern than angry. He was non-profane, reassuring, complimentary, concerned.

Given the circumstances, the level of force exhibited in the first rape was minimal. The victim reported that the offender seemed to care about her welfare.

The victim resisted the first rape. She resisted the offender verbally. She resisted passively by not taking off her nightgown. And she resisted him physically by moving away to avoid intercourse.

It is clear that even though the offender possessed the victim sexually, he did not intimidate her emotionally. His lack of violent reaction indicates the desire or intent to harm the victim physically was absent.

However, after the first sexual assault, the offender

exhibited marked personality changes. His level of increasing violence was presaged by the nature both of his threats and the nature of the second assault.

It is interesting to note the sequence of events in the second assault. Verbally the offender went from "We're going to make love" to "I'm going to fuck you in the ass."

The anal attack was followed by fellatio. The order reveals a clear effort to demean and humiliate the victim. The stern threats escalated to "I'll cut your goddamn head off" and the use of moderate force—cutting the victim's neck enough to cause blood to flow. After beating the victim severely, the offender taped her mouth and cut her twice more across the back of the neck.

The victim was unable to determine if any sexual dysfunction occurred. She said the rapist had no difficulty in obtaining or maintaining an erection. She said the first sexual attack "lasted about an hour. He wouldn't stop." Her lack of sexual experience does not enable her to know if the offender ejaculated during the first attack. He did not ejaculate during fellatio. The paraphilia of retarded ejaculation may affect the offender.

The first attack included, in the sequence reported by the victim, these acts: (1) kissing mouth and breasts, (2) digital manipulation of the vagina, (3) cunnilingus, and (4) vaginal rape. The activity and sequencing suggests an attempt to stimulate the victim, to "involve" rather than "use" her. Such was not the case in the second attack, which included (1) vaginal rape, (2) anal rape, (3) fellatio. After thoroughly cleaning the victim, the offender then engaged in brutal force.

The mind dictates what is or what is not sexually

arousing or pleasing. It is significant that during the first attack the offender wanted the victim to express affection, ("Tell me you love me,") and involvement ("Move your ass for me,") and that afterward he stood nude with the victim on an open porch, combed her hair with his fingers, and asked that she tell him he was a "good boy."

The attitudinal change on the part of the offender is particularly noteworthy. Although he was substantially larger than the victim, much stronger, and had a knife, he met substantial resistance during the first assault. Yet he was stern rather than brutal; he manifested some concern for the victim, i.e., as when he tried to avoid hurting her during the rape. The rapist engaged in a battle of wills with the victim and lost.

This case is filled with actions taken by the offender to protect his identity, facilitate his escape, and deny investigators evidence. He wore surgical gloves. He wore a ski mask. He checked the lock upon entering. He unplugged the telephone. He covered the victim's head before removing his mask. He turned apartment lights off. He forced the victim to shower and douche. He carried a "rape kit" containing, at least, tape, condom, two tape recorders, and—upon leaving—sheet and pillow cases and possibly personal items owned by the victim. Most of what he took was evidentiary material. He possesses a knowledge of forensics far beyond the layman level. He knows about fiber tests, and he knows about phosphotate tests. He used the words vehicle *and* transport *as they are used by police officers.*

The first attack was "unselfish" while the second was "selfish." His abrupt shift indicates how he is perceived by those who know him. He presents different images to different people. Some would describe him as re-

spectful and quiet with a "good personality," while others would say he is hostile with deep-seated anger. His fruitless attempts to dominate the victim suggests that he thinks of himself as a macho individual. He is self-centered and does not accept criticism. He demands instant gratification of his needs and desires. The attitudinal change strongly suggests that he does not like losing in his dealings with women. He dislikes authority, especially in females. he thinks of himself as superior yet associates with those he considers less than equal to him. Associates would describe him as cool and aloof. He reacts negatively when his authority is challenged. Some would say he is short-tempered. He is glib and manipulative.

The offender is a white male. He is a polished, experienced, and dangerous criminal. He is between 28 and 32 years of age. He lacks confidence in dealing with women and therefore would choose a victim as much as ten years younger.

The offender's knowledge of forensics indicates he may have been arrested for rape or for B&E. His anal assault and upper-body development indicates he may have been incarcerated.

The amount of time he spent with the victim provides two significant pieces of information: (1) he was familiar with her routine, and (2) he felt comfortable in the socioeconomic environment in which the attack occurred. Therefore he lives in similar-type property (rental and middle-class), perhaps even in the same part of town.

When he defecated on the floor, it was an act of contempt against her and against all women.

The offender's verbiage and the victim's opinion of him indicate that he is educated beyond high school.

As a student he achieved high grades. But because he dislikes authority, it is unlikely his education has been fully utilized.

Considering his age and dislike for authority, it is unlikely he served in the armed forces. If he did, it was probably as an enlisted person. He may not have served a full tour. And his desire to project a macho image suggests he served in the ground forces, the army or marines.

He is working in a job for which he is overqualified. His performance may reflect an attitudinal problem.

His car is 3–5 years old, but is well maintained, neat, and appears almost new.

He is a very neat individual. He takes a great deal of pride in his personal and physical appearance and is critical of those who don't. He exercises regularly and is physically fit. He is meticulous about body cleanliness.

There was more. Nigel rubbed his back. He needed time to assimilate all the information. But several things were quite clear. The victim had dark hair. The single blonde among the six victims must have been a diversion. That was the only explanation. That meant the U.C. people at Emory should be increased in number and should focus on dark-haired women who fit the profile. It meant Sarah must come home. She had to come home. Clearly the offender had a job that enabled him to be in contact with numerous students. He is either a law enforcement officer or is connected to law enforcement in some fashion.

In addition, while the victim had received no phone calls or notes that would indicate she had been under surveillance, and while there had been no break-in of her apartment or her car, and while she had seen no prowlers or peeping toms around her apartment, and while she had no feeling of being watched or followed, nevertheless, there had been something familiar about the rapist. She felt she had met him, perhaps briefly, at some point. Perhaps it was his voice. But he was not a stranger. Of that she was certain.

Why had the offender not used brutal force until after the first rape? Was it for punishment? What non-sexual need did it fulfill to brutalize the victim after there was no resistance, after he had raped and humiliated her? Why does he want to punish his victims?

Sudden and unexpected behavior changes indicate weakness and fear on the part of the offender. Rape can be as stressful to the offender as it is to the victim. How the offender reacts under stress is crucial.

When she asked him why he was doing this, he smiled and moved a lamp. What did that mean?

Nigel closed his eyes and visualized a man moving a lamp.

It returned, that faint and distant memory, that gossamer cord stretching back to something he had read. He knew it was important. For a moment he almost retrieved the memory. Then the cord disappeared and the memory was gone.

Why had the offender not only released the victim but made the 911 call for her? It had something to do with what she had written in blood: "I God's Child." Was he a religious person?

This was Saturday, June 22. Dates were important. Did his releasing her have something to do with the date? If so, what?

The ritualistic aspects of the attack were disturbing. A sexual offender's rituals have only one purpose: psychosexual gratification. The ritual may improve, but it will not change. It is offender-specific. It is his signature.

Two other things bothered Nigel. Every time the offender used the knife, it was on the back of the victim's neck. Not on her face or arms or body.

When a serial rapist begins murdering his victims and a victim is found with cuts on the back of her neck, it means only one thing: the offender had planned to cut off her head but had not yet gotten enough courage to do so.

This was a practice run.

Even more portentous, the offender had closed the windows in the apartment and turned the air conditioning to the lowest setting.

There was only one reason for that.

Colder temperatures slow decomposition.

18

Lucifer was not happy.

It had not gone well last night. He had gone adventuring and his plan had worked perfectly until the woman who wanted him wrote "I God's Child" on the shower wall. He should have ignored it. He should never have let her explain what she was doing.

Memories.

Memories.

Too many memories.

He had never meant to hurt Fiona. It had been an accident. He had been doing penance ever since. Last night the woman wanted him. But if there had been an accident, it would have been reliving that day with his sister.

Lucifer's plans had been thwarted. But there was another woman on campus who wanted him. He knew her name. He knew her schedule. He had planned for such a contingency. He knew how to let her find him tomorrow tonight.

As for tonight, he already had plans.

The end was near. There were only three more women to whom he would show his kingdom and explain his glory. And then the plan would be fulfilled, and he would sit on the right hand of Him.

The other two had not yet revealed themselves to him. Perhaps they would do so Friday night.

The rock concert on campus would be the ideal place. God was leading the way. And Lucifer would bend to God's will.

Lucifer thumbed through detective magazines for more than an hour, studying each page, each picture of women tied with ropes or chains or handcuffs. He also liked pictures of women who were being tortured with hot instruments or threatened with cudgels. But his favorites were pictures of woman being threatened with a knife. He studied the wide eyes and the twisted mouths of the women and knew the pictures were fakes. They were not as good as what he had seen.

But they would do for the time being.

Lucifer stripped off all his clothes except for his blue silk shorts. The tape recording from last night had been edited, and the good parts, his favorite parts, were still there. He inserted the tape, then walked across the room and covered his hands with lotion. He sat down, rubbed his hands together for long moments, then pressed the Play button on the tape recorder.

He leaned back in the chair, looked in the mirror, and admired his reflection. He had a splendid body. He teased and flexed his muscles, smiling at his image. Then he cradled the small gold cross around his neck and listened to the music.

Wagner and me. Together. Outstanding.
I hear her moans of pain.
I feel the power.
I have control.
Wagner created the music.
I created the chorus.

My work is superior.

I have done wonderful things to please my God. But why can't there be another way? Why can't this cup be taken from me?

I know what they call me. They say I am the Arch Fiend, the Evil One, Lord of the Flies, Ruler of Hell, and a Foe of God.

These are perilous times. There are wars and rumors of wars. I must protect myself against the incursions of the ungodly.

They don't understand.

All I want is to liberate them.

All I want is to evict them from their bodies.

All I want is for them to share my glory.

19

All I want is to take care of my wife, to make her as comfortable as possible, and to protect my daughter until she gets a good start in the world. If I could do those two things, and have time for my flowers, I would be content.

Nigel cradled his head in his hands. The case files were spread across the top of his desk, and a yellow legal pad was in front of him. On the wall was a map that included the Emory campus, Atlanta, and DeKalb County. Colored pins were stuck at various sites. Red pins denoted locations where bodies had been found. White pins denoted rapes. A legend on the edge of the map revealed distances between the sites.

Nigel looked up and moved his notes around until he found the legal pad where he had written the names of the victims and a few words about each.

Victoria Kennedy, brunette, 18, freshman. Columbia, SC.

Jan Archangeli, brunette, 20, junior. McKeesport, PA.

Monaco Jackson, brunette, 20, junior. Manhattan.

Kathleen Powers, brunette, 18, freshman. Trenton, NJ.

Anne Justice, *blonde*, 19, sophomore, Scarsdale, NY.
Virginia Blair, brunette, 21, junior. Decatur, AL.

Nigel closed his eyes. Something was stirring in the back of his mind, a flitting, ephemeral hint about the case, that distant memory of something he had read. He concentrated, trying to retrieve the memory that, like a forgotten scent born on a faint breeze, tantalized him with its elusiveness. He sensed but could not invoke its presence. He could not grasp it before it disappeared.

Nigel sighed. He struggled to remember all that he had read about killers. What was it Ralph Stone had said about anger in the offender? He was terribly angry at a woman in his past. he wondered if Emory had enough details in the files of its white male employees—that is, the names of mothers and sisters— to run a computer check to see if there was something in the names of those women that would release a clue. He knew the killer was connected to Emory. And he knew the killer had a strong connection to law enforcement. But how?

Even with Ed Medlin's computer printouts, the universe of potential offenders was too big. It was going to take several weeks to check out those names. That was far too long. He had to hasten the process.

Nigel shook his head. Smart crooks were the most difficult to catch. Some never got caught. It was like fishing for a big old lunker every fisherman in the state had heard about. The fish didn't get to be a lunker by snapping at every bit of bait dangled in front of it. Maybe he had been snagged a few times. Probably had. But almost getting caught had only made him more wily and more difficult to catch.

The telephone rang.

"Officer Trench."

"Hey, Roach. Norris here."

"Hello, Major."

"Roach, you remember that list of names from Emory you gave me?"

"Yes. The preliminary list we need to look at a little closer. Find something already?"

"Well, I talked to the chief and she put the fugitive squad and intelligence unit on it, and we narrowed it down to a half-dozen possibilities. Then when we had that forty-nine last night, the mayor called. He says that what's good for the goose is good for the mice that play when the cat's away."

Nigel thought for a minute. "Major, would you run that last one by me one more time?"

"Mayor is raising hell. He asked the chief and the chief called. They both on the line. 'What you got?' he wants to know. I told him about the list. He wanted some rather detailed info about several of the names. he asks good questions—former U.S. attorney, you know."

Nigel could see what was coming. He put his hand over his eyes. "Major, you didn't . . .?"

"Emory's got a bunch of sex offenders on the payroll. Fucker butts out there like you wouldn't believe. The mayor believes strongly that one of them, fellow who works in the president's office, is a strong suspect. Right age. Was here five years ago. Muscular fellow, works out all the time at the Emory gym. Had some sex offenses as a juvenile. You know how hard it is to get juvenile records unsealed on short notice? And we talked to some people at Emory who say he is suspected of having homosexual relationships with a couple of Emory freshmen."

"Fresh*men*, Major. Fresh*men*. I don't care about gay guys. Our offender is not gay. He's a psychotic serial rapist. He's a sexual sadist. He's a killer. He's a lot of things. But he is not gay."

"Six of one and three dozen of another far as the mayor's concerned. Or vice versa. He's so upset he's spitting metal."

"You're way off base."

Nigel heard Major Morris blow out a puff of cigarette smoke. "Mayor disagrees with you, Roach. It's out of my hands. He said this case has to be cleaned up because of the Olympics. Hell, reporters from all over the world start arriving in the next few days. We have to show them our good side."

"You're not . . . ?"

"Roach, you got two days. Three at most. That's all I could get for you. And I wouldn't have been able to do that if it weren't for waiting on the juvie records. Good thing it takes a day or so."

"Norris, this is the very thing we talked about that day when you came to my house . . . to my apartment. No investigation can go forward under these circumstances. My job is to find this guy, and your job is to cover my back."

"Roach, you got to understand something. This thing is political and I have no control at all over it. None at all. The chief gets her marching orders from the mayor, and I get my marching orders from the chief. I say, 'Yes, ma'am,' and do it. If I don't, she'll retire me and put somebody in my desk in five minutes who will."

"She doesn't think this is the guy, does she?"

"I don't know what she thinks. I only know that I have been working for her long enough to know that there are two or three days every month when, if a man has walking-around sense, he stays out of her way. Every senior officer in the department keeps a calendar with those days marked on it. According to the calendar I'm looking at, she's on day two of her three-day cycle as the chief from hell. I wouldn't question her right now if she told me that sun was going to come up outta the south tomorrow. Or vice versa."

"So what happens at the end of the three days and this guy is still running around loose? The guy who attacked my . . ." His voice faltered.

"That's the end of the delay time, Roach. After that, if there is even the slightest amount of evidence, I'm arresting that fucker butt in the president's office. Mayor's already got his press man working on it."

"Working on what?"

"The press conference where he's gonna announce the arrest of the rapist."

"Rapist? Rapist? How about sexual homicide? How about serial killer? Since when does rape take precedence over homicide? Is that only during the Olympics?"

"Roach, listen up. A few weeks before the Olympics, Atlanta does not have a serial killer. He's a rapist. That's bad enough. That's all the mayor wants to talk about."

"What about the two bodies at the Carter Center?"

"We're talking about a rapist. That other stuff is way down in the press release."

"Major, have you gone absolutely crazy? I don't know that this man you're talking about is the offender. You haven't even briefed me on what you found."

"You do believe the perp is at Emory?"

"Yes, but ..."

"You do believe he might be included in the list of names you gave me?"

"Yes, he could be. But ..."

"And, according to your memo, you believe he has great anger toward women?"

"Yes."

"You are the expert on this case, the man in charge?"

"Yes."

"Then don't cry over milk under the bridge. This will be a righteous bust."

"There are some questions you didn't ask."

"What?"

"You should have asked, 'Do you know how this guy is picking his victims? Do you know his motive?' "

"Mayor says he has thought this thing down one side and around the other. He says that will be evident when we arrest this asshole."

"The mayor's an idiot. There are several obvious things he hasn't factored into his wacky equation."

"Yeah? What's that?"

"First and most obvious, that the offender might not be on that list."

"You know that for certain?"

"No, I don't."

"Then if we arrest this fucker butt we are killing three birds with one rock. We are taking him out of circulation. With his record, he ought not to be at Emory anyway. And there is a good chance he is the perp."

"Won't fly, Major. You think Buchanan will buy this crock? You think your wife will buy it? You think the public will buy it? Unless you got a hell of a lot I don't know about, this whole thing reeks of a setup."

"Don't know about Buchanan. Marie, well, the woman's Italian. What can I say? That newspaper will let her write whatever she wants. She might wig out for a day or so. But even she knows a bird in the bush is worth two in the nest. Besides, that kinda stuff is for the major's press guy to deal with. He says if we can reveal the motive and how he picked his victims when he has the press conference that it will head off any possible criticism."

"There's one more thing, Major. One more thing you haven't considered."

Another drag off the cigarette. "Yeah?" came the guarded voice. "And what would that be?"

"Haven't you Rhodes scholars considered the most fundamental flaw in your little scenario? What happens when he rapes and kills another student?"

"Mayor's thought of that, too," Morris said.

"Tell me."

"Happens after the mayor's press conference, it's a copycat killer."

"And the next time?"

"Mayor says it won't happen."

Nigel laughed.

"Roach, let me change the subject here. I put Maytag on permanent morning watch and assigned him to Grady. He's out of your hair."

"I gotta go." Nigel hung up the telephone and stared at the files on his desk.

He shook his head. That zephyr of an idea about

the case, that distant hint of how the killer was select-
ing his victims, was gone. There was nothing.

Nigel rubbed his back.

Even after three years he did not always know how
to talk with her. Foremost in his thinking was what
the doctor had said about her fragility and how he
must protect her from the past. Most of the time she
seemed normal. Her conversation could be bright and
bouncy, as when she inquired about the apartment
and his flowers and what he was doing to occupy his
time. She always asked about Sarah.

Granted, she was quite pale, but that came, or so
he thought, from her being indoors almost all of the
time. Her eyes seemed dull, as if covered with a film
that protected her from seeing too much. But it was
her hands that bothered him most. She used the nails
of each finger to dig into the cuticles of other fingers.
Her hands almost writhed as her nails dug into her
fingers. Sometimes blood oozed from around her nails.
At times she would catch herself and use one hand to
seize the other as if to keep it from misbehaving. But
after a few moments her attention would wander and
her fingers would again begin their restless digging and
picking and scratching.

Usually she was up and walking around when he
arrived. If only a few patients were in the big dayroom, they would wander down the hall and sit in the
sun and talk.

He opened the door to her room slowly and was
relieved to see she was in bed. He did not want to
go to the dayroom today. He pulled one of the big,
comfortable chairs from across the room and placed

it near the bed. Slowly he sat down and reached for her hand. Her head was turned toward the windows.

"I'm here," he said softly.

"I didn't smell beer on you the other day."

"What?"

"When you came by with Norris. He looked good, by the way. Growing older like all of us. But he looked very handsome in his suit."

Nigel waited.

"He's still smoking," Rachel said. She moved her head slowly from side to side. "I don't see how you could be in the car with him. I know how you detest that odor."

"He's my friend."

"But I didn't smell beer on you."

"I don't understand."

"You two came in here talking about running into each other at Manuel's and having a beer, and neither of you had been drinking." She turned her head and looked at him for the first time.

"We were talking about going to Manuel's for a beer," he said lamely.

She squeezed his hand and smiled. "Oh, Nigel. You are so transparent when you try to hold something from me." She paused. "I believe I could ask you any question in the world, you would tell me the truth."

He said nothing.

"If I didn't know you so well, there would be some questions I would be afraid to ask you."

"Why?"

"As I said, you would tell me the truth."

"What do you want to ask?"

Her filmy eyes stared at him for a long moment,

and she did not answer. Then, very slowly, she moved her head from side to side. "I'm not sure."

He waited.

"I know you and Norris had not been drinking beer. But you were together." She paused. "He said he is still with the police, a major now."

Nigel nodded. He had to change the subject. He stood up quickly, too quickly, and a wave of pain washed across his face. Involuntarily, he squeezed her hand very hard while, with his other hand, he clutched his back. He smiled and put his right hand in his pocket, rattling his change. "Want a Coke? Let me go down the hall and get us something to drink."

"What's the matter?"

"What do you mean?"

"You grabbed your back. Are you having back problems?"

"Those things never really go away. Sometimes I feel a twinge. You want a Coke?"

"You never had back problems except when you were working on a big case."

"I stood up too quickly." He smiled ruefully. "Like you said, we're all getting older." He squeezed her hand. "Want a Coke?"

She smiled. "Okay, Nigel. I'll drink a Coca-Cola with you. Lots of ice in mine. You remember."

"Of course." He turned for the door, using every ounce of his strength to stand erect and to make sure his left foot moved properly.

He was almost to the door when his pager sounded.

Goddammit all to hell.

He should have turned it off when he arrived at the hospital. But, then, no one was to page him when

he was here. And he had left his location with the
task force.

He turned.

Rachel's eyes were wide. "Nigel?" She sounded
bewildered.

He rushed across the room to her side. He winced
and he knew his left foot was dragging. He reached
for her hands.

"Nigel?"

He sat on the bed beside her. He did not know
what to say.

"When did you get a pager? Why do you need a
pager?"

"Some people are having a problem, and they asked
me to do some consulting work with them." He tried
to laugh. "They must want me to meet them for lunch.
That's why they're calling. It's the only reason anyone
could be paging me."

Her eyes roamed over his face.

"Nigel?"

"Yes, my love."

"I want to see Sarah. I want my daughter."

20

For several years they had been noticed around Atlanta, these ordinary people with jobs—usually administrative—connected to the Olympics. They were easy to identify, since their little picture ID's always swung from chains about their necks. Anyone who has ever lived in Washington or in any city where there are high-security defense contractors knows that most White House staffers and most defense workers take off their ID badges when they are in public. Not Atlanta Olympic workers. They strutted about town and blazed in and out of bars and restaurants with their ID's swinging. They were masters of what many level-headed people predicted would be the worst debacle in Atlanta since Sherman went through.

Hundreds of thousands of visitors were expected every day in Atlanta during the summer Olympics. They would spread out and virtually take over every restaurant and every historical site and every park and every form of entertainment in the metropolitan area.

In anticipation of the unprecedented number of visitors, a maintenance worker was taking the empty sky lift to the top of Stone Mountain, testing it for smoothness of operation before that day's visitors descended on the large state-owned park east of Atlanta. He had done this every morning for the past few weeks. After reaching the crest of the mountain he looked west, toward the skyline about fifteen miles away. He had grown used to the sight. But this morning there was an anomaly, something that wasn't usually there, something that jarred his consciousness. From a distance it appeared to be a small lump atop the highest part of the mountain, a small, dark lump sitting alone there in an expanse of gray granite. And there was something about the shape that worried the maintenance worker. He stared, moving about for different perspectives. It could not be what he thought it was.

He stepped out of the sky lift, walked through the large public rooms, and took the steps down to the surface of the mountain. He walked slowly, walking around or stepping over the countless washbowl-sized depressions made by lightning strikes, and he was careful not to step on any of the flowers that grew atop the mountain.

He drew closer, his eyes locked onto the object. Now the shape was more clearly defined.

It couldn't be what it appeared to be.

Where was the rest of the . . . ?

A few more steps. Now there was no doubt. Horrified, he walked around his discovery to look at it from the other side, to look it full in the face.

The maintenance worker had discovered the severed head of the seventh victim.

The heavy makeup she wore did not cover the massive bruises on her face. Her hair was combed perfectly. Every hair was in place. Even the wind that always blew atop Stone Mountain could not ruffle her hair.

But that wind did ruffle the silk scarf looped from her chin around her head.

Her head faced away from Atlanta, toward the east, toward the morning sun, and on her face was an expression of unendurable agony and otherworldly horror.

"She was an Emory student. Her name is Susan Bishop. From Squirrel Hill, Pennsylvania. Junior. Prelaw." Nigel squeezed the telephone against his shoulder and looked at his notes. "Twenty years old."

Major Morris sighed. Nigel could hear him lighting a cigarette. "Mayor's not gonna be happy about this. He's gonna want to know what you got."

"Tell him I got a body at the foot of the mountain. A body without a head. Tell him the medical examiner is trying to separate the bruises she got from a beating before she was killed from the bruises she received when she was thrown off the mountain. Tell him the medical examiner believes she was raped before she was killed. And tell him it can be his job to notify the parents."

"I ain't telling him all that. Give me something I can tell him."

"Tell him there's a little pool of rainwater on top of the mountain, one of those formed when lightning strikes, that is filled with soapy water. It's close to where we found her head. Smells as if it's dishwashing detergent."

"Soapy rainwater?"

"Yes. And the M.E. has found what appears to be soap film around the vagina and on the legs of the victim."

"You mean . . . ?"

"You can tell him her nipples were cut off. And you can tell him I believe the offender had sex with her body after the head was removed."

"Oh, shit, Roach. Nobody does that."

"Serial killer did it down in Gainesville, Florida."

"That's one. He was a whacko."

"Remember the guy about eight or ten years ago whose fiancée died two days before their wedding? He went out a week after she was buried, dug her up, and had his wedding night right there by the grave. He was holding her and crying when I found him."

"Okay, okay. That's two. I don't want to talk about them. Let's talk about this case." Major Morris grimaced and took a deep puff of his cigarette. "Things are moving too fast. This case has reached terminal philosophy."

"If you have to tell the mayor something, tell him I don't know why Stone Mountain was picked."

Morris sucked on his teeth. "Maybe the guy is a Civil War buff. What's special about the mountain otherwise? Didn't the Klan used to burn crosses out there? Isn't it the biggest hunk of rock in the world?"

Nigel remembered the hype about Stone Mountain. Everyone in Atlanta knows the hype about Stone Mountain: "Biggest piece of exposed granite in the world."

Nigel stopped. Stone Mountain. Mountain. A high mountain. There were two bodies on a high hill near the Carter Center. Then this one at Stone Mountain. A rape victim in second-story apartment. Height. Altitude. Up high. High places.

There it was again, that ephemeral something, that elusive memory, something about the victims. For a moment he almost had it. Morris spoke again and broke the spell.

"What else you got?"

"She was facing east."

"You think that's important? Maybe he just put her head that way."

"This guy doesn't do things in a capricious fashion. Everything is planned. Everything. If he put her head facing that direction, there is a reason. She was facing away from Atlanta." Nigel paused. When he spoke it was as if he were talking to himself. "Away from Atlanta. Her back would have been toward Atlanta. She had her back turned to the city. Is that it? Or is it significant instead that she faced the morning sun?"

"Symbols. Symbols. Just give me something for the mayor."

"Okay, Major. Tell him Buchanan is at the crime scene and that I gave him everything. Tell him that in the afternoon paper he's gonna read a serial killer is targeting Emory students."

Silence. Then, "Good God, Roach. You didn't ... you did ... I ain't telling him that."

"Buchanan has known since we found those two bodies at the Carter Center. You were right. Somebody dropped a dime. But I convinced him not to go with it until we had something. But we can't keep a lid on this anymore. Somebody would break it. And somebody would tie it all together. I gave Buchanan everything. Everyone else, the other papers, radio, TV, will all follow what he writes. That way we have some control over the story."

Morris was horrified. "Do you realize what you've done? A lot of sheep will come home to roost about this."

"I've done you a favor."

Morris snorted into the telephone. "You're in a pissy mood."

"I'm getting pissier. Your man Popcorn paged me at the hospital. Now Rachel suspects I'm on The Job again. I don't know what that will do to her, but it won't be good. You keep Popcorn away from me. And if you don't like my mood, I can be a civilian again in about as long as it takes me to drop my badge on your desk. If it weren't for reasons you know all too well and for the fact I'm afraid for my daughter, I'd do exactly that. In fact, if I could get my daughter out of Emory until this is over I'd leave you people on your own."

"Roach, Roach. I understand how you feel, but—"

"One other thing," Nigel interrupted, "I want whatever analysis the mayor thinks he's come up with from the fugitive squad and from intelligence. I want everything he's got, and I want it now."

"A copy will be on your desk when you get back."

"Major?"

"Yeah."

"One more thing."

"What?"

"Tell the mayor to read the paper."

Morris hung up and stared at the telephone. The case was causing Roach to lose his judgment. The guy was falling apart.

21

It was still dark when Lucifer slid on a pair of jeans, stuck his feet into spotlessly clean white tennis shoes, and padded down the long driveway to the street, where he picked up his copy of *The Atlanta Constitution*. He pulled the paper from the clear plastic sleeve, annoyed at the pieces of grass that slid away from the dewy surface onto his hand. He wadded up the plastic sleeve, tossed it into the neighbor's yard, and walked with long strides back toward the house, taking deep breaths in the cool morning air.

At his door he carefully wiped his tennis shoes on a thick mat, looked at the bottoms to make sure he was taking no grass inside, and opened the door. The bacon cooking on the stove was done. He knew that bacon was not good for his body. But he had never had bacon as a child, and now it was his one weakness. He lifted three strips of bacon from the pan and put them on a paper towel to dry. Then he poured the bacon grease into a can on the rear of the stove. The paper was tucked under his arm and a glass of orange juice in one hand and a saucer of bacon in the other as he trotted lightly up the wide stairs toward the large room on the second floor. He sat down, took a long drink of juice, and shook open the paper, studying the front page at length.

The story he sought was played on the right side above the fold. A four-column story with a two-line head. The byline read Dan Buchanan. Lucifer did not like Buchanan. But it was appropriate that the most famous reporter in Atlanta was covering the story. Lucifer nodded in approval, picked up a slice of bacon, and began reading.

A serial killer who is stalking Emory University students struck again when the head of the third victim was found atop Stone Mountain on Tuesday morning. The student's body was found at the foot of the mountain, beneath the Confederate carving on the north side.

"This is the third Emory student he has killed in recent weeks," said Detective Nigel Trench, who was called out of retirement to head up a task force investigating the case. The bodies of Two Emory students were found last week near the Carter Presidential Center.

Trench said four other Emory students have been assaulted by the suspect but were not killed.

"The common element in each of these attacks was Emory University," Detective Trench said. "The man we are looking for has a connection to Emory."

A worker who was testing the skylift at Stone Mountain discovered the dismembered Emory student. She has been identified as Susan Bishop, 20, a junior from Squirrel Hill, PA, and a pre-law student. Miss Bishop's apartment in Decatur has been examined, but no clues or evidence were found there, according to Detective Trench.

"We believe the offender kidnapped the student, possibly from her apartment, and took her to an as-yet unknown location, probably his house or apartment. The evidence indicates the mutilation occurred atop Stone Mountain," said Detective Trench.

"We are utilizing every investigative and forensic tool at our disposal," said Detective Trench. "In addition, the task force assembled to investigate this case is being assisted by numerous police departments. The assets we have pulled together are such that we expect to identify and arrest the perpetrator within a matter of days."

A spokeswoman for the president's office at Emory said that until the summer session ends next week, the campus will remain under heavy guard. She said Emory police are working double shifts and that DeKalb County officers are assisting in patrolling the campus.

"About three hundred" students have withdrawn from school, the spokeswoman, who did not want to be identified, said.

Lucifer snorted. "Blah, blah, blah." He read the remainder of the story, and then he reread the part quoting Trench and the impending arrest. Trench was alluding to the computer search now being conducted at Emory. He knew all about that. He knew all about the research Major Morris's office had conducted. The fruitless research. They had developed a profile and were scanning employee lists to see who fit the profile. And they were wrong on everything. They still thought the color of the hair on those who had chosen him was important. They thought women with dark hair had picked him out. He laughed. In addition, when they finished the computer search, they would be no closer to him than they were now. His name was not in the computer.

Lucifer smiled in satisfaction. He ate the last slice of bacon. He knew virtually every undercover officer on campus. He could spot them from a hundred yards away. Some of the U.C. officers he had talked with. They were all young and fresh out of the academy, and they thought because he wore a uniform that they could confide in him. He knew how many of them were working on each shift. He knew their duties and he knew their radio frequencies. He even knew the commanding officer of each shift.

He knew everything.

He folded the paper carefully and lowered it to the floor. He sipped his orange juice and stared out the large window over the grove of pine trees.

By the time Trench figures it all out—if he figures it out—God's work will have been done. The woman I took to the mountaintop was particularly rewarding. It was necessary to leave part of her there looking away from Atlanta—which has become my city, Pandemonium. And then she experienced what I experienced. She was tossed down from a high place. Only two more remain, two more who are seeking me out, two more with whom I will go adventuring. Two more who will feel the breath of God. Only two more and my work will be done. What my work will be afterward, I do not yet know.

But it will be glorious.

It will be unprecedented.

It will be something all the world will recognize.

For to have accomplished what I am on the verge of accomplishing will render all the rewards of heaven open to me.

He smiled at the thought of Nigel Trench. He knew the name. Already he had talked to some of his comrades in uniform at Emory, and he had discovered that Trench's wife was in a private hospital, a mental institution. He wondered if she was as pretty as she had been three years ago. Ahhh, the things she had done for him. She was an older woman, and he did not care for older women. But she had done wonderful things for him.

Lucifer looked at his watch. Two students, the final two, were searching for him. The two who were closest to God and who were the most important had not yet found him. He knew their names from the student directory. He knew their pictures.

Perhaps tonight would be the night.

They see me and they do not know me.

I am here to clear the path. God is returning to earth, and I am His Wayshower. I am the Light Bearer.

And I must punish those who tried to keep me from the paths of righteousness.

Lucifer finished the orange juice in a long gulp and walked down the stairs to the kitchen, where he washed the glass and saucer and placed them on the counter. Then he went into his bedroom, pulled his uniform from the closet, and began dressing.

22

Members of the opening act, a band called DRE, were fingering their instruments when Shari and Sarah approached the gate at McDonough Field. They could see the band members atop the stage across the field. If one had to pick a single word to describe the band it would be "loud." If allowed two words, one could add "dirty."

Pepsi scampered along with Sarah and Shari, licking every hand he could reach.

"That singer reminds me of Mick Jagger," Sarah said, standing on her toes and looking across the crowd at the gate. More than a few male students looked at her. She wore cutoff jeans and a flaming red knit top.

Shari, who was wearing a plain blue blouse over jeans, shook her blond hair. "He doesn't have the moves. Nobody can move like Mick Jagger. For an old guy, he has the greatest moves ever."

Sarah looked at the placard on the fence. "DRE. Funny name for a band. What does that mean?" She had to speak loudly to be heard over the noise of the band.

Shari shook her head. "I have no idea. Probably

doesn't mean anything. The featured band is Spewing Turkeys. You like them?"

Sarah laughed. "I heard them once downtown at the Somber Reptile."

"Did you get down in the mosh pit? Do any slam dancing?"

Sarah shook her head. "That's kid stuff. I'm too old for that." She laughed. "When the lead singer blew his nose on the crowd, I did join in throwing shoes at him. I hit him with a tennis shoe."

"I went down there once. Big mistake."

"What happened?" The two young women pushed their way through the crowd toward the gate, Sarah always keeping an eye on Pepsi.

"They picked me up and I went body surfing. All across the top of the crowd. I was terrified." Shari looked around. "This crowd is almost as bad. Let's don't go down front. I don't want to get anywhere near the pit."

"Suits me. Some of the fraternity guys will be in there using their elbows."

"And their hands."

The two young women stopped and dug into their pockets for their ID cards as they approached the security guard at the gate. He smiled. He was wearing sunglasses.

"May I see your ID cards, please?" He stood close so they could hear him.

They stuck out cards and would have kept walking, but he said, "Just a moment, please." He took the cards and stared at them, studying the faces and then looking at the two young women. His heart was pounding.

He had found them.

The final two.

He returned Sarah's card.

"Is your father a policeman?"

She was surprised. "Well, sort of. He's retired. Do you know him?"

The officer smiled. "Everyone knows your father." He could not believe his good fortune. He looked at Pepsi.

Pepsi's tail stopped wagging. He backed up a step and growled.

"That your dog?"

"Yes." Sarah was embarrassed. "I don't know why he's growling. He likes everybody."

"Maybe he thinks I won't let him in without an ID card." The security guard pursed his lips in mock concentration. "Looks like a grad student to me. Probably forgot his card."

"Thanks," Sarah said. She snapped her fingers, then slapped her thigh and Pepsi ran to her. "Come on, boy. You can go to the concert." She picked him up and laughed when he licked her face. "Why are you growling at the nice man?"

The security guard returned Shari's ID card. He looked at Sarah and Shari. "You are together."

"Yes," Sarah said. "Is that against the law?"

The officer smiled. "No. On the contrary. It's wonderful."

Shari and Sarah looked at each other. The young security guard laughed. His gaze lingered on Shari. She blushed. She was not used to such attention from such a handsome man, particularly when she was with Sarah. Sarah was the one who always received the attention.

"Just asking. Have to make sure of everything these

days. My boss said check every card. It's because of the troubles." He looked at each of the young women. "That reminds me. You two have your security devices?"

The two women nodded. "Just got them," Shari said. She pulled the small alarm device from her pocket and held it up. "Want me to press the buttons and see if it works?"

"No. Better not." The young man's face was very stern. "Keep them with you at all times." He smiled. "We're going through a bad time. You know Emory almost canceled the concert tonight?"

"Yeah, we heard," Sarah said. "Glad they didn't." She nudged Shari, and the two young women moved with the crowd. They took a few steps and Sarah whispered, "I think he likes you."

Shari laughed. "Don't be silly."

But when she looked over her shoulder the security guard was giving cursory glances at the ID cards of passing students while his attention remained on her. He nodded. She blushed and grabbed Sarah's arm.

"He's looking at me."

"Go with it. You never know."

"How can you say that?" She looked over her shoulder again. "Wonder what he looks like behind those sunglasses? Eyes are important."

Three hours later, the crowd of several hundred Emory students emerged from McDonough Field. About a dozen uniformed Emory police officers were standing at the gate. Ed Medlin was there with a bull-horn. He put the horn to his lips as the crowd approached.

"Could I have your attention, please? We have uni-formed officers here, and we have cars available. We will provide escorts to your dormitories. Simply ask any officer for an escort. That is why we are here."

"You getting an escort?" Shari asked.

Sarah picked up Pepsi and looked around. "I better carry Pepsi, or one of those officers might take him." She waved to a group of students. "No, I see some people here from my dorm. Besides, nothing has happened on campus since that first attack. It's all off campus."

When Shari did not answer, Sarah looked at her. "What about you? Want an escort?"

Shari shook her head. "No, it's not far over to Turman. There will be someone going that way." She looked around.

"What's the matter with you?"

Shari giggled. "I have to go to the bathroom."

"Come with us. My dorm is close."

"Okay." Shari fell in with a group of students, and she and Sarah walked toward Harris Hall. They saw numerous uniformed officers patrolling the campus on foot. And Sarah noticed several young men whose demeanor was too serious for them to be students.

She pointed out one of the young men to Shari. "I'll bet he's an undercover officer."

Shari looked at the young man and then at Sarah. "How do you know?"

"My dad's a . . . was a policeman. He told me about those things. You can always recognize them if you know what to look for."

"What do you look for?"

"I don't know how to explain it. It's the way they walk. The way they carry themselves. Their eyes. Body language. But mostly the eyes. They act as if they own the world, even the young ones."

"All I see is people. A lot of them. And I'm glad."

At the dorm, the two young women talked until almost two a.m., when Shari looked at her watch.

"I have to run. It's late."

"Why don't you stay over? Pepsi won't mind if you take his bed."

"I would. But my parents might have called while I was out. If I don't return their call, they will be over here looking for me."

Sarah laughed. "God, I know what you mean. Come on, I'll go with you to the front door."

At the front door they looked out. "You taking the tunnels?" Sarah asked.

Shari nodded. "They're full of people. And when I get out, I'll walk across the parking lot and I'll be at the dorm."

A series of tunnels cuts under the hospital at Emory. The wide, well-lighted tunnels are designed to move patients from various parts of the hospital without having them cross Clifton Road. The tunnels connect various parking lots to the hospital and are used daily by hundreds of people.

Shari had taken no more than a half-dozen steps away from the dormitory when she was suddenly illuminated by the bright lights of a car emerging from the parking lot adjacent to Harris Hall. She stopped to let it pass and noticed the insignia on the door. It was an Emory car. The car stopped, and the window on the passenger side rolled down.

"You going to your dormitory?"

"Yes." She recognized the driver as the young man who had been checking ID cards at the gate. He was still wearing sunglasses. "Oh, hi," she said, momentarily nonplussed.

"Which one?"

"Turman."

"Jump in. I'll give you a ride."

"No thanks, I'll take the tunnels. I'm okay."

"Get in," the young officer insisted. "The chief said we should take students to their dorms. Particularly this late. I'll be in trouble if he hears that a female student was allowed to walk across campus alone. You don't want to get me in trouble, do you?"

Shari paused a moment, then opened the car door and slid inside. "So I'm being rescued from the boogey man by a man in uniform?"

The young officer laughed and pressed a latch that locked the car's doors. "You found me," he said as he pulled from the driveway and turned right.

Shari looked at him. Her smile was quick and nervous. She pointed over her shoulder. "Excuse me. You're going the wrong way. Turman is that way."

Lucifer laughed.

23

The computer searches yielded nothing. Sure, there were staff members who had been hired before Emory began running background checks who were found to have records for everything from assault to auto theft, but nothing that would indicate they were the offender Nigel sought. And there were faculty members who had committed offenses that were not contained in Ed Medlin's files, offenses usually of a different nature than those committed by staff members, offenses alleging the faculty members were shoplifters, peeping toms, flashers, and pedophiles. There were minor dope convictions and charges of being protesters, demonstrators, animal-rights whackos, and involvement in gay and lesbian activities. The faculty was a squirrely bunch of misfits. But there was nothing that would prevent tenure and nothing like what Nigel sought.

He looked at a copy of the files sent over from Major Morris, files the mayor's minions had gone through. Some of the stuff was titillating, and some of it should be known by Ed Medlin, but there was nothing to point to anyone who fit the profile of the person he sought.

The GCIC computers and NCIC and several federal

data bases had yielded nothing about any faculty or staff member that would indicate a strong suspect.

The human resources people at Emory had taken the information from Ed Medlin, information that would fit the profile of the offender, and entered it into their own computer. Nothing.

Nigel sighed, stood up and rubbed his back, and paced back and forth behind his desk. He walked slowly. His left foot was beginning to drag. Nigel tried to ignore the pain as he wondered about the offender.

What was he overlooking?

The offender was connected to Emory. He was a cop buff, maybe even . . .

Nigel pursed his lips. He sat down, looked at his notes, and dialed a telephone number.

Ed Medlin answered.

"Ed, Nigel here. You're working Saturday morning, too?"

"I'm here seven days a week."

"Ed, we've checked out both the staff and faculty. Is there anyone else? Anyone who works at Emory who is not in the computer?"

"What do you mean?"

"I'm not sure. People who work there, especially in law enforcement, on maybe a part-time basis. People who are not listed on employment records. People who are not in the computer."

There was a long pause.

Then Ed Medlin spoke. His voice was slow and portentous. "Yes. I should have thought of that. Security guards. Contract people. The hospital alone uses several private security companies. Their people are at the emergency entrance and around the hospital. The clinic uses a private—a different—security firm.

Emory parking decks use still another private security firm. Woodruff Library has its own full-time security patrol. The Carlos Museum uses a private firm, but those guys wear blue blazers. And there is cross-fertilization that complicates this."

"What do you mean?"

"Some of the security guards moonlight for other security companies. We have outside contracts for part-time security guards at different campus functions. Distinguished visitors on campus. Graduation. Concerts. Major athletic events."

Nigel was taking notes. "Anyone else? I want it all."

"Let me think. Hmmmm. The community-service people, the ones who check parking stickers and do other jobs, are Emory employees and part of the system. But they are a mixture of Emory employees and private hires. For instance, if a student is working part-time for community service, he is considered a student and not a regular employee, so he wouldn't be in the computer as an employee of community service."

"Where would the students come from? Any particular school or division?"

"A number of those people are from the Theology Department. Older students there. Many of them on a second career as a preacher. And a surprising number of them came out of law enforcement."

Neither man spoke for a moment as both considered the number of police officers who are conservative Christians, avenging angels, hard-liners who follow the Old Testament precepts of an eye for an eye and a tooth for a tooth. They have been washed in the blood of the lamb, and they will kick your ass from hell to breakfast and do it for all the right reasons. They are out to enforce the Ten Commandments rather than the law. They investigate sin rather than crime. The meanest guys in law enforcement are the Sky Pilots. Both men knew of police officers who, in mid-career, had switched to divinity school and become preachers. Few of them went to Emory, as it was considered far too liberal. But those who did go went as missionaries among the savages, believing it was their sacred duty to show Emory theology professors the way, the truth and the light.

"How long will it take, Ed?"

"It's Saturday. I'm going to have to roust some executives to get what I need. And there are a half-dozen or so different private security firms to check, plus the students working in community service."

"How can we narrow it? Do all these people wear uniforms?"

Ed thought for a moment. "Yes. And most of the uniforms are close enough to the Emory Police Department uniform that most people couldn't tell the difference. The only significant difference is that security guards don't carry weapons." He paused. "Although I'm not sure how many civilians would even notice."

"Radios?"

Ed sighed. "Yes. They usually use their own frequencies. But since they work on campus, their radios are modified so they can call us if they need to do so."

"They can monitor your radios?"

"Yes."

Neither man spoke for a moment.

"What about computer access? Do they have access to your main computer?"

"Not the security guards. But the community-service people would."

"Could a security guard get access through one of your people or through the computer center or through an Emory employee?"

"I doubt if they could do so through my people. We don't exactly consider security guards as professional colleagues. More like rent-a-cops. But, yes, if a security guard was halfway smart, he could go through someone else and get access to the computer."

"He's known every step we've taken."

"Before we took it."

"Ed, we're close to him. I feel it. How long to get those new names to me? I'll run them through NCIC here so he won't know what we're doing."

"And I'll impress on the security company executives the need for discretion on this one." Ed paused. "I'll start calling. But this is Saturday. The people at the security companies who can release the personnel records may not be around. It could be Monday noon before I get all the names."

"Let's speed it up. I'll detail someone to be at this number full-time this weekend. It will be arranged for him to have instant access to the computer. Anyone who looks promising, we will check out immediately. Just feed us the names as quickly as you get them."

"Tell him to stand by. I should have some names within an hour."

"Do you need help tracking down the security company executives?"

"No. I think because they want to keep our business that they will move faster for me than they will for you. Let me take care of that."

"Okay."

Nigel paused. "You feel it?"

"Yes. We have him."

"I know you'll move fast."

"As soon as I can get you off the phone."

Nigel laughed. "Bye, Ed."

He stood up and turned to stack the files on his desk when there was a sharp pain in the lower left side of his back. He froze, hoping he was wrong, that it was not what he feared. Then he tried to move and the pain was even greater. It was the first time in three years this had happened, but he knew what he had to do. God knows, he had been through it enough in the past.

He picked up the phone, easily remembered the number, and began dialing.

24

Mid-afternoon Saturday, June 29, 1996.

Nigel was sifting through case files and computer printouts of the Emory faculty and staff, and wondering what he had overlooked, when his pager sounded. He lifted his elbow and looked down at the top of the pager. A number with a 727 prefix—Emory University. He stared. Then he recognized it. Sarah was calling. Cops usually remember telephone numbers and auto tag numbers the way a mother remembers birthdays. What was the matter with him? He should have recognized it instantly.

"That's my daughter," he said aloud.

Police officers, particularly in homicide and sex crimes, must be remote, detached, and clinical. They must not be absorbed by a case. The thinking among sex crimes officers is that if the bad guy, the sexual sadist, is not affected by what he does, why should a cop handicap himself by becoming emotionally involved? Nigel understood the concept. But for him it had never worked.

He had always been affected emotionally, behaviorally, and physically. The pain and the increasing problem with his back told Nigel he was being affected physically. But he could deal with the pain. He did not look forward to becoming virtually incapacitated and to dragging his left foot around behind him as he had done in the past. But what worried him the most was becoming emotionally or behaviorally affected. Those symptoms were more difficult to recognize. And they were more dangerous. He tried to tell himself that he kept his emotions under control and that he would not be affected emotionally. And he willed himself to be slow and steady and not lose his temper; he would not let his behavior be affected.

But he was being affected. For a moment he had not recognized his daughter's telephone number.

He dialed and the telephone at the other end was picked up on the first ring.

"Daddy?"

"Sarah. Yes. How are you?"

"Daddy, Shari is missing."

Nigel's white eyebrows clustered together. "Shari who?"

"My friend Shari. You met her the other day."

"Oh, yes. Girl with the baby face. Glasses." Nigel paused. "What do you mean, she's missing?"

"She was in my room last night after the concert. Until about two o 'clock. She left and said she was going to her dorm. I called this morning and she didn't answer. I called later on and she still didn't answer. So I went over there and knocked, and no one answered the door. I called the Emory police and told them what happened, and they sent someone over to open her door. Her bed had not been slept in."

"Could she have gone anywhere else?"

"No. I told you, she was going to her room. There were calls on her answering machine from last night while we were at the concert, and mine were on there from this morning. She never got home last night. I just know something has—"

"What did the Emory police say?"

"I don't know. They said they would check around campus. I heard one of them say he was going to contact the task force. Is that you?"

"Yes. But no one has called."

"Daddy, something has happened to her. I know something has happened."

"Did anyone check the hospital or clinic? Maybe she was sick? Was she okay at the concert."

His mind was racing. He tried to remember the details of Shari's face. She had blond hair, as he recalled. How was her hair parted? What did she have in common with the other victims, other than being an Emory student? What was there about her that made her a victim? Why had she been picked?

"Daddy, she was fine last night. Don't try to make me think she just wandered off somewhere in some irresponsible fashion or that she might be sick. Something has happened. She made a big thing last night of telling me she was going home in case her parents called. I tried to get her to stay with me because it was so late. But she didn't want her parents to worry. It's only a few steps from my dorm to the hospital and the tunnels. Once she got out of the tunnels, it's only a few steps to her dorm. I just know—"

"Tunnels?" Nigel interrupted. "What tunnels? I don't know anything about any tunnels."

"The tunnels under the hospital."

Nigel was surprised. "I didn't know there were tunnels under the school."

"Oh, Daddy. We use them all the time. But nothing could have happened there. They are patrolled. Lots of lights. Lots of people. Daddy, I don't think she ever got to the tunnels."

"Why?"

"I saw the Emory police talking with the woman in the lobby. She made a call and had the police talk to someone. The officer was shaking his head. Daddy, I keep telling you: something happened between my dorm and the hospital."

"Sarah, that's only a few yards, less than a minute. That's not enough time for coincidence, for someone to have been passing by who might have stopped her. She could have easily run back to the dorm or into the hospital."

Nigel stopped, not wanting to say what was so obvious.

"Sarah, did you and Shari plan earlier that she would go back to the dorm with you?"

"No. She wanted to use the bathroom. Then we talked for a while. But she came here to use the bathroom. She was going somewhere else. I invited her over."

Nigel paused. "That means he was waiting outside the dormitory. It means that he followed her from the concert."

"Daddy, there were hundreds of people around."

"Sarah, listen to me. If . . ." Nigel paused. His pager was sounding again. He looked at the digital display. Major Morris was calling.

Suddenly he sensed Sarah was right.

Something had happened to Shari.

And now her body had been found.

"Sarah, I have to go. The major is calling me."

"Daddy, can I go with you?"

Nigel flinched. "You know I can't let you do that."

"Will you call me as soon as you know something? As soon as you find out anything about Shari?"

"Yes. Will you be in your room?"

"No." Sarah paused. "Daddy, I want to come home. I didn't know the first three victims. But I knew Kathy Powers from my Yeats class. And now my best friend. This is too much. I'm scared and I want to come home. Now. I can get my stuff later."

Nigel sighed in relief. "Can you get a ride? I can have a police officer pick you up."

"No, I'll get a cab. It will only be three or four dollars."

"I'll call you at home. I have to go."

"Daddy, I'm scared. Call me."

"I will."

25

Her blood announced her presence.

Because her body was high in the air, no one noticed her for much of the day. she was nailed to the junction of the vertical support and the crossbar on the pole vault in the middle of Olympic Stadium. The stadium, the primary Olympic venue and Atlanta's new centerpiece, is alongside the downtown connector snuggled up against the heart of the city.

Her ankles were crossed and nailed to a vertical pole, and her right arm trailed out on the crossbar. A large, shiny new nail penetrated the palm of the right hand and held it to the crossbar. Her left arm hung limply. Her blond hair was neatly combed. She was nude except for the blue scarf around her neck.

A groundskeeper raking the sawdust at the foot of the pole-vaulting area saw two small circular objects on the ground; objects with a dark spot in the center. His brows wrinkled in disbelief. Then he noticed a spattering of brown spots around the bottom of the vertical pole and saw a dark, shiny material glistening on the pole. He sniffed, and when the sweet, coppery odor assaulted his nostrils he looked up and stood in open-mouthed horror as he gazed upon the mortal remains of Shari Kaufman.

Her breasts had been severed from her body and were placed neatly at the foot of the pole.

Her body was covered with dozens of knife slashes and was in tatters. On her stomach, scrawled in block letters of her own blood, was the word EVIL.

Nigel stared. He stood inside the yellow crime-scene tape and did not move for long moments. He knew from the relatively small amount of blood that she had been killed somewhere else and then brought here. He knew, again from the small amount of blood around the two gaping spots on her upper torso, that her breasts had been cut off after she was dead.

Nigel stared at the neat fashion in which Shari's hair was combed. He looked at the blue scarf around her neck.

What is it about you that appealed to him?

Nigel did not notice the arrival of three cars and the anxious cluster of people who disembarked, all staring at him. And he did not hear when someone called his name.

Then there was a voice beside him. "Well, I see your boy is having himself a grand old time agin." Nigel jumped, his reverie interrupted. It was Lieutenant Raines from Homicide.

"Hello, Kenny." Nigel's gaze returned to the body.

Kenny looked over his shoulder at the people standing by the cars. "Roach, there's more brass over there than in a Salvation Army band. I'm the lowest-ranking man on the totem pole around here, so I've been ordered to bring you a message."

"How did he pick her, Kenny?"

Kenny followed Nigel's gaze. "Don't know. But looks to me like she fell into a Cuisinart."

Kenny looked over his shoulder. The mayor was

there. Chief Beverly Harvard was there. And Major
Norris Morris was there. Major Morris waved his arm
and motioned for Kenny to continue.

"It won't be much longer, Kenny," Nigel whispered.
"I'm close. And he knows I'm close."

"Roach, the mayor and the chief are over there."

Nigel began moving slowly in a circle around the
pole-vaulting area, his eyes never leaving the body of
Shari Kaufman. As he walked, his left foot turned
outward and dragged slightly. He was stooped from
pain. He had been on the way to a physical therapist
when this call came. The therapist would have to wait.

"Mayor wants the body down, Roach. Somebody
talked too much on the radio and the press picked
this up. They are on the way. Mayor wants the body
down before they get here." He paused. "I got the
SWAT team and special equipment standing by."

Nigel continued his slow pace around the body.
He nodded.

"She was a friend of my daughter," he said. "Did
you know that, Kenny?"

"No, I didn't, Roach. I'm sorry."

"Bright kid. I met her several days ago at Emory.
The whole world was in front of her. She and my
daughter were very close."

"Roach . . ."

"Kenny, your eyes are better than mine. And I can't
lean back far enough to see. You notice any flecks of
white material around her mouth or on her ankles or
wrists; anything to indicate she was restrained?"

Kenny peered up at the body. "Not from here,
Roach. It's too far. But the M.E. is on the way. Be
here in a couple of minutes. He can tell you." Kenny

paused. "By the way, my people are sketching the scene. You mind if we take our measurements now?"

Nigel stopped pacing and looked full into Shari's face. "Go ahead."

Where did he take you to do this?

What sort of place does he have where he can do this kind of thing?

Where is his slave chamber?

Nigel willed himself not to think of what Sarah's friend had experienced. He willed himself not to think of the horror she had known in her last hours on earth.

Kenny's radio blared. He turned down the volume and put the radio to his ear.

"Yes, sir. Roach, Major Morris says he's giving you an order to take down the body now."

"He must have used heavy plastic sheets. Or old carpet. But whatever he used, he got blood all over something. We might find fibers ..." Nigel's voice trailed off. The offender was too aware of forensics. There would be no fiber evidence.

Nigel paused. "Tell Morris this is my crime scene. The M.E. is not here. And in case the major and the chief and the fucking mayor have forgotten, it's against the law in Georgia to move a body until the M.E. has examined it. You tell him if any of them even steps inside the tape, I'll arrest him and personally take him to jail."

Kenny grinned. "Maybe I better walk over and relay that in person."

"Use the radio."

Kenny nodded. The Roach wanted every police officer in Atlanta and everyone with a scanner to hear what he said. Insurance.

A few moments later Major Morris walked to the edge of the tape and motioned for Nigel. He looked at Kenny and said, "Dammit, Lieutenant, I see you laughing and I'll have you in uniform working morning watch at the airport."

"Major, I'm not laughing. I'm just waiting for Officer Trench to finish his investigation and turn this crime scene over to Homicide."

Morris stared at Nigel. His face jerked in a mad dance. Even the muscles in his neck were dancing like guitar strings being plucked by an invisible hand. "Roach, don't do this to me."

"Am I the lead investigator on this case?"

"Goddammit, Roach."

"Am I?"

"Roach, the mayor is standing over there. So is the chief. They want the body down now. The mayor's afraid reporters will take pictures that will go out all over the goddamn world a few days before the Olympics."

"What about the victims, Major? You see that kid up there? She was my daughter's friend."

"Roach, I'm sorry, but I just don't give a shit about that."

"Well, goddammit, I do. The Olympics will come and go, but rape victims will still be here."

Morris looked at Kenny. "He's lost his fucking mind."

He turned back to Nigel and shook his head. "You used to be a good cop, Roach. But look at you now. You're a goddamn mess. All bent over and dragging your foot. Your clothes look like you slept in them. You've lost weight. You need to see a doctor. Maybe get a KGB. You need to go home. The mayor thinks you're incontinent. If I'm lying, I'm standing here."

Nigel stared at his old friend.

"Roach, you let yourself get personally involved. That has always been your great strength and your great weakness. You let this become your life when I thought you would make it a job."

"Am I the lead investigator on this case?"

"Yes. Yes. Yes, dammit. You know I can't take you off right now. We got bodies decorating this city like Christmas tree ornaments. But don't cut off your nose to save your face."

"You tell the chief and you tell the mayor that her body stays up there until I say take it down."

Morris nodded. "I made a mistake recommending you for this job. I should have left you in that grubby little apartment tending to your grubby little flowers."

Nigel stared at his old friend for a long moment. He was about to answer when the slender bearded figure of Dr. Randy Hanzlick stepped over the tape. The M.E. winced as he looked up at the body. "Roach, I'm looking forward to doing the autopsy on the guy who did this when you catch him."

Nigel turned to Kenny. "Did an ID tech take pictures before I arrived?"

Kenny looked at Major Morris and then at Nigel. "No. She is here, but she did not take pictures."

Nigel looked toward the cluster of uniformed officers and homicide detectives standing some yards away from the mayor and chief. He waved, caught the eye of the ID tech, and motioned her forward.

"Yes, sir," said the breathless young woman. She looked nervously toward the major.

"Shoot it," Nigel said. "Get it all. Don't stop until you got everything you need. Stills and video."

"Yes, sir," she said, unlimbering her cameras.

Nigel walked closer to the body; to where Dr. Hanzlick was standing.

"Trench. Trench," came an urgent voice.

He brought you here in the early morning hours, four-thirty or five o'clock, not long before dawn. He was pushing his luck and he knew it. He was caught between having enough time with you during the night and getting you here before dawn.

He had to put your body on display. He had to show his contempt for us.

"Trench, you will answer me," came the strident voice.

Nigel turned. The mayor, slender, dapper, and mustache quivering, was standing at the yellow crime-scene tape.

Nigel stared. He motioned for the mayor to come forward.

"Can I help you?" Nigel's voice was remote.

"What are you doing? Who do you think you are? Just exactly what are you doing?"

"I'm standing at the foot of the cross."

The mayor looked at Major Morris and then back at Nigel. "You're what?"

"He put her on the cross. He crucified her. He . . ." Nigel's voice dwindled away. That faint memory was stirring again. That distant glimmer of reason that hinted at how the offender was picking his victims was there. Nigel wanted to relax, to let it come to him unhindered. But he tried too hard to tug the memory out of the distance, and it faded before he could seize it.

The mayor's voice pulled Nigel back to the present.

"Get her down, Trench." The mayor motioned toward the photographer. "You got your pictures. The M.E. is here. The press is coming."

"Mr. Mayor, you're very close to being arrested for obstructing justice. You want the press to have that story?"

"I am what?" the mayor sputtered. "I'll have your badge for this. You're ..."

Nigel looked over the mayor's shoulder. He nodded.

The mayor turned as the satellite trucks of three television crews came through the stadium gate. It was followed by a marked car from *The Atlanta Constitution.* As if on cue, a red helicopter appeared overhead, a cameraman in harness standing on the skids shooting with a telephoto lens.

"The Fox station," the mayor said. He smoothed his coat.

"You want me to arrest you in front of the press and tell them you destroyed a crime scene?" Nigel asked. "How'd you like to see one of Buchanan's stories on that? Or better yet, one of Marie Morris's columns?"

Major Morris winced.

Randy Hanzlick looked away.

Kenny Raines grinned.

The mayor looked at the reporters streaming across the field. He looked at Nigel.

An aide leaned toward the mayor. "They all have long lenses. They're shooting this now."

The mayor squared his shoulders, straightened his tie, and glared at Nigel. He turned toward Major Morris. "Your job and your pension are riding on how this turns out." He turned to meet the press, a big smile on his face.

The ID tech motioned to Nigel. He looked at Dr. Hanzlick. "Randy, you ready to have a look at her?"

The M.E. nodded.

"Kenny, would you have your men take her down? Cut off the bottom of the post and lower her. Try to keep the crossbar attached until she is on the ground. Dr. Hanzlick will examine here and then she's all yours."

"Okay, Roach." Raines turned toward a group of detectives and black-uniformed officers. He motioned them forward.

Nigel reached toward Major Morris. "Major, before you lose your pension, let me use your portable phone."

Morris pulled the small collapsable telephone from his shirt pocket and handed it to Nigel. "How much longer?"

"I'm close, Major."

He dialed. "Ed, Nigel. Anything yet?"

"I've cleared the personnel at two of the private security companies," said the calm voice of Ed Medlin. "The top people at several of the security companies are out of town for the weekend. I'm tracking them down. It's frustrating, but it will be Monday morning, maybe as late as noon, before we run them all and see what pops up."

"Another day and a half." Nigel sighed. He looked across the stadium. "I hope that's not too late."

"What will you do until then?"

"He's still out there."

"You're right. But look at his pattern. He won't

strike again soon. We've got two or three days. And by then we will ID and arrest him."

"I hope so." Nigel watched Dr. Hanzlick leaning over the tattered remains of Shari Kaufman. "This one is with the medical examiner. Nothing else I can do here. Nothing I can do to help you. I'm going to have my back worked on. Then I'm picking up my wife at the hospital and bringing her home so my family can be together tonight."

"Have a quiet weekend."

26

The muscular young man opened the door of the Atlanta Back Clinic, took one look and said, "Mr. Trench?"

"How'd you know?"

"Rich described your problem. Said for me to put some heat on you and loosen up your back before he got here. He's on the way. You want to come down to the first treatment room?"

"Sure." Nigel walked slowly through the office. "You get the fax?"

"Yes, sir. Your doctor sent it out. We're okay." The young man opened the door of the treatment room. "I understand you are a former patient. You have your shorts or bathing suit?"

. Nigel held up a bathing suit. The only place it had ever been worn was at the Atlanta Back Clinic.

"I'll give you a minute to change and then I'll be back with the heating pad."

Nigel nodded. He took the bulldog edition of the Sunday paper from under his arm and dropped it on a chair. He undressed, put on the bathing suit, and slowly crawled atop the table. With a sigh he wrapped his arms around the top of the table.

A gentle knock came at the door.

"Come in."

The young man opened the door. A heating pad wrapped in thick towels was in his hands. "You comfortable?"

"Yes."

Slowly the young man placed the heating pad on Nigel's back. He looked at it, then pulled it down a few inches. "How's that?"

Nigel sighed. "Come back in a month or so."

The young man laughed. "Relax until Rich gets here."

"Ummmmmm."

Nigel reached out, hooked the chair with his hand, and pulled it under the top of the table. He picked up the front section of the newspaper. His head was over the top of the table, and he looked down at the paper. Marie Morris's column was on the front page. It was in a box above the fold, had a double-decked headline, and was spread across four columns. A one-column colored picture of Marie Morris was in the upper left-hand corner of the story.

Nigel squinted to read the "Editor's Note" above the piece.

"Because of the expertise of Ms. Morris and because of the newsworthiness of the topic, her column is appearing on the front page rather than in its regular position on the op-ed page."

He skimmed the column, a few phrases jumping out.

I will not again go into what I think of those who work on the Interpersonal Violence squad, as my feelings about them are long-standing and well known. . . . The only thing uncertain about his next victim is her name. . . . Perhaps I could offer the

police a few guideposts toward identifying, locating,
and arresting the twisted soul committing these hor-
rible and repugnant acts of violence.... If he is
caught, it will be because he makes a mistake. If
he makes no mistake, he will be among us until he
decides to stop or until he realizes he needs help
and seeks rehabilitation.... If he will call me and
tell me he wants counseling, I will see that every
effort is made to provide rehabilitation rather than
incarceration.... What police officers do not know
or will not acknowledge is the connection between
normal behavior and the extremes of psychological
behavior as manifested by this lonely and pain-filled
man.... He seeks the love that has always eluded
him. But because he has so little experience with
love, he does not know how to give or to receive
that most priceless of emotions.... Lonely soul,
pain-filled one, whoever and wherever you are, call
me at 526-5431 and I will introduce you to professionals who will ease your pain, who will bring
you relief.

I promise.

Call me.

Now.

Nigel understood the fascination that the offender
held for Marie Morris. After all, when someone goes
to the zoo, it is the snakes they want to see. They talk
about the monkeys and giraffes and the elephants. But
all the while they are trembling in anticipation. What
they really want, what they came to see, are the
snakes. Why? Because snakes are evil incarnate. Because snakes are deadly. Because snakes are cold and

implacable in their willingness to strike; to release their poison; to do what they do.

Nigel sighed. She meant well.

The door opened. "You okay?" the young attendant asked.

"Yes. Thanks. It feels better already. Can you continue the heat a bit longer?"

"Yes."

Nigel's eyes remained fixed on the column.

Marie Morris, in the middle of her nonsense about providing counseling, had touched on a crucial point. She was right in hinting that the offender wanted to memorialize his erotic adventures with mementoes. But they were not souvenirs, as Marie Morris said. They were trophies. Trophies of his victories. Just as a big-game hunter brought home trophies of his victories.

She was right, too, about wanting to keep the young women and that was why he had mutilated them.

When Jeffrey Dahmer had been arrested, that was one of the things he told the police officers who interviewed him. But mutilation had been only part of Dahmer's evolution as a sexual killer. After he used them sexually, he dismembered them. He stored their body parts around his house. But even that was not enough. What better way to bring about the mystic conjoining of lover and loved, or lover and worshiped one, than to take them into one's own body?

So, like primitive religions who believe that by eating a victim, one absorbs the victim's virtues and strengths, Dahmer began practicing ritual cannibalism.

While cannibalism is considered repulsive and backward by Western standards, it is, in metaphor, a fundamental part of various religions, including Christianity.

Take, eat, this is my body.

Nigel flipped the paper over to see what was on the lower half and saw the sidebar to Marie's story. The mayor had ordered the police department to take the rapist alive. The rapist, not the serial rapist or serial killer, but the rapist. Marie had called him, told him about her column, and gotten him to agree the offender needed counseling. Now the task force members and the SWAT team were being issued TASER's. "This proves we can make humane arrests in this Olympic city," the mayor said.

Nigel sighed. If the offender was taken alive, and that was a big if, he would enter an insanity plea and the case would be tied up in courts for years. It was possible that the guy could even be back on the street one day.

The door opened.

"Sorry to hear you're having trouble again," came a soft voice. Nigel knew without looking up that it was Rich Nyberg, owner of the Atlanta Back Clinic. If one word could be used to describe Rich, it would be comforting. You knew when you looked at this guy that he was going to help you. He was tall, slender, wore black-framed glasses, and had a very sober mien. He always wore a tie, not something done by most physical therapists. But perhaps it was his voice that engendered the most confidence. His voice was soft and deep and soothing. It was a natural rather than a cultivated confidence and for that reason was all the more powerful to his patients. And his hands. My God, what hands. Even when probing the most sensitive and inflamed part of a person's back, his hands were lighter than the landing of a butterfly. Sometimes he would stand for long minutes with only a fingertip

touching a person's back as he closed his eyes and
waited until the angry, excited muscles of a person's
back spoke to him. It was almost metaphysical the
way he listened to a person's body and knew exactly
what to do to relieve the pain.

He took the paper from Nigel's hand. "I want your
undivided attention while you're here."

He questioned Nigel at length about the pain in his
back. Then he talked of Nigel's history of back problems. He asked about the aggravating factors of the
pain, what caused the pain and when Nigel most noticed the pain. He asked what exercises Nigel was
doing and shook his head when Nigel said he did no
exercises.

"You have to participate," Rich said. "You are sitting a lot. Sitting causes compression of the spine. You
need to walk. You need to exercise."

"I know."

"Do you believe this is the same as when you were
here last, three years ago?"

"I know it is."

"What do you mean?"

Nigel told him about the Emory case. He finished
by saying, "I'm worried about this guy. I'm worried
that my wife might find out about what I'm doing. I'm
worried about my daughter. I know that when the case
is over, the back problems will be over." He snapped
his fingers. "Just like that."

"You could be right. In the meantime we have to
calm down your back."

He had Nigel stand. He took a position behind
Nigel and ordered him to bend forward and backward
and to the side, all the time his eyes watching Nigel's

spine, seeing how it moved and if Nigel was favoring any particular spot.

Then he had Nigel lie on the table again, and he began what he called "provocation testing," seeking to determine what was tender, where the trigger points were.

He touched and probed and sometimes he hurt.

"It's the old L5 again, isn't it?" Nigel asked.

"That's the weakest link in the spine, the very last mobile segment, and it bears the most weight," Rich said. "About ninety percent of lower back problems are at either L4 or L5."

A half hour later, he sat down. "I'm almost certain it's a return of your previous problem. A bad disc aggravated by job stress and lack of exercise. I'm a bit worried about the foot drop. That means there may be a neurological problem. For that you need to see a medical doctor. Soon. We can't do much about the disc problems until the muscular inflammation is alleviated. We have to go for the soft tissue problem first. I'm going to work on that. But you must exercise. You have to stay vertical as much as possible. You must support your lower back when you are sitting. Try to avoid long periods of sitting. Do the backward bending exercises. Those are progressive. They get tougher and tougher."

"What can you do right now?"

Rich motioned for Nigel to lie on his stomach. He put his magic hands on Nigel's lower back. "I'm going to do some soft-tissue-release techniques," he said. "We need to get this area to calm down."

He began his work.

A few moments later, only ten or fifteen minutes,

Nigel could feel a difference. "My God, what are you doing?"

Rich continued. "For the muscle to release, there must be a signal. The muscle is saying, 'I'm tight. I'm hurting. I will stay tight as protection.' I'm saying to it, 'Relax a bit.' I'm using soft contact to do that."

"Ummmmmmm."

Rich probed. "Feel the tension here?"

"Yes."

"Let it go." A moment later Rich spoke again. "Let it go."

So it continued for more than an hour. Then Rich put Nigel under the heat pad for another half hour.

Finally he went into another room and returned with a package. From it he took a piece of white material about fourteen inches wide that fastened at the ends with Velcro.

"This is for your back," he said.

"When can I come back?"

"We need a day or so for your back to settle down from the treatment. How about Tuesday?"

"Wednesday."

"Okay, I'll check the calendar. But plan on Wednesday morning." He pulled a piece of hard white plastic from the container. "I'm going to warm this, soften it a bit, and then mold it to your back. It slides into the pocket on the back of this corset. It keeps you straight."

Nigel sighed. "A corset? I have to wear a corset?"

The plastic was heated, molded to his back, and then inserted into the corset. Nigel stood up and wrapped the device tightly around his waist. He was surprised. "That feels good."

He took several steps. He was standing straight up. The dragging of his foot was hardly discernible.

"Get dressed," Rich said. He opened the door. "I'll be up front."

"Rich, you're a miracle worker."

Nigel looked in the mirror for a long time. He stood up straight and squared his shoulders. "Okay, Mr. Offender," he said softly. "It's not much armor. But it's all I have. This is the end game. I'm coming after you."

27

Lucifer waited all day for the news. He had turned on the police radio scanner as soon as he returned home that morning. He listened as he cleaned his house and took a shower. Then he sat down to wait and to listen. This was important.

I bent her to God's will.

Lucifer grew exasperated at the controlled chatter on the radio and burst out with "Blah, blah, blah." would the police never find the body? He was giving serious thought to making an anonymous call telling them a crucified body was hanging over the pole-vaulting area when, finally, his vigilance was rewarded. He grinned in satisfaction as he recalled the radio chatter, especially when Nigel Trench had threatened to arrest the chief and the mayor. The police force was falling apart.

He had little to fear. Then, a half hour ago, Trench had radioed he was "eighty-nine"—out of service—for about two hours.

But to make sure he telephoned the task force. He used the name of homicide detective Kenny Raines. And he asked for the Roach.

Popcorn answered the telephone. "Hey, Kenny," he said. "It's me. Popcorn."

"How's it going, guy?"

"Great. Hey, the famous Roach man is eighty-nine. He's out getting his back worked on. You know how it is with the old guys. I think after he has his back worked on, he's picking up his wife at the hospital. Whatever you do, don't call his pager over there. I almost got my ass run off for doing that."

"Thanks, guy," Lucifer said. "I'll remember that." He hung up.

Popcorn stared at the phone a moment, then looked longingly at the fiberboard paneling over his desk. He looked around the office. No one else was in.

Why not?

He stood atop his desk and lifted the fiberboard and reached inside and found the bottle.

The police officer parked in front of a private hospital off the I-85 access road in northeast Atlanta. The quiet building was located on the edge of a residential area. No sign was displayed out front. Only a discreet metal plate on the door gave the name of the hospital.

The officer looked in the rearview mirror and adjusted his sunglasses. He snugged the hat down a bit tighter over his head. He adjusted the weight of the pistol on his right hip and checked the Velcro patch on his shoulder.

He didn't need a mirror to know how he looked. Crisp. Clean. Professional. Plus a little intimidation and a lot of command presence.

He would have no trouble.

He stepped from the white car marked with the logo of Emory University. He was parked in front of the hospital. The most invisible things are those which are most obvious. Little would be remembered about his car except that it was a police car. He strode confidently toward the door.

You will not recognize me. It has been three years. This time I am in uniform. When we have arrived at my special place, I will prod your memory. I know things about you. I remember things about you. And before I begin my work I will reveal myself to you.

Your accident will cause great confusion in my city of Pandemonium. Only your husband will understand. But he can do nothing. I know more about him than he knows about me. When the time comes, I will meet him. I reside over the Angels of Quaking, the Masters of Howling, and the Lords of Shouting.

And I will prevail.

He is nothing.

The officer cut across the flower bed lining the walk, trampling several flowers, and strode swiftly toward the door of the small two-story hospital.

He did not remove his sunglasses as he entered the building.

"Afternoon, Nancy," he said with a smile. "I'm here on behalf of officer Nigel Trench."

He smiled when he saw her questioning eyebrows.

"Officer Trench—Nigel Trench—told me your name."

The officer unbuttoned his shirt pocket, took out a sheet of white paper, and handed it to the receptionist.

She looked at the letterhead of Emory University. Then she read the brief typed note:

Nancy. As you know, Rachel is to come home tonight. I can't get away right now, and I don't want to disturb her by being late. So I have sent this officer to pick her up and bring her home. Please help him in any way you can. Give him her medication. I'll bring Rachel back at the time we planned. Thanks.

The signature was scrawled.

Nigel Trench had been very busy of late.

Nancy looked up at the handsome young policeman.

"Several days ago I met another policeman who was a friend of Mr. Trench. Major Morris. You know him?"

The officer smiled easily. "I'm just a patrolman. I don't know him. But I know who he is."

"I guess all you fellows know about each other?"

"Law enforcement is a close-knit group." The officer looked at his watch.

Nancy stood up. "Sorry. Sometimes I talk too much. Mrs. Trench is doing real well today. She's dressed and ready to go. You want me to go with you?"

"No. Don't want to take you away from your work." The officer seemed suddenly embarrassed. "Nigel told me her room number, but I can't remember it."

"Sixteen." She pointed. "Right down the hall. Fifth door on the left."

"Thanks."

Nancy smiled at the officer's back. What a good-looking man. A little serious. But all policemen seemed serious.

The officer paused in front of the door with the small number 16 in the upper right-hand corner. Across the middle of the door was a name plate on which had been inscribed RACHEL TRENCH. This was some hospital. He knocked softly.

After a long moment there was a hesitant "Come in."

Lucifer entered.

Rachel covered her eyes. For a moment Lucifer was afraid she had recognized him. Then she looked up and slowly shook her head. She shuddered. She was sitting in a large, overstuffed chair to the left of the door. A small suitcase stood by the chair. As is the case with almost all such rooms, the lighting was subdued and came from several lamps.

"Who are you?" She was confused at the sight of the police officer. What was a uniformed officer doing in her room?

"Your husband sent me."

"Is he okay?"

"Of course."

"I don't understand. How could my husband send you?"

Lucifer smiled and shrugged. "He asked me to pick you up and take you home. Said he would meet you there."

"But how could he send a police officer? He's not in law enforcement anymore. He doesn't have the authority to send a police officer here to pick me up."

Rachel's suspicions, the suspicions aroused during her last conversation with Nigel, the suspicions she had dismissed, came rushing in.

She knew.

Nigel was working somehow for the Atlanta Police Department. But he had always worked in sex crimes. What could he be doing?

Lucifer was having his own epiphany. This was a mental hospital. He had never made the connection. That meant . . . And that must be the reason the detective who answered the telephone—Popcorn, he said his name was—had said not to call Trench on his pager when Trench was at the hospital.

"I don't know, ma'am. I just know I was sent over here to pick you up." He saw the suitcase and nodded. "I see you're ready. Shall we go?" He reached for the suitcase.

Rachel's brow was wrinkled. There was something odd about this young officer. What was it?

"Is my husband working for the Atlanta Police Department?"

Lucifer paused. Another problem. He had not expected this. He had assumed Trench's wife would know what he was doing and that she would see nothing unusual in a young officer coming to pick her up and take her home.

He moved a step closer. "He's tied up. I think he's having treatment for his back. Anyway, he called Major Morris, and the major asked me to pick you up and take you home."

Rachel stiffened. "His back? His back? I thought the other day he was having back pains. But he hasn't had trouble with his back in years. Not since . . ." Her voice dwindled away.

"Are you ready to go?"

"Where is he?"

"I don't know. I just heard he was having his back worked on. I don't know anything else about it." He looked at his watch.

But Rachel Trench was not concerned about the

time. Too many things were bubbling just below the surface.

He looked at his watch again. "Ma'am, we need to be going. Major Morris said your husband would meet you at your residence."

She shook her head in bewilderment. What was there about this young man?

He held out his hand. Her eyes were locked on his sunglasses, trying to see behind them. Slowly, ever so slowly, her quivering hand extended. Her eyes never left his face. Their hands touched. His fingers closed around her hand to lift her, and her heart was gripped with bands of ice and steel.

"What is your name?" she asked.

When he did not answer, she looked over his right pocket. No name tag. That's what was missing. No officer would forget his name tag. Uniformed officers took off their name tags only when they did not want to be identified.

He held her suitcase with his left hand and pulled her slowly toward the door.

She followed, eyes still locked upon his sunglasses.

"What is your name?" she repeated.

Because he held her suitcase in his left hand and because she moved so swiftly, he could not block her hand when she suddenly reached up and tore his sunglasses away. To avoid her hand, he arched his head backward, a motion that pulled the sunglasses away all the more quickly.

The two stood there in a frozen tableau, staring into each other's eyes.

He moved closer and seized her elbow and began to pull her slowly toward the door. He smiled to reassure

her. But her closeness, the touch of her arm, the memories, turned his smile into a rictus of anticipation.

She dropped the sunglasses.

Something was wrong. She shook her head as if to
clear away the kaleidoscope of pain.

His eyes were a watery pale yellow.

Only one man had eyes like that.

She sniffed. There ... beneath the cologne ... she
smelled him.

Her eyes widened and her breathing increased and
she flinched in horror.

He knew that she was about to know. Suddenly he
realized she was in the hospital because of him, because of their adventure, and he felt himself growing
hard. His grip tightened upon her arm. He would have
to go out the side door.

"Do not make a sound," he whispered. "Or I shall
hurt you very badly. You remember how I can hurt
you, don't you?"

It was *him*.

Her past collapsed upon her, and her face gleamed
as if lit by a great inner light.

"Let me reveal myself to you," he whispered. "Let
me reveal myself to you in all my glory."

He moved closer and breathed full in her face.

"Feel the hot breath of the Heavenly One."

She was too filled with horror to make a sound. As
she looked at his face and into his eyes, it was as if
that day were being replayed in her mind. Everything
she had blocked away cascaded upon her. The doors
in the closets of her mind were thrown open, and everything therein came tumbling forth. She was overwhelmed by the volume of torment. And in that

moment everything that Nigel had feared came to pass.

Her mind snapped.

Finally, and without a doubt, she was irretrievably destroyed by the events of three years earlier. She vanished into a place from which she could never return.

She giggled. She looked up at Lucifer and giggled.

His pale eyes narrowed.

"I am of the Faithful. And now I am going to release you to Abbadon, Sovereign of the Bottomless Pit."

Again she giggled. With her free hand she began pulling at her clothes. Before he realized what she was doing, she had pulled the buttons from her blouse and jerked her blouse open and broken her bra and pulled it from her body.

Lucifer paused. Someone could come in at any moment. He looked about the room for a raincoat, anything to put around Rachel Trench. There was nothing. Only a sheet.

He dropped the suitcase and pulled her across the room and snatched the covers away from the bed and jerked the sheet.

Rachel pulled down the zipper of her skirt and then pushed the skirt and half slip down her hips.

What is the matter with her? Why is she doing this?

Fear he expected. Fear he enjoyed. And fear he could have dealt with. But this giggling, coquettish woman taking off her clothes? This was not what he wanted. His nose wrinkled in disgust.

She pushed her panties down her hips and stood with only her blouse hanging from one shoulder.

What was that look in her eyes? That blankness?

Lucifer realized he had made a mistake.

Now he could not take her with him.

As she looked at him and giggled, it was as if a giant hand swept across her features and changed her face forever. Suddenly her body jerked and quivered. Her eyes closed in confusion and bewilderment and the sure and certain knowledge that something terrible and something powerful was happening inside her chest. As her heart went into ventricular fibrillation, perspiration broke out across her brow. She clutched her left breast and sagged to her knees.

Lucifer tried to pull her upright, but she was limp. Her head lolled to the side, and her eyes rolled backward until he saw only the whites.

He shifted his grip on her wrist so he could feel her pulse. He moved his fingers again. There was nothing.

Rachel Trench was dead.

Lucifer let her sag to the floor. He reached down and picked up his sunglasses, adjusted them and stepped back. He thought quickly. There was nothing here that could point to him. The woman at the desk would remember only that a police officer had appeared. Like most civilians she could barely make a distinction between officers of various jurisdictions. She lived and worked in Atlanta. Therefore, when she looked up and saw a police officer, it had to be an Atlanta cop.

He backed toward the door, took another look around the room, and then looked briefly at Rachel Trench's body crumpled in a heap in the middle of the room.

Then he picked her up and carried her to the bed. Her blouse fell from her shoulder. He put her in the bed and turned her body to the side, facing away from the door. He pushed the tousled sheet around her body and pulled the covers over her shoulders.

He backed away. Perfect.

What about her clothes? He paused. Then he picked up her clothes and opened the bathroom door. No. Not the bathroom. Women did not toss their clothes into the bathroom and leave them. He opened the closet door. There. In the clothes hamper. He tossed them into the hamper in the reverse order that she might have taken them off, saving the bra and panties for last.

Again he looked around.

It appeared she was asleep. The room was unruffled.

He looked longingly at the back of Rachel's head.

Too bad. He had had plans for her. But the end result was the same. Trench would know what had happened. That was all that was important.

He turned off the lamps and backed through the door, looked down the hall, then closed the door, turned, and walked toward the receptionist.

He smiled and shook his head. "Nancy, it's one of those days. Mrs. Trench decided she would wait for Nigel. She said she was more tired than she realized and that she wanted to take a nap."

She smiled and smoothed her hair. "Okay. We'll let her sleep until dinnertime." She paused. "Will you come back for her?"

He shrugged and cocked his head to the side. "Depends on what Officer Trench wants me to do." He smiled. "But I hope so."

"When he calls, is there anything special you want me to tell him?"

"No, we will talk later."

"He knows who you are?"

Lucifer smiled. "Yes. He knows who I am."

Lucifer walked to his car, slid inside, and drove away. As he drove, he smiled.

The battalions of hell are on the march.

The earth shakes.

28

It was late that afternoon when the senior physician at the small private hospital in northeast Atlanta walked down the hall toward Rachel's room. She walked with the same brisk professional pace she always used. The charge nurse, as she always did, walked a respectful half step behind.

But the patients knew.

They always knew when something happened to one of their own. Several of them peered from open doorways and watched the doctor, who was a surprisingly young woman, as she entered Rachel's room. The doctor knew they would be waiting when she emerged, and she knew they would demand answers. Patients in private hospitals are that way.

The nurse closed the door, nodded toward the bed, and said, "That's the way I found her. Nothing was touched."

Now the doctor moved faster. She crossed the room and stood for a moment beside the bed. She leaned over and pushed Rachel's head to the side and peered at her neck. No sign of neck compression. She peeled back an eyelid. No petechia.

It did not strike her as odd that Rachel was nude. She slept in the nude herself.

The doctor picked up Rachel's medical record and went through it slowly, page by page. "She was in good physical health," the doctor mused. "Taking heavy doses of Thorazine." The doctor shook her head and stared at Rachel's body.

"Cardiac?" asked the charge nurse.

The doctor nodded. "Undiagnosed hypertension. Ruptured aneurism. Cardiac-conduction disturbance. It could be any one of a half-dozen or more things. The M.E. will have to make that determination. He will check for drug levels to make sure it's not a suicidal drug overdose."

She turned to the nurse. "Did you find any pill bottles? Syringes?"

"No. Nothing."

"Good. This was probably a natural death. I'm calling it a malignant neuroleptic syndrome."

The charge nurse nodded. When a patient on heavy doses of a tranquilizer dies suddenly, unexpectedly, and in an unexplained fashion, a doctor thinks "malignant neuroleptic syndrome." That or "cardiac dysrhythmia." Both are good for explaining the unexplainable.

The doctor looked at her watch. "I'll call the M.E. and the next of kin."

"Will the next of kin be coming here?"

The doctor thought for a moment. One of the problems with running a small private hospital was that when a patient died the next of kin expected to hear the news from the doctor and not from a medical examiner or from the police. That would be particularly true when the next of kin was a retired police officer. She would call him. But she would wait until the M.E.

did his work and the body was moved. It was always a balancing act.

"No. I'll make sure the M.E. is through and she has been moved. The next of kin can view her at the funeral home."

Nigel arrived at the clinic about an hour later. He waved at Nancy as he turned the corner. "Hello, Nancy. I'm here to pick up Rachel."

She stared. Her eyes grew wide as he walked down the hall.

"Mr. Trench. Mr. Trench."

He stopped. "Yes."

"No one called you?"

"About what?"

"We've been trying to reach you."

"Why?"

She held up her hands. "Could you wait just a moment? The doctor wants to talk with you."

"Is this about Rachel?"

She motioned for him to follow her. "If you could just wait right here by my desk for a moment. The doctor will be right with you."

No one told Nigel about the young police officer. It did not seem important.

29

Sunday morning, June 30, 1996.

It was barely daylight, and Nigel was hunkered down, sitting on his heels, pulling weeds from the flowers at his front door. The purple day lilies were at their peak. The cleome was too tall and too full. By July or August it would take over the little garden unless he chopped it back. The europsis was scraggly, and the lower leaves were beginning to blacken, probably because it had not received enough water.

Nigel pulled the water bucket closer, carefully measured two small cups of fertilizer from a plastic container, and dropped them into the bucket. He picked up the bucket and stretched, wincing from pain. With his left hand on the small of his back, he slowly poured the water, greenish blue from fertilizer, around the plants. It was difficult to work while wearing a corset.

He stood up, still holding his back, then used his foot to slide the small hoe, the snips, and the fertilizer across the walkway. He stretched, trying to get the kinks out of his back, then again hunkered down and slowly and meticulously began cleaning out the second bed.

Behind him the door to the apartment opened. He did not turn around.

"Morning, Daddy," came Sarah's soft voice. She wore a white cotton sweater and jeans. She was barefoot.

He mumbled something she did not understand.

"You have a phone call." She paused and looked away. "From a Dr. Hanzlick."

Nigel froze. He sighed, stood up, and walked inside. Sarah stayed outside, staring out across the apartments, looking at the sky.

Nigel picked up the telephone. "Randy?"

"Nigel, I'm sorry to have to make this call."

"That's okay. What have you got?"

"The official report hasn't been written, but based on what my associate found, I have no reason to differ with the doctor's opinion at the hospital. There is nothing to indicate this was anything other than natural causes."

Nigel exhaled. "I guess she just got tired."

"That's possible, Nigel. In fact, she wasn't feeling well late yesterday afternoon."

Nigel thought back. When he had been at the hospital, no one had said Rachel had not felt well. He had been told that the supervising physician had tried unsuccessfully to reach him at home. Knowing he was a former police officer, she then called the police station. The call was forwarded to the task force, where Popcorn, who was half in the bag, refused to page Nigel even after the doctor told him it was a death message.

"How do you know that?"

"The receptionist told my assistant that a police officer came by to pick Rachel up and take her home.

But he left after just a few minutes. Said she was too tired and that she would wait for you. They found her an hour or so later."

"I didn't send anyone to pick her up. I wouldn't do that. Who was the police officer?"

"I don't know. The receptionist just said a police officer. She didn't get his name."

"He was in uniform?"

"Yes."

Nigel grunted. "Randy, something is wrong. You know what happened to her three years ago. Even when Major Morris visited her, he wore civilian clothes."

"You have no idea who this could have been?"

"None. I'll call Norris."

"Let me know if I can do anything."

"You're convinced it was natural causes?"

"I have no reason to think otherwise."

"Thanks, Randy."

Nigel hung up. He dialed the task force. He was right. Major Morris had sent no one to see Rachel. Morris put Nigel on hold. A moment later he returned and said, "Ed Medlin says none of his officers were there."

"Major, can you send someone out to the hospital, track down that receptionist, and ask her if she saw what kind of car the officer was driving? I'm betting it was an Emory car. If so, get a detailed description of the guy."

"I'll call you back."

Nigel hung up. He had a sudden terrible feeling about what had happened.

It was *him*.

Nigel's knees trembled and he almost collapsed. He

shook his head as if to fling away the realization of what his work had brought to his wife. He looked around the small apartment, took a deep breath, and opened the door. He avoided looking at Sarah as he crouched among his flowers.

Sarah looked at his white hair, at his back. He had lost weight. He appeared almost frail. She wondered what was going on in his mind. He had changed so much during the past few weeks. And now this.

"Daddy?"

"Yes."

"Did you make all the plans?"

He pulled out several weeds. "Tuesday afternoon. One o'clock." He paused. "Your Uncle Rick in Pittsburgh, he can't get here before then."

"Where will it be?"

"In the chapel at the hospital. A memorial service." He pulled more weeds. "She'll be cremated today."

Sarah paused. She wrapped her arms around her waist and rolled her shoulders forward and stared at the ground. "Not in a church?"

Nigel shook his head. "Your mother . . . there won't be many people there. I just want to get it done. Your mother would agree."

"Will you be moving?"

Nigel sat back on his heels and looked at his flowers. "I don't think so. This place is not much. But I'm comfortable here." He picked up his clips, opened them, and idly began sharpening one of the blades on the sidewalk. It made a dull screeching noise.

"Daddy."

He stopped. "Sorry." He studied the cleome and began trimming the uppermost branches. "Your mother's gone. You're graduating soon and may be leaving town with a new job." He duck-walked a few steps so he would not have to reach so far. "I'm comfortable."

Sarah wiped a tear from her cheek. "I'm not leaving you. Not now." She looked at the morning sky, bright and clear. It was going to be very hot today.

"Shari's funeral is tomorrow."

Nigel nodded.

"She's Jewish," Sarah said. She shook her head. She *was* Jewish. There's a memorial service for her on campus at ten o'clock. The religious service is tomorrow afternoon."

Nigel cut several branches off the cleome and stacked them neatly. "Too many funerals."

"Daddy?"

"Yes?"

"Would you go to Shari's memorial service with me? Will you take off from work?"

Nigel looked up at Sarah. "Of course."

Nigel did not tell his daughter that he suspected the offender would be there. Not for the reasons usually expressed in fiction or in the movies. Not out of curiosity or guilt or even arrogance. No, the offender would be there for sexual reasons. At the memorial service the offender would relive the crime. For the offender the funeral was a sexual event. After all, these people were gathering together because of him. They were there to talk about his work. Everything would again be fresh for him. His face might reveal those emotions. Nigel planned to examine every white male face in the audience tomorrow morning and again at the synagogue.

"Shari was my best friend. College won't be the same without her."

Nigel stared at the cleome. He had cut it closer than he intended. But it would grow back.

"You going to stay at home until you finish school?"

She nodded. "Yes. If you let me use the car, I'll go over tomorrow morning before the service and pick up my things."

Nigel nodded.

"I need to pick up Pepsi, too." Sarah's face brightened. "A boy down the hall said he would take care of Pepsi until I picked him up. Is it okay if I—?"

"He's house-broken?"

Sarah nodded. "Never had an accident. Not one."

Nigel grunted in approval. "I'll get Ed Medlin to send one of his uniformed officers to your dormitory with you." He began pulling at the dark, stringy leaves hanging from the europsis.

"Don't worry about me, Daddy. Everyone at Emory looks after me. Ed Medlin must have told his officers to keep an eye on me. They treat me differently. Even the security guards at Emory know who you are."

"What do you mean?"

Nigel looked up. The sudden twisting motion caused him such pain that he forgot what he was going to ask Sarah.

"Your back?"

"Yes. Getting old."

"Daddy?"

"Yes."

"What do you think happened?"

"When?" Nigel knew what she was talking about.

"With Mom."

"Your mother was very fragile, Sarah. She was tired."

"Did she know you had gone back to work?"

"I don't think so. I thought once that she did. But she never asked me." He paused. "Why?"

Sarah shrugged. "I just wondered."

She waited a moment. "I'm going to fix us some breakfast. You hungry?"

He pulled at the europsis. "You go on in. I'll be there in a minute."

She leaned over and kissed the top of his head. "I love you, Daddy."

"I love you, too." He waited until he heard the door close, and then he sat back on his heels and stared at the flowers.

Why Rachel? Why? She is entirely different from the other victims. Why did you go back and pick someone from the past, someone who would have recognized you? Why such a radical departure in your M.O.?

Why such a radical departure from your fantasy?

Nigel stared unseeingly at the garden. Tomorrow, Tuesday at the latest, he would find the offender. He felt only anticipation. He had difficulty moving, he had become almost frail, and the offender had about twenty years on him. None of that mattered to Nigel.

"I'm coming after you," he whispered. "You must know how close I am."

He put his hand on the small of his back and pushed hard, relieving the discomfort.

"God, give me the strength to kill this son of a bitch."

30

Most of the Emory police, the Atlanta police assigned to the task force, and the DeKalb County officers are tied up on a research project. They are trying to locate me. And I'm not even in the database.

Lucifer smiled in contentment. He had been ordered to the center of the Emory campus, away from the parking decks where he usually worked. Today he was in the center of the campus, in the center of action where he belonged.

The vertical creases down the front of his shirt were lined up precisely with the sharp creases in his trousers. His black leather belt and his black leather shoes glistened in the morning sunlight. His hat sat squarely atop his closely cropped blond hair.

He reached into a rear pocket and pulled out a freshly ironed handkerchief. Then he carefully took off his sunglasses, wiped the inside of the frames where they contacted his nose, and then wiped hard along the edges of his nose to take away any oil. The glasses must ride high and not slip. He carefully tucked the handkerchief into his pocket, making sure it remained smooth and made no unsightly bulge in his rear pocket and that no bit of white protruded.

He slowly looked around. The campus was begin-

ning to come to life. About twenty-five hundred journalists from Third World countries had come onto
campus in the past two days. They were here for the
Olympics. They could not afford the big downtown
hotels and were being billeted in Emory dormitories.
Groups of them were ambling toward the front gate,
where they would catch buses for the Olympic Stadium. He smiled. A few students were making their
way toward White Hall, where the memorial service
would be held.

He was supposed to be at the southwest corner of
the quadrangle, directing journalists toward the bus
stop and simply being a presence for students—showing the flag, as it were. But he had moved away from
the quad, down past the corner of the Administration
Building, where he had a clear view of both the front
and side entrances to White Hall.

He watched the somber students entering the building, and he felt himself growing warm. They were
there because of him.

On the rare occasions that memorial services were
held for students, they were most often held in Can-
non Chapel. But because the woman who had wanted
him had been Jewish and because the expected crowd
was so large, today's ceremony would be in White
Hall, Room 206, the big assembly room. And it was
all because of him.

Lucifer squared his shoulders and preened.

He watched the gathering students and thought of
the memorial service, and in his mind's eye he saw
the girl as he had left her atop the crossbar in Olympic
Stadium. She should never have gone to that concert
on campus. The Spewing Turkeys was a group of per-
verts. He remembered all he had told the girl when

she was in his house, in his high place, before he went adventuring. He remembered how he'd had to punish her. He remembered the accident. He watched the students and the faculty and the staff slowly walking into White Hall, and he remembered how he had been forced to use his knife on her. Those incisions had been so smooth and so symmetrical; a doctor couldn't have done it better. He was so respectful of her and so mindful of her.

He remembered the tape recording he had listened to this morning before coming to work, and he felt himself growing hard.

Then he saw an old white Ford pull up in front of White Hall. Out stepped Nigel Trench. White-haired. Stooped. Ill-fitting clothes. Dragging his foot as he walked around the front of the car. Good God, a cripple, an old man, running this case. Lucifer, had he not known Nigel's reputation, would have been offended.

Lucifer chuckled. Maybe Nigel was a token hire, a disabled person.

Then *she* stepped from the passenger seat.

The Burning One.

She was wearing a dark red suit, almost burgundy. But it was red. He liked that. Appropriate. Her black hair shimmered in the morning sun. And as she walked in long strides around the front of the car, he involuntarily sucked in his breath at her beauty. She appeared in a hurry. The two of them talked only a moment. Nigel gestured over his shoulder at White Hall. She nodded impatiently, looked at her watch, then slid into the car and drove up the hill toward him.

Why wasn't she going to her friend's memorial service?

The Ford turned left at the main gate, and Lucifer

suddenly realized she was going to her dorm, to Harris
Hall around the corner on Clifton Road.

This was his chance. This was a gift to him. The
dormitory would be empty. Everyone would be at
White Hall.

Lucifer stared at Nigel. Now he could be found by
the last one and his mission would be complete. He
would have prepared the way. All would be as it had
once been. He would again be on the Right Hand
of Him.

At that moment Nigel stopped. He had been slowly
climbing the steps into White Hall. He felt something.
Slowly he turned.

Lucifer ducked and turned around and began walking toward the corner of the quad. He almost ran into
one of the young U.C. officers on campus. He smiled.

"Hey, man," he smiled.

The officer, a wiry young man carrying a book bag
that Lucifer suspected contained a semi-automatic
weapon and extra ammunition, nodded.

Nigel's gaze roved up toward the Administration
Building, around toward the quad, and across the
open plaza, where students were coming in increasing numbers.

Only students and uniformed officers.

But he had felt something.

As Lucifer strode north on the quad, he pulled his
radio from his waist and whispered into it. His pace
quickened.

Less than ten minutes later, he was driving a
marked car along Clifton Road. He smiled as he approached Harris Hall. The old white Ford was parked
at the front of the dormitory, doors open. *The Burning
One* was loading the car. She had a lamp in one hand

and clothes in the other. She placed the lamp in the rear seat and draped the clothes alongside it. She turned and in three or four steps was inside the dorm.

Lucifer slowed, then swung into the short driveway behind the white Ford. He stepped out and looked around. No one in sight. He walked inside.

He listened. Down the hall he heard conversation. A woman was talking. Then he heard a short bark and her lilting laugh and he knew. He strode down the hall.

The dog was in her arms and her back was to him as he approached. Over her shoulder he saw the room was empty.

"No dogs allowed on campus, miss," he said, pushing her inside the room and closing the door.

"What? Don't push me." She jerked her arm away and glared at him. The split second of defensiveness about the dog was gone. "I'm taking the dog with me now," she said.

She stared. "I know you."

He smiled. His hands were on his hips, and he rocked on his toes.

"The concert," she said. "Friday night when Shari and I ..." She paused. Suddenly she was frightened. She looked at his uniform. "You're a security guard. What are you doing here? You have no authority here."

"You'll have to come with me," he said softly.

"No, I will not." She backed up a half step. "Get out of that door and let me pass."

He smiled.

She looked at the telephone. They reached for it at the same time. He seized the cord and jerked hard, pulling it from the wall. She lunged for the door, but he seized her arm. Pepsi fell to the floor and began barking. He backed up several steps, staring at Lucifer. His barking increased.

Without seeming to tense his muscles, Lucifer's right foot lashed out and caught Pepsi under the stomach, lifting him and hurling him against the wall. Pepsi fell to the floor, yelped once, and was silent.

Sarah ran to his side. Pepsi raised his head and licked her hand.

"Oh, Pepsi," she said. She looked over her shoulder. "You hurt my dog. My father will—"

"Your crippled father will do nothing," Lucifer said. His voice was lazy, but it had an underlying edge. He wondered where she kept her security device, the little palm-sized electronic device the university had recently issued to students.

"Where's your purse?"

"Is that what this is? A robbery? Well, you'll have to get it out of my car. I left it there."

"Thank you."

He reached for Sarah. At that moment Pepsi rallied, popped to his feet, and with an almost comical growl latched onto Lucifer's hand. The dog's teeth caught Lucifer's left hand in the fleshy part between his thumb and forefinger. The dog sank its teeth harder, shook its head several times, and tried to back up, as if it wanted to pull Lucifer away from Sarah.

Lucifer winced in pain. He reached out with his right hand, seized Pepsi by the neck, and began squeezing. The dog released Lucifer's left hand. The dog whimpered in pain.

Lucifer and Sarah stood up at the same time, their eyes locked on each other.

"Please don't hurt my dog," she said. "I'll go with you."

"I know." He squeezed harder.

Sarah leaped for the door. But she was not quick enough. Lucifer seized her arm, and pulled hard, twisting her in a quick circle so that suddenly she was in the crook of his left arm. His hand, oozing blood, was over her mouth.

He turned his attention back to Pepsi. He continued squeezing. Pepsi could no longer whimper. His body was limp. Suddenly there was a sharp snap. Lucifer flung the dog's body across the room.

Sarah began wiggling frantically, muttering threats under his hand. But he easily held her. With his right hand he reached into his shirt pocket and removed one of the gold ballpoint pens. He reached for her left hand, put the pen between the forefinger and middle finger, and pushed it tightly between the fingers. Then he slid his grip down to the lower part of those two fingers and squeezed, forcing her fingers tightly around the pen.

She was seized with a pain she did not know existed. She moaned and her body arched.

"We are going to walk out of here now," he whispered. "If we meet anyone, you will look at them and smile. You will get into my car, parked behind yours, and you will make no sound and you will not attempt to escape."

She nodded.

He took his hand away from her mouth and at the same moment slapped her with such force that her head rocked. She would have fallen had he not suddenly squeezed her fingers around the pen and pulled hard. The pain in her fingers and the semi-unconscious state into which she had been rendered by the slap made her instantly compliant.

Lucifer looked at his left hand. It was bleeding profusely. He muttered a curse and pulled a handkerchief from his pocket and wrapped it around his hand.

"Let's go," he said.

"Pepsi," she whispered.

At the front door of the dormitory he paused. No one was in the hall. No one was on the sidewalk.

"Go straight to the car and get in. Do not raise your head. Do not look at anyone." He squeezed her fingers.

She moaned and nodded.

"That is only a sample," he said.

He opened the door and pulled. She walked quickly to the car, opened the front door, and slid across the seat. He appeared to be assisting her.

Inside the car he pressed a lever that locked the doors. The windows were rolled up. He held onto the fingers of her left hand. "I can drive with one hand," he whispered. "Don't even think of getting out."

He eased from the driveway, turned left on Clifton, and slowly drove away. As the car drove down the long hill past Wesley Woods, she looked at him.

"Where are you taking me?"

"Angels do not ask questions."

"What?"

"You are the seraphim, the brightest of all the angels, the one closest to God. Among all creatures you have the most perfect understanding of Him."

For a moment she was silent. She turned to look at him. "What are you talking about?"

"Questions proceed out of not knowing. An angel cannot be curious. You have nothing to be curious about. You do not wonder. You know all there is to know."

"Sometimes I forget. Tell me where we are going."

"To a high place."

"Where is that?"

He smiled. "I will escort you across the Fifth River, and there you will forget the troubles of this world. You will enter my kingdom."

For a moment her fear passed. She was her father's daughter. "Your kingdom?" She snorted. "Where is that? Oz?"

He turned. For a moment he did not speak. "See if you laugh later. See if you laugh when you are bent to God's will." He paused. "I live in the high capital of Pandemonium."

Sarah's fear returned. She knew she was in the presence of a madman.

"You have found me," Lucifer continued. "You will see. You will understand. In the end you will understand."

"Who are you?" she whispered.

"I am what I do."

31

Nigel looked at his watch.

Where was Sarah? The service was about to begin. His eyes roved over the crowd surging into White Hall. He looked toward the Administration Building and down the hill toward the rear gate opening onto Oxford Road. Thinking the offender might be using binoculars, he peered beyond the rear gate toward that strange blue-gray house sitting on the creek bank on Oxford Road. Nothing. No one was in sight whom he could pick out as possibly being the offender.

He felt someone pulling at his arm. Turning, he saw a solicitous face hovering above an outstretched hand. "Hello. My name is Milton, Jack Milton, and I'm conducting the service. It's time to begin. Would you care to come inside?"

"Yes. Certainly." Nigel was annoyed. He knew what Milton was thinking. The man had seen his bent-over posture and noticed his left foot and thought he was some handicapped old fart.

The two men walked down the hall. At the auditorium Nigel held back.

"I'm waiting on someone," he said softly. "I'll sit here in the back."

Milton held out his hands. He was about to ask

someone to give up their seat, but something in the man's eyes stopped him. He wasn't as old or as handicapped as he appeared. Milton nodded and slowly walked down the steps toward the dais, threading his way among the crowd. Students and faculty and staff members and parents and even local merchants filled every seat and stood along the walls.

Nigel stood at the door. He looked around, wondering if the offender had come in another door and was sitting in the crowded auditorium. His eyes systematically roved the faces.

He looked at his watch. What was Sarah doing? She didn't have that much to pack.

Milton raised his hands, and the soft mutter of the auditorium ceased. He waited, drawing out the silence, letting those in the audience realize why they were there.

"Friends of Shari Kaufman, students, faculty members, and all others in the Emory family. We draw together today to pay our respects to one of our own. We are here to remember her and all that she stood for. We are here to celebrate a brief but oh-so-promising life."

Nigel looked around again. He slid a few steps to his left, inching through the throng so he could get a better look at some of those sitting on the right side of the auditorium. The reverend's words became white noise as he searched for the offender, for the man whose presence he felt. The man *had* to be here.

Nigel walked farther, eyes probing, searching, row by row, face by face, not noticing how some of those along the rear wall were staring at him.

He walked a few steps farther.

Suddenly his eyes widened. He turned toward the stage. What was Milton saying?

"... yes, I knew Shari. She had been in my office. She was a brilliant young woman. She liked to wear blue. She had big eyes and a face that could only be described as that of an angel. She was a cherubim. She ..."

Nigel froze.

A cherubim? There it was again, that quick half remembrance of something read long ago, that feeling he was at the door, that he was about to understand. This time the feeling was overpowering.

Nigel gasped. His hands pushed on his stomach as if trying to force up the answer. He wanted to see clearly the rush of memories.

Milton continued.

"... yes, she was an angel walking among us. So were they all angels, all those bright and talented and gifted young women who have been untimely plucked from among us. Plucked from among us by a person who has bedeviled this university and bedeviled this city. These young women, these harbingers of light, symbolized our hope of the future. They ..."

Nigel was not listening.

Angels? Angels? What was the name of the first victim? Victoria Kennedy. But everyone knew her as "Angel." The second victim was Jan Archangeli. The third, Monaco Jackson.

Nigel grunted as if struck a powerful physical blow.

He remembered. The ephemeral dream, that elusive memory of something read long ago, this time would not be denied. It tumbled through his consciousness and hammered on his memory. Milton had opened the door to the past, to a book on angelology he had read three years ago. "... *she was an angel walking among us. So were they all angels ...*"

Nigel struggled to put the fragments into order.

Nine orders of angels.

They are divided into three groups.

The first of the lowest group is known simply as Angels. Then there are Archangels ... Jan Archangeli. Principalities are the third group, Principalities. Monaco Jackson. Monaco is a principality.

That's how he chose them. Not by the color of their hair or how they looked or any other physical feature. Not even because of age or availability.

He picked them by their names.

He is killing the angels.

In the second group of angels, Powers are the lowest order. Kathleen Powers. Then Virtues. Anne Justice? Anne Justice? Of course, justice is one of the virtues. What was next? Which order of angels came next? Dominions. That was it. Virginia Blair.

Nigel stopped. He was stooped over, looking at his fingers as he went through the orders of angels. Was he right? Now it didn't make sense.

Dominions. Virginia Blair. Dominions. Virginia Blair.

He snapped his fingers and stood upright. That was it.

Virginia is called the Old Dominion. What was next? What was the first order of angels in the third and highest group? Thrones. That was it. And the next victim had been Susan Bishop. Susan Bishop?

The words of Milton again hammered into his consciousness.

"... they have ascended to the throne of grace. They were among us ..."

Throne of grace. That was it. Thrones. Bishops sat on thrones. My God the man was diabolical. But that was it. Who is next? What is second from the top? Cherubims. Yes. Cherubims. Shari Kaufman.

This time Nigel did not stop and wonder if he was wrong. Instead he instantly searched for the connection.

How was Shari a cherubim? It was her face, her appearance. Of course. When he met her two nights earlier, he had thought she had a cherubic face. The preacher had seen it, too. What was it the preacher said? ". . . a face that can only be described as that of an angel. She was a cherubim."

What is next? What is the highest order of angels? Seraphims. Seraphims?

Dear God.

Sarah.

32

Nigel's groan of pain could be heard throughout the auditorium. Even Milton paused as his eyes darted to the back of the room. The undercover cops in the audience tensed and turned around. Several stood up. Many in the audience turned to look over their shoulders as Nigel pushed through the crowd, eyes wide in anxiety as he rushed for the door.

As he reached it an unusual and unexpected sound echoed eerily through the cavernous auditorium: the sound of a pager.

Nigel's pager was beeping. He glanced down at the display window.

Ed Medlin's number blinked at him.

Nigel knew the call was about the offender. Medlin had probably identified him. But it would have to wait. As he ran down the steps, the pain in his back returned with a vengeance. He scurried from White Hall and up the western edge of the quadrangle and past the Candler Library. He cursed his foot and he cursed his bad back and he cursed the fact he could not move faster and he cursed the fact he had not realized earlier how the offender was picking the victims. He cursed the fact he did not have a cellular phone. He cursed the offender.

He was crossing Asbury Circle when he saw an athletic young man carrying a book bag. The guy's eyes gave him away; he was one of the U.C. guys. In fact, he was the same officer Lucifer had spoken to an hour earlier.

Nigel flashed his tin and said, "Nigel Trench. APD. Head of the task force. You have a radio?"

"Yes, sir."

"Emory or APD frequencies?"

"Both. Plus the feds and the Olympic tactical frequencies."

The young man opened the book bag. Inside were stun grenades, a sawed-off double-barrel twelve-gauge shotgun with a pistol grip, a .357 Magnum, and a MAC-11 with a long clip. Extra ammunition for the weapons was in the bottom of the bag. There was a pistol-shaped device with two needle-like protuberances. There was a boxy, pistol-shaped device. And there was a small leather-covered item nestled in an inside pocket.

Nigel looked up in astonishment. "I thought you people were right out of the academy. The city didn't issue you this."

"No, sir. The cuffs and the TASER are city-issued. Rest is from my own stock."

"You SWAT-trained?"

"No. Something better."

"What?"

"I was a Navy SEAL. SEAL Team Six."

Nigel shook his head. 'We could invade a Third World country with what you got in here."

"Never can tell what you'll run into these days, sir."

Nigel looked at the young officer. "You know the mayor said take this guy alive?"

The young officer stared back. "Mayor ain't on the street, sir."

Nigel picked up the radio. He pointed at the inside pocket of the book bag. "That a cellular phone?"

"Yes, sir."

"I'll use that."

The young officer handed him the telephone.

"What's going on?" the young officer asked. His voice was calm.

"Follow me." Nigel quickly pressed Medlin's number. He turned and began walking.

"Ed. Nigel."

"We've got an I.D."

"What do you mean?" Nigel turned to the young U.C. officer. "I'm going to Harris Hall. Is this alley the shortest way?"

"Yes, sir. This will put you on the ground floor of Harris."

Medlin continued. "Subject's name is Luther Brumley. Native of Dahlonega. Twenty-nine years old. Went to work here about four months ago. Was in the army the past three years. Served as an M.P. in Germany. Before that he was in Atlanta. Went to Georgia State. Didn't graduate. Works as a security guard in the parking decks."

Nigel's mind was racing.

It was *him*.

At last.

"Any priors?"

She was a cherubim . . . all it takes is an ID card . . . I didn't see anyone but students and uniformed officers . . . even the security guards know who you are . . . throne of grace . . . his eyes were a pale, watery color . . . the seraphims are the highest order of angels, the

*ones closest to God, the ones so filled with God's glory
they are known as the fiery ones or the burning ones . . .*

"Negative. Appears to be clean."

"He on duty today?"

"Yes. But he went eighty-nine less than an hour
ago. Reported to his supervisor that he was ill."

Nigel pushed open the heavy metal door of the
dorm and climbed the stairs as fast as he could. He
was breathing hard when he put the phone to his
mouth. "Ed. Stand by a moment. I'm in Harris Hall.
U.C. with me. Send backup."

Nigel saw his car parked in the driveway of Harris
Hall, front and back doors open. The rear seat was
piled high with clothes and topped with a lamp. The
keys were in the ignition. For a moment he felt a flood
of relief. Maybe Sarah was still inside, finishing her
packing, and had lost track of time. No, she wouldn't
do that. She would have been at Shari's memorial service. Nigel pushed open the front door and limped
down the hall.

"What you got?" Medlin asked.

"I'm going in. Stand by." Nigel slipped the telephone into his pocket and turned to the young officer.
"What's your name?"

"Price. Carl Lee Price." The young officer pulled
the .357 from the book bag and stuck it in his belt.

"Well, Carl Lee Price, stay behind me and be careful. My daughter is in there."

Price moved the backpack around front so he would
have quick access to extra ammo and the other weapons. He moved closer to the wall. Nigel nodded in
approval. The kid knew what he was doing.

"I'll go first, sir. I'm wearing a vest."

Nigel shook his head and motioned for Price to stay behind him. He tiptoed down the hall.

Sarah's door was open. Nigel looked over his shoulder at Price. The young officer nodded.

Nigel swung around into the open door and dropped to one knee. A raincoat and a small suitcase were on Sarah's bed.

He saw Pepsi's broken body, limp and lifeless on the floor.

Then he saw the blood. Blood on one wall and across the ceiling. A small puddle of blood on the floor.

"Sarah!"

No answer.

Nigel did not go inside. There was no place for anyone to hide in the tiny room. Sarah was not there.

He put the telephone to his lips. "Ed, get an officer over here. We have a crime scene. Block it off. Call the task force for an ID tech. We got blood here and I want a DNA. And—"

"Stand by," Medlin interrupted.

Seconds later he was back on the phone. "There should be an officer walking in the front door about now. APD notified and en route."

"Give me Brumley's home address."

Nigel repeated the street address Medlin gave him. He looked at Price.

The young officer nodded. "Got it. That's an Atlanta address."

"Ed, I need one of your cars."

"Stand by."

Nigel heard Medlin call an Emory unit, presumably the officer parked out front and entering the dormitory. Then Medlin was back on the phone.

"The officer coming down the hall will give you his keys."

"Thanks, Ed."

Nigel turned to Price. "Give me that radio."

He put radio to his lips and called dispatch. "Lose the three-way," he said.

Then, having blocked the radio message from being picked up by scanners, he asked for APD backup to be sent to Brumley's address. "If they get there first, tell them to wait for me. No one goes in until I get there. Notify Atlanta SWAT. Dispatch an ambulance."

"Roger." The dispatcher's voice was laconic.

An Emory officer appeared. He was running down the hall toward them, hand outstretched. Nigel seized the keys.

"Nobody enters this room."

The Emory officer nodded.

Nigel turned to Price. "Let's go."

"Yes, sir."

As the two men jumped into the Emory police car parked behind Nigel's car, Nigel turned to Price. He was breathing hard. He winced. Sitting was painful. Nigel looked at the book bag. "That shotgun loaded?"

"Yes, sir. Double-ought buckshot." He pulled it from the backpack and placed it on the seat.

Nigel pulled the shotgun closer.

He backed up, tires squealing and throwing gravel. A car coming down Clifton Road veered wildly to avoid him. Then he was off, racing at high speed down Clifton Road.

Price looked at him. "How do you want to play it?"

"We're going in hard."

33

Lucifer could not stop the bleeding. The dog had bitten and then torn the flesh between his thumb and forefinger, a particularly difficult spot to bandage. Blood continued to seep through the bulky bandage. Lucifer was growing angry. He had work to do. This was the last one, and it had to be perfect. He could feel stiffness creeping into his hand and forearm.

Lucifer looked down at the *The Burning One,* the one who wanted him the most, the one who had been seeking him, the one who wanted to go adventuring.

Sarah was spread-eagled on the floor under the enormous wall of windows that occupied the east side of the house. She was bathed in the glare of the hot mid-morning sun, an effect increased by the heavy piece of clear plastic under her body. Tape secured each wrist—neatly wrapped and precisely measured tape. Yachting line, a soft and expensive rope, was secured over the tape and ran across the plastic to hooks in the baseboard. Sarah's ankles also were taped and then restrained with ropes. The ropes were pulled so tight she could barely twist her body. She stopped twisting after only a moment because the motion rucked her skirt high up her legs. Her mouth was taped. Her eyes followed every move Lucifer made, and although her sounds were muffled, it was clear she was angry.

Lucifer squeezed his hand and looked down at Sarah. A pillow was under her head, a plastic-cover pillow that could be washed. Lucifer was proud of the pillow. It proved he was considerate of women.

It proved he was a good boy.

You are the last one. Once we have had our adventure, my quest will be over. Together we will ascend. I shall return to the Right Hand of Him. We will go together. Then all will be as it once was. I will rule over the one true kingdom.

Lucifer smiled at Sarah.

I am your master, I am your God. I am your absolute ruler. You are nothing but a helpless object of my will. I will do as I please with you. The only thing you can do is experience the humiliation and the pain.

Lucifer looked into Sarah's eyes and saw that fear was beginning to overshadow the anger. He knew he could do anything he wanted. He grew hard. He smiled.

"I'll be back in a minute."

He went down the steps and crossed the kitchen to his bedroom. Slowly he took off his shirt. He hung it neatly on a coat hanger, smoothed it carefully, then hung it in the closet. He took off his mirror-like black shoes, blew imaginary dust off the left one, then wrinkled his lips in disgust. The toe of the right shoe was scuffed and dull; no doubt where *The Burning One* had stepped on it while he was taking her up the stairs. He could not leave the shoe like that. He reached into the closet and pulled out his shoe-shining gear. Then he sat down on the floor, stuck his left hand into the shoe, and picked up the cloth. It was difficult because of the bandage. But the shoe had to be polished. He opened the polish, took a bottle of distilled water, and poured a splash into the upturned lid. He dipped the soft cloth into the water, then into the polish and slowly and methodically began shining the shoe.

Ten minutes later, he was done. Satisfied, he eased shoe trees into the shoes and placed them in the closet. He took off his pants, carefully placed them on a hangar, and placed them in the closet. He had worn the uniform only for several hours. The creases were still sharp.

He was stripped to his blue silk underwear. Although the air conditioner was on, his body was covered with a sheen of perspiration. He carefully unwrapped his hand. The wound was still bleeding though not as much as before. He walked across the room, muscles bunching in his shoulders and legs. He picked up a small tube of Super Glue. In the other hand he picked up his 9mm Beretta. It was loaded with fifteen rounds of Hydra Shok ammo.

He walked up the stairs, turned on a lamp, and, with Sarah's horrified eyes full upon him, began to work on his hand. He took the top from the tube of glue and squeezed a blob into the open wound. Then he placed his wounded hand on the floor and used his other hand to push together the edges of the wound. The burning pain caused his mouth to jerk.

Sarah stared.

"Learned this in the army. The army learned it from terrorists. Quick way to stop the bleeding and close up a wound."

Lucifer waited several minutes for the glue to harden. Satisfied, he held out his hand, wiggled the fingers, then put a piece of two-inch-wide adhesive tape over the wound. Again he wiggled his fingers and examined his hand, as if studying a newly repaired piece of equipment.

Lucifer opened the wooden chest where he kept his trophies, reached inside, and pulled out a knife he had bought from a special forces soldier in Germany. Some people liked fancy knives with curved blades and ornate handles. But if it had been used by special forces, it was good enough for him.

He pulled the blade down his arm, examined his arm, and made a grimace. The knife should have left a smooth, denuded track, like a scythe through high grass, as it moved through the hair on his arm. But it was too dull. He had forgotten to sharpen it after he went adventuring the other day. No, he hadn't forgotten. It's just that the joy of that adventure so filled him that he had delayed. He would do it now. It would take only a minute.

He glanced at *The Burning One*. She was going nowhere.

Lucifer savored these delays. Every delay proved his control, his domination, and heightened his anticipation. Her terror grew by the moment. What better way to demonstrate to her that she was helpless before his power than handle a few mundane chores.

From inside the chest he took a whetstone and a small can of oil. He squirted a drop of oil on the stone, spread it with his finger, then began slowly pushing the blade down the stone. A flat, dull scratching noise sounded from the stone.

The sound horrified Sarah. She rolled her eyes and tried to twist her head, but she could not see him. He was behind her.

Eventually the sound stopped.

Lucifer walked across the room. He straddled Sarah, standing at about her waist, holding the knife in his right hand. She looked up at him. She could see him growing.

The Burning One has found me.

I have the power.

I have the control.

In her agony I shall find my glory.

He slowly pulled on a pair of rubber gloves. With each pop of the latex Sarah flinched.

Lucifer flexed his fingers. He smiled at Sarah and held his open arms toward the big window. "Do you like my florida room?"

From inside his black gym bag he pulled a ball of string, measured off about four feet, and cut it with his knife. He coiled the string and placed it by Sarah's head.

Then he walked across the room and pressed the button on a small tape player.

Music blared. It was Wagner—"Brunhilde's Immolation." Lucifer closed his eyes and listened. He swayed gently. He turned up the volume. From the black gym bag he pulled another small tape recorder, placed it near Sarah's head, and pressed the Record button.

He stood over her. With his left hand he adjusted his growing bulk. He smiled. Slowly he knelt until his knees were under Sarah's arms. He leaned over until the small gold cross on the chain around his neck was touching her chin. His massive upper body covered her, and she felt as if she were being smothered.

The sound of Wagner throbbed inside the room.

Lucifer's yellow eyes glowed. He leaned closer, pressing against Sarah. He placed his lips against her ear.

"Are we ready to go adventuring?"

34

The white car raced at high speed across North Decatur Road, lurched and screeched through a red light at Briarcliff Road, then rocketed down one hill, then up another toward North Highland Avenue. Nigel was too close to turn on his siren or the flashing lights. Instead he turned his headlights on and off and forced his way through the red light and turned left on Highland.

"Check the numbers," he said to Price.

"They're going down. It's this block. On the left."

This part of North Highland is a curious mixture of new apartments, smaller and older homes that are being yuppified, and those comfortable old homes—usually brick—in which the residents have lived for many years. In some of the older two-story homes, the owners rent out the upper floor or the basement, often to Emory students or employees. The neighborhood is ten minutes from Emory. The route between the neighborhood and the university is crosstown and free of the heavy stop-and-go traffic that immobilizes most of the direct routes into the city.

At the corner, Nigel turned left and pulled to the curb. He looked around.

"See any APD units?"

Price twisted around. "Negative. Want me to call?"

"Don't have time." He opened the door and grabbed the shotgun. "Give me some extra shells."

Carl Lee handed him a half-dozen shells.

Nigel dropped them into his pocket. "Let's go."

Price stuck the .357 Magnum in his belt and seized the MAC-11. He raced ahead. Then he looked over his shoulder. Nigel could not move so fast. Price slowed down and looked over his shoulder.

"You having problems?"

"No. I'm having to wear a . . ." He did not want to say "corset." "I'm wearing a back brace."

Price smiled the smile that very physical young men have for anyone who doesn't wear a cape and have a big S on the front of his shirt.

He looked ahead. "Fifteen fifteen is three doors ahead on the left."

"Move over closer to the houses."

The two men moved from the sidewalk and across the lawns of several houses.

Price pointed. "That's it."

"I want you to walk down the sidewalk, check the number, and be absolutely certain. Hand me your weapon."

Price nodded and handed over the MAC-11. He pulled his shirt over the .357, slung the book bag over one shoulder, sauntered out to the sidewalk, and began walking down the street. He passed the house, rounded the corner, and then cut across a lawn toward the alley that ran behind the houses. From there he raced back toward Nigel.

From behind a blooming forsythia bush, Nigel waited. He took out his badge and hung it over the breast pocket of his suit. The shotgun he tried to keep hidden under his coat.

He looked up anxiously as Price appeared.

"Guess what?" Price said as he pulled his badge from the book bag and hung it around his neck.

"What?"

"It's a boarding house. Four different residences in there. It's on the mailbox. Apartments one, two, three, and four."

Nigel nodded. "The owners will live on the main floor. Top floor and basement rented out. Did you see any names? Which is his apartment?"

Price shook his head. "No names. They might be inside on the doors."

Nigel nodded. "Is the basement underground or does it have windows on the sides. I don't want him to see us coming if he's in the basement."

"I couldn't tell from the street. But if we go in the front door, he won't see us."

"It's locked."

"Not to worry." The smiling young officer took the book bag from his shoulder and reached inside. He removed something that looked like a battery-powered drill. But on the end, where the bit would have gone, were two thin bands of steel. Price grinned. "Battery-powered lock pick. Three seconds, maybe four, and that door is mine."

"What the hell is law enforcement coming to?" Nigel grinned.

"Let's do it."

Price held the MAC-11 against his body with the book bag. The lockpick was held against his leg. Nigel stuck the shotgun into his trousers. The two men walked across the yard, then approached the front door of the targeted house.

The lockpick made a brief whirring noise and the door was open. As the two men quickly stepped inside, Nigel pulled the shotgun and Price slid his arms through the straps on the book bag so it would be open and in front of his body. He clicked the safety off the MAC-11 and held it vertical, finger alongside the trigger.

"Basement apartments first," Nigel whispered. "There will be an inside entrance somewhere back in the back."

The two men moved down the hall, walking on their toes but moving fast. Nigel tried not to drag his left foot.

Two doors were at the end of the hall. One was open.

"Me first," Price whispered.

Nigel shook his head. "No. Back me up."

He stepped inside, shotgun leveled, and took two steps. He was in a kitchen. A gray-haired woman was at a table around the corner. She was drinking coffee. She looked up with a smile. The smile abruptly disappeared when she saw two men with guns. Her eyes widened.

"Police," Nigel whispered. He pointed at his badge.

She stood up. "What? What do you want?" Her hand went to her throat.

Nigel lowered the shotgun, smiled, and motioned for her to sit down. "Don't be afraid. We're police officers. We're not going to hurt you. We're looking for Luther Brumley. What's your name?"

For a moment she did not speak. Then she shook

her head. "Peggy Haefele. This is my house." She paused. "Luther. Do you mean Lucifer?"

Nigel and Price looked at each other. Price's eyes widened. "Lucifer?"

Nigel was remembering.

He moved the lamp across the dressing table . . . Lucifer is the Light Bearer . . . When Monaco Jackson asked why he was hurting her, he said, "Because I am the Son of the . . ." Lucifer is the Son of the Morning.

Peggy nodded. That's what he told me to call him. Said that's what his family always called him and that I was like family. He was such a nice young man."

"Was? What do you mean, was? Where is he?" Nigel snapped.

"He's not here." She looked at Nigel as if he should apologize for his tone of voice.

"Where is he?"

"I just don't know. But he's not here."

"When will he return?

"He won't."

"Why not?"

"He moved several weeks ago. He doesn't live here anymore."

35

"Give me that phone," Nigel said. The two men were walking rapidly toward the white Emory car parked around the corner. "You drive." He passed the keys to Carl Lee Price, quickly punched in the numbers for the APD radio and identified himself to the dispatcher.

"This is an emergency," Nigel said. "Call security at the phone company. Get the phone number and address of subject known as Luther Brumley. No middle initial. New phone. Maybe three weeks old. Previous address was 1515 North Highland Avenue. White male. Employed by a private security company, but he may have listed his employment as Emory University."

"Roger."

Price unlocked the door of the Emory car and opened the door. Nigel slid inside and continued talking. "Also, contact SWAT and my backup en route to the Highland Avenue address. Tell them to stand by for a new address."

"Ten-four."

"Contact security or the police contacts at Atlanta Gas Light and at Georgia Power. Get home address of the subject. Just in case."

"It's going to take maybe fifteen minutes with the phone company. Same with the others."

"We don't have fifteen minutes. Tell them it's a police emergency. Top priority. Do it now."

"Stand by."

Nigel gave the dispatcher the phone number for the cellular phone and the phone number for Ed Medlin in case a radio message had to be relayed. "If you call on the radio, lose the three-way."

"Roger."

Price turned on the ignition. "You want to wait here?"

Nigel thought for a moment. "I'm betting he lives somewhere near Emory. He needs privacy for what he does. He has to come and go without people seeing him. A house, maybe a remote apartment."

"Could it be a house or a condo?"

"He can't afford a house. A condo is not right for him."

"You certain about that?"

"Hell no, I'm not certain," Nigel exploded. "I don't know any more about it than you do. If I was certain, I wouldn't be sitting here sucking my goddamn thumb while my daughter is out there with him."

Price ignored the outburst. He nodded. "What I was getting at was whether you wanted to wait here, or do you want to make a guess and start driving?"

"I can't sit here."

"Okay. You don't think it could be a regular apartment?"

"No. Maybe a garage apartment. There are lots of those around Emory. Graduate students like them."

"Where are most of the garage apartments? Any particular place around Emory?"

Nigel thought for a moment. "Yes. Between Emory and Ponce de Leon. On Lullwater, Springdale, or Oakdale. Lots of big houses set back from the road on big lots with garages behind them. Lots of trees, too, that would give him even more privacy."

"That's five minutes away. Want to go that way?"

"We'll be close to Briarcliff and North Decatur, so if we have to, we can go the other direction in a hurry. Yes. Let's go."

He redialed the telephone. Dispatch answered.

"Anything from the phone company?"

"They're working on it. I'm keeping an open line to their office."

"I'm standing by. Let me know something as soon as you can."

The car was crossing Briarcliff when the cellular phone sounded. Nigel punched the Receive button before the first ring ended.

"Trench."

"I have the subject's address. Ready to copy?"

"Go."

Nigel listened, grinned, and turned to Price. "It's on Lullwater." He waved his hand forward.

Price accelerated rapidly. "Any apartment number?"

"Negative. It will be a carriage house. People there don't advertise that they are renting an apartment."

Nigel was back on the cell phone talking to dispatch. "Contact SWAT and backup and give them the address. Tell them not to go in until they hear from me."

"Roger."

The dispatcher punched several buttons to go from a three-way broadcast to two-way.

"We're only five or six blocks away," Price said. H

flipped on the car's flashing lights and turned on his headlights. Ahead, at Springdale, was a major intersection. The light was red.

"Don't use the siren," Nigel said.

"I'll use the horn." Price flashed his lights. As a car peeped from Springdale, Price tapped the horn. The other car squealed to a stop, and Price careened through the light. At the bottom of the hill, as North Decatur swung to the left, he slowed and made a hard right turn onto Lullwater.

Nigel was looking at the house numbers. He pointed across the road. "That side. Another couple of blocks. Don't get too close."

Price nodded. His eyes were locked on the road. His hands were light on the steering wheel.

Nigel pointed. "About four or five houses ahead. Pull over."

Price eased to the curb.

The two men stepped from the car. Nigel picked up the shotgun.

"That's a big house," Nigel said. "He doesn't live there. It will be out back."

"Think there's another way out?"

"Not with these houses. The Druid Hills golf course is back there."

"Want to go through the backyards again?" Price checked the clip on the MAC-11. He adjusted the backpack so it was over his chest. He stuck an enormous plug of chewing tobacco into his mouth, grinned round the plug, and pushed the .357 Magnum more securely under his belt. The earplug for the radio was in his ear.

"No. I'm betting that garage apartment is so far in

back of the house that he won't be able to see us until we're in the front door."

The two men walked up the road, Price moving at Nigel's pace.

"Want a walker?"

"Don't be a fucking smart ass with me right now."

The two men climbed a steep driveway. About a hundred yards from the road they slowed as they passed the main house, a three-story mansion. No one was in sight. Nigel paused to wipe perspiration from his brow. A three-car garage was in the backyard. It appeared relatively new, far newer than the house.

The driveway continued through the backyard and wound into a thick clump of pines.

Nigel nodded. "On up the hill."

Once the two men passed the house, they held their weapons at the ready.

"Scout ahead," Nigel said softly. "But be careful. Don't let him see you. And don't do anything on your own. I go in first."

Price spat an enormous dollop of tobacco juice into the rose bushes, nodded, and began an effortless trot around the corner and up the steepening hill.

Two minutes later, he returned, loping as effortlessly as a young deer. He skidded to a stiff-legged stop, spat again, and nodded.

"Well?" Nigel said. He was breathing hard.

"House is about fifty yards ahead. Looks like an old barn that's been remodeled. Around the next corner. You come up on it all at once. Sits on the crest of the hill. There's one door on this side, but it looks like the front of the house overlooks whatever is on the other side of the hill. A car is there."

"See anyone?"

Price shook his head.

"That it?"

"I heard music."

"You what?"

"Music. Inside the house. Somebody's there."

Nigel's mouth tightened. "We'll be working in close quarters. I need another weapon."

Price opened his book bag.

Nigel picked up the TASER. "Two shots? Fifteen-foot range?"

Price nodded. "You got it. That'll light him up."

Nigel slid his coat off one arm, hung the TASER from his shoulder, then put on his coat. The TASER was hidden. He pushed past Price.

As the house came into sight, Nigel slowed. He stared, catching his breath and planning his attack. He heard the high-pitched music.

"Any word on SWAT or the backup?"

Price plucked the radio from the book bag and whispered into it. He listened intently, then turned to Nigel. "They're pulling up behind our car. What do you want them to do?"

"Tell them to come up the driveway until they can see the house but to stay out of sight. They're not to move until I say so."

Again Price whispered into the radio.

"Let's go," Nigel said. "There's a window on this side of the house. We'll cut through the woods here and come out behind the house in case he's watching the driveway. I don't see any windows on the back of the house."

Five minutes later, the two men were standing at the rear of the house. The music was louder. It was coming from the upper floor.

The offender was at work.

"We've got to get him away from her," Nigel whispered. 'Here's what I want you to do."

Minutes later Lucifer's head snapped up. He held the gleaming military knife in position. He sliced the buttons off Sarah's jacket, slowly and one by one, and watched the terror in her eyes and heard her tape-muffled groans. He worked slowly. To prolong her pain was to prolong his pleasure. He nodded and hummed along with Wagner.

He cut the jacket from her body and watched it fall away.

He sliced the buttons from her blouse and split it down each arm.

He sliced the button from her red skirt, slid down the zipper, then slowly inched the blade down her leg and through the seam. The skirt now was now only a piece of red material draped across her body. She was afraid to move, knowing it would fall away and expose her body.

He sliced her bra in front and, despite her efforts to control her breathing, she gasped in fear. The bra pulled aside until it barely covered her breasts.

Lucifer stopped humming.

What was that odor? Something was burning downstairs in the kitchen. But there was no reason for anything to be burning. He had not cooked for several days. And he had been gone for hours this morning.

With the agility and speed of a jungle animal he leaped upright, knees flexed, holding the knife at the ready. His head pivoted back and forth. His nostrils flared.

On tiptoe he trotted across the open upstairs room to the window overlooking the driveway. His back wa against the wall and his head turned over his left shoulder toward the window. He slid closer to the window, looking at an angle through the sparkling panes. Nothing. He moved out a bit. Nothing. He stepped back and moved out farther, and then he saw it—there, back in the trees were black-clad men with long guns. They wore black ski masks.

He snapped back against the wall.

A SWAT team.

On the tape player, Wagner was in full voice.

Nigel peeked again. The men were still in the woods. If SWAT was holding back, that meant someone was closer. Someone was inside the house. Either a SWAT fire team or . . . no, it wasn't SWAT, it was Nigel Trench. Trench was downstairs. SWAT would not come in until Nigel gave the order.

Lucifer grinned.

This would be fun.

He trotted lightly across the big room. The hot summer sun blasted a white light through the enormous wall of windows.

The odor from the kitchen was stronger. Smoke was wafting up the stairs. What was Nigel burning to lure him downstairs? That was the oldest trick in the book.

He lay the knife on the floor above Sarah's head, picked up the 9mm pistol, slowly pulled the pillow from under Sarah's head, and then slowly walked down the room until he was over the kitchen. He closed his eyes and imagined where Nigel would be in the room. Almost certainly behind the stairs, where he would be out of sight but where he could see anyone who came down the stairs. Lucifer slid over a few steps, moving lightly. He did not want the floor to creak. He spread his legs, wrapped the plastic-covered pillow tightly around the pistol with his left hand, and pointed the weapon at the floor.

Quickly, so quickly that the shots of the heavy pistol sounded like rapid coughs, he fired into the floor, walking the bullets across the floor, placing them every six inches, as neatly as if he had measured. He moved the pistol over several feet and again walked it across the floor for several feet. He counted twelve shots when he heard a sharp exclamation of pain.

Nigel flinched when he looked up and saw the floor splintering overhead and a series of neat holes appearing. He tried to move, but the bullets were coming too fast. A bullet caught him on the edge of his left shoulder and knocked him to the floor. He shouted and dropped the shotgun.

Price dropped into a crouch, swung the MAC-11 upwards and was about to stitch the floor when Nigel waved and shook his head. Sarah was upstairs. He pointed across the kitchen to the bedroom door.

Price looked, understood, and ran swiftly across the kitchen and into the bedroom. He left the door open.

The smoke was growing thicker. Price had picked up the morning newspaper from the table, pulled it from the plastic wrapper, shook it a few times to loosen it up, spread it across the top of the stove, and turned on two gas burners. The newspaper was blazing. A can of grease on the rear of the stove was smoking.

Nigel looked at the stove and saw Marie Morris's picture crinkle and blacken and disappear in flames.

When Price ran across the room, he held the MAC-11 at the ready. He looked over his shoulder to make sure Lucifer was not coming down the stairs. The barrel of the MAC-11 brushed the burning newspapers as he raced past and pushed them to the rear of the stove. Flames nibbled around the bottom of the curtains.

"Officer Trench," came a voice from upstairs.

Nigel wanted a moment. He lay on the floor trying to reach the shotgun.

"Your daughter is here."

"Don't hurt her." Nigel's hands closed over the shotgun, and he looked upward, waiting to see the legs of the offender.

"Throw your weapon across the room."

Nigel looked at the bedroom door. Price peeped around the corner. The barrel of the MAC-11 was level. Nigel motioned for him to get out of sight.

"Okay." He cracked the breech on the shotgun, plucked the two shells out, and put them in his pocket. He closed the breech and slid the gun across the floor so it was visible from the top of the stairs.

"Now the pistol."

"I don't carry a pistol. That's it."

Lucifer paused. "Okay, move out where I can see you. Keep your hands over your head."

"I'm hit," Nigel said. He coughed. The smoke was thicker. He looked across the room. The curtains were blazing and licking at the ceiling. The can of grease was bubbling. In seconds the old house would be on fire.

"Your house is burning," Nigel said. "We've got to get out. Let my daughter go."

Lucifer laughed. "I like the fire. Move to where I can see you."

Nigel stood up and limped across the room, his right hand clasped to his bleeding shoulder.

Lucifer nodded when Nigel came into view. He ignored the smoke billowing across the room. The sound of flames could now be heard crackling over the sound of Wagner. But the police officer in front of him and the young woman behind him were all that mattered.

"Open your coat."

Nigel pushed back his coat on the left side and then the right. Lucifer saw he wore no holster. The TASER was hidden in the folds of Nigel's coat.

"Hands behind your head," Lucifer ordered.

Nigel tried. His right hand he placed behind his head. But his left hand would not go that high. The pain in his shoulder was too great. His left hand hung limply, blood dripping from his fingers.

Lucifer pointed the Beretta at Nigel. His eyes were locked on the police officer. "Do not move," he said as he came slowly down the stairs, his slow approach made all the more malevolent by the smoke swirling up the stairs and wrapping around his body.

At the bottom of the stairs he paused. His eyes never left Nigel's face.

"Where is my daughter? This place is burning."

In a move of indescribable speed Lucifer back-handed Nigel's face with the heavy Beretta, splitting his cheek and knocking him semi-conscious to the floor.

He leaned over Nigel, shoved the pistol under his chin, and smiled. "I'm going to do three things," he said. "I'm going to tell you about the little accident your wife had the other day. I'm going to tell you my plans for your daughter. And then . . ."

Lucifer paused.

Nigel looked at him. He had never seen eyes that color.

Lucifer nodded. "And then I am going to send you to hell."

The fire crackled. The heat was intense.

Smoke curled around Lucifer.

The horns of Wagner were rising to a crescendo. The thundering drums and clashing cymbals resounded.

36

Lucifer's words cut through Nigel's pain.

"It *was* you at the hospital."

Lucifer arched his eyebrows and smiled malevolently. He stood over Nigel, looking down at him. "I wanted to see your wife again."

"Price. Now," Nigel shouted. He flung his injured arm to the side, knocking the pistol away, and at the same time he reached up and seized Lucifer's testicles and twisted with all his strength.

Lucifer screamed. The Beretta fired, the bullet missing Nigel by about six inches. Lucifer was about to pull the trigger again when Price leaned around the door of the bedroom. He could not see Nigel. He had only a glimpse of a half-naked figure with a pistol. The MAC-11 was on full auto when Price stitched half the magazine through the smoke. One of the bullets caught Lucifer in the edge of his stomach, below the ribs, in a neat through-and-through shot. It was not a dangerous wound. But the searing pain was such that Lucifer flung himself backward freeing himself from Nigel's grasp. He snap-fired the Beretta toward the source of the shots. He fired until the magazine was empty, then dropped the pistol.

In the bedroom, Price was crouched and shouting

into his radio. "Move in. Move in. Subject wearing only shorts. If he comes out, kill him. Two officers and female civilian in here." He dropped the radio and leaned around the corner.

Lucifer heard Price. He snarled in anger and picked up the shotgun.

Price jumped from the bedroom, MAC-11 at the ready. But the smoke was too thick. He could see nothing. Fire was racing up the walls.

Lucifer pointed the shotgun at Nigel. "I never hurt a woman," he screamed. "Never was I unmindful of them. I will comb Sarah's hair and she will wear a red scarf."

He pulled the trigger.

Click.

He pulled the other trigger.

Click.

Lucifer screamed in rage and flung the shotgun across the room. It landed atop the stove, bounced to the floor, and skidded across the room.

Lucifer bounded up the stairs.

Price spun, gun leveled, when he heard the noise at the stove. The pan of grease was melted and smoking. He kicked the shotgun across the room toward Nigel.

"Price, he's going up the stairs," Nigel shouted. "Stop him." He forgot the TASER. With his good hand he reached for the shotgun and flipped open the breach.

Price saw a flash of bare skin. He picked up the can of bubbling grease and threw it across the room toward the middle of the steps. The can was still in the air when he followed it with one of the flash-bang grenades from his book bag. Then he popped the little

automatic into position and emptied the clip toward
the top of the stairs. He jammed his hand into the
book bag, grabbed another clip and snapped it into
the MAC-11 and ran toward the steps.

The hot oil hit Lucifer on the shoulder, sprayed
across his bare body, then ran down his legs. He
screamed. The concussion from the flash-bang caused
him to jump back against the wall. It also saved him
from being cut in half by another fusillade from Price's
MAC-11.

Those few seconds were all Nigel needed. With his
bloody fingers he could not load the shotgun. He remembered the TASER and pulled it from under his
body. He fired straight up the stairs. Nothing.

He moved the TASER to the right and fired again
as Lucifer spun from the wall at the top of the steps.
The two darts slapped into Lucifer's shoulder. Nigel
pressed the button and, like a bolt of lightning, the
electrical charge surged through the wires. The tre-
mendous jolt ignited the oil on Lucifer's body. He
virtually exploded in flames. Liquid fire ran from his
shoulders and down his back and onto his legs.

At that moment Price fired again. A dozen bullets
tattooed Lucifer's body, causing him to twirl and
dance and spin, hands over his head. His burning body
was silhouetted against the enormous glass windows.
The gold cross around his neck glistened in the
sunlight.

Lucifer made no sound as his fiery dance and the
force of the bullets propelled him across the room
toward the windows and the light. He never slowed.
He leaped through the windows, spraying glass, arms
and legs outstretched as the SWAT team approached
the house.

Sergeant Luke and his SWAT team were about to enter the side door when they heard exploding glass, looked up, and saw a figure clad only in shorts leaping through the window.

"Pull," Luke shouted.

Lucifer's body jerked and twisted as bullets from three automatic weapons ripped into him.

Lucifer fell from a great height. He kept falling. His burning body hit the lip of the sixty-foot drop-off and bounced and again was falling. He landed at the bottom of the steep gully, on the blood red Georgia clay, his body still burning.

Members of the SWAT team ran to the edge of the precipice and peeked over the side, rifles at the ready.

Lucifer's body, blackened and burning, was crumpled in a small heap.

Smoke and a few small flames curled from the remains.

Major Norris Morris watched the EMT's loading Lucifer's body into an ambulance. Dan Buchanan stood nearby, tapping his notebook on his chin, watching the body being loaded. Mayor Campbell was at the rear of the ambulance, nodding at a photographer from *The Atlanta Constitution*. Norris turned to Nigel.

"Well, Roach, it's over. The mayor is happy." He nodded wisely. "I think we've reached the ajax of this case."

Nigel did not speak.

"Roach, the mayor wants me to tell you he appreciates your using the TASER. But did you have to flambé the guy?"

Nigel said nothing. He stared at the ambulance.

Morris was not deterred. He looked at the trees and the summer sky and rocked on his heels and said, "You know, I love this city. Forget about the rapes and the homicides, and we live in a city with the lowest crime rate in the country."

Nigel looked over his shoulder. Sarah sat in the backseat of a nearby police car. She wore his suit jacket. Price's shirt covered her legs. Price stood by the car. He had appointed himself Sarah's protector and had kept reporters and photographers away first by advising them to "think about tomorrow. There will be other days and a lot of other stories. You fuck with me, and I'll close you down like a two-dollar whorehouse."

But reporters cannot see beyond the next deadline. There were those who sought to steamroll the young cop. Price let tobacco juice dribble down his chin, widened his eyes, raised his voice to a high pitch, and said, "I'll beat the dog shit out of the first person who points a camera at this car."

No one took pictures.

Morris turned to Nigel. "Sarah okay?"

Nigel looked at the still burning remains of the old barn. he looked at the police car. He nodded. "Her mother's funeral is tomorrow. It will take a while. But she is young. She is strong. She will be okay."

Morris shook his head. "My friend, you don't know how sorry I am about Rachel."

Nigel looked at the sky and blinked his eyes rapidly. He wiggled his bandaged shoulder. Then he sighed. "In a way she is better off."

"What are you going to do?"

"I'm taking Sarah home. Then I'm calling Mr. Jackson in New York to tell him what happened. I promised him I'd do that. We'll get ready for the funeral. Then we'll get on with our lives."

"Sarah be glad to graduate?"

"Yes. She's moving in with me for the time being. But she'll leave in a few months. She doesn't know it yet. But she will want to move out and have a place of her own."

"You okay with that?"

Nigel shrugged. "That's the way it is."

He slowly unbuttoned his shirt and pulled off the back brace.

"You still in pain?"

Nigel shook his head. "For the first time in days there is no pain." He stretched. "I never felt better." He stood up straight and twisted back and forth. Then he handed the back brace to Morris.

"Here, take this. You need it more than I do."

"I resemble that remark." Morris looked around. He rattled the keys in his pocket. Then he pulled out a cigarette and lit it. "That little old lady who owns this place. She have insurance?"

"Yeah. I asked her. She didn't seem to mind that the place burned down. Said she's going to put a garden up here."

Morris looked down the hill where the ambulance had disappeared in the pine thicket. "I guess all this is behind us. Or vice versa."

"It'll never be behind us."

Morris reached out and shook Nigel's hand. The two men stared at each other for a long moment.

"Good-bye, Roach."

"Bye, Norris."

The major turned and walked toward his car.

"Hey, Major."

Norris stopped and looked over his shoulder.

"Yeah?"

"Let the games begin."

EERIE SUSPENSE

TERROR . . . TO THE LAST DROP